FALLEN ANGELS

FALLEN ANGELS

Kendal Grahame

This book is a work of fiction.
In real life, make sure you practise safe sex.

First published in 1994 by
Nexus
332 Ladbroke Grove
London W10 5AH

Copyright © Kendal Grahame 1994

Typeset by TW Typesetting, Plymouth, Devon
Printed and bound by
Cox & Wyman Ltd, Reading, Berks

ISBN 0 352 32934 3

Chapter One

Lisa watched her friend in disbelief. It was happening again! Oh, true it wasn't Janet's fault, she was a very beautiful girl, but it seemed so unfair somehow.

She'd arrived at Janet's flat unexpectedly, finding her friend in the company of two distinguished-looking men in their early thirties; diplomats, apparently. It was obvious, however, from her friend's blushes and her guests' apparent embarrassment, that diplomacy was not what was on the agenda. Janet certainly moved in exclusive circles these days, and probably didn't welcome Lisa's intrusion.

She had wondered though, even hoped, that as there were two of them, maybe, just maybe, one of them might be interested in her; Janet surely couldn't cope with two men at the same time!

She was wrong, of course. Janet could cope perfectly well with them both, and Lisa was in the way, at least as far as the men were concerned.

Not that she could blame them, of course. Compared to her friend she must have looked like something from a horror movie. Janet was stunning, simply stunning. She was tall, slim but with firm, apple-sized breasts, a narrow waist and gently curved bottom. Her legs seemed to make up most of her height, and she used their remarkable length to full advantage, wearing exceptionally short skirts or skin-tight jeans, and rarely bothering with underwear. Her hair was dark, cut in a short bob style, framing her lovely face, with her large doe-like eyes and pouting mouth which seemed to be permanently smiling.

1

Lisa could not have been more different. She was short, a little over five foot, dumpy with straggly, carrot-coloured hair topping a freckly, plain face. The only area of her body that couldn't be considered in any way plump was her bust, which she had always felt was most unfair, her insignificant little breasts resting almost comically on her flabby chest.

She tried to do something about her looks, of course, but no amount of exercise seemed to have any effect on her shape, and the handiwork of the most expert make-up artist wouldn't have been able to do anything to conceal the homely look of her face.

Janet had always been very kind, telling her that looks weren't important, that personality counted much more. Easy to say, of course when you are so gorgeous that you could stop traffic, Lisa often mused. They were great friends though, and had been since early school-days when they were inseparable.

It was when they reached adolescence that things started to change. Janet had been travelling abroad with her parents for about six months and when she returned she'd changed from a little girl into an utterly devastating, man-hungry woman, whilst Lisa had stayed plain, overweight and exceptionally naïve.

Her friend discovered the pleasures of sex very early and had developed quite a reputation for herself, often recounting stories of her many conquests to an ever more envious Lisa, who had now reached the age of eighteen without losing her virginity.

Not that she didn't want to, of course. She was sure it was her looks alone that stopped the boys in their tracks, leaving her to take nightly solace with her finger as she fantasised herself starring in the latest of Janet's adventures. If only they knew how compliant she would be, how willing to do anything to please them; surely then they would want to tear her voluminous pants from her large thighs and bury their greedy faces in her hungry warmth.

* * *

2

Lisa stood awkwardly in the lounge, looking uncomfortably at Janet and her guests, desperately trying to think of something intelligent to say. Her friend was smiling, of course, but her eyes betrayed her wish to see Lisa leave her alone with her two prospective lovers.

'I'm sorry I disturbed you, Janet,' she said, quietly. 'I just thought you might like to come out for a drink.' She shuffled awkwardly from one foot to the other, wishing that she was anywhere but there. Her friend hadn't even offered her a seat, and didn't look like she was going to.

'Well, as you can see, I have company,' said Janet, with an expression of almost benign sympathy.

'Yes, er, sorry,' said Lisa. There was a long, silent pause as she waited for the invitation that she knew in her heart wasn't going to come.

'I suppose I'd better go,' she said finally, turning with marked reluctance towards the door.

Janet smiled again. 'OK, Lisa,' she said, her relief apparent, 'I'll call you tomorrow.'

'Right, yes, erm . . .' Lisa looked again at the seated men, almost in desperation. Surely it wouldn't matter if she stayed; the four of them could have such fun together. The frustration building within her was making her perspire. 'Oh, sorry Janet, could I use your toilet before I go?'

Without trying to conceal her impatience, Janet walked back into the centre of the lounge. 'Go on then, you know where it is.' Lisa hurried out, closing the door behind her.

She stood for a moment with her back to the door, breathing heavily. The visit to the toilet was just an excuse, of course. She wanted to give Janet time to change her mind, to invite her back to join in with the fun.

There was no call from behind the closed door, the only sounds were those of muffled, male voices and Janet's co-quettish giggles. Lisa decided to give her friend one more chance.

She quickly returned from the bathroom where she'd been preening, attempting to make herself look reasonably presentable in a last-ditch effort to persuade Janet and her guests to invite her to stay. She opened the lounge door cautiously, to find both men with their arms wrapped around Janet, kissing and cuddling her whilst their free hands groped up her short skirt, feeling at her naked sex.

'Lisa!' exclaimed Janet, angrily, pulling the two busy hands from between her long legs. 'I thought you'd gone!'

'I'm sorry, Janet,' said Lisa, tears beginning to trickle from her eyes, 'I, I was going to call a cab. It's raining hard outside.'

Janet's attitude seemed to soften as she responded to her friend's tearful expression. 'That's all right, Lisa. You can use my phone to call the cab and wait here for it. I'll take John and Peter into the other room.' She walked over and kissed her friend lightly on the cheek before disappearing with the two grinning diplomats, leaving Lisa to sob her heart out on the sofa alone. .

She decided that she wouldn't get a cab, at least not yet, resolving that even if she couldn't have the satisfaction of having a screw herself, she would watch her friend, to see what two men might get up to with her.

She waited about five minutes, then crept to the bedroom, opening the door slowly and carefully; just enough to gain a full view of the proceedings, hardly daring to breathe.

Janet hadn't wasted any time. She lay naked on her back across the bed, watching with unconcealed lust as the two handsome studs struggled to strip off their clothing. It was the first time that Lisa had seen Janet naked since they had left school, and even then she had been beautiful. Now she looked simply gorgeous as she lay there, waiting for sex.

Lisa let her fingers trail inside her frumpy, smock-like dress and under the waistband of her knickers as she feasted her eyes on the lithe, young body of her friend, knowing that she was about to witness Janet have sex with two good-looking men. She began to tremble with excitement, realising that she was about to see not one, but two naked men at close quarters, to view their bodies; to see their

4

erections as they took it in turns to make love to, no, to *fuck* their lovely conquest.

She'd always been physically attracted to Janet, and knew she would give anything to join this threesome; to enjoy the bodies of both the men and the enchanting child who, even now, was caressing herself between the legs as she watched the strong nakedness of her two lovers slowly revealed before her.

Peter was the first to be completely naked, almost tearing off his briefs in his effort to get at Janet. He stood next to her, his long, thick manhood jutting out from his smooth, tanned body, the thick, purple head oozing the wetness of his excitement.

Janet reached out with one hand and grasped his rigid stalk, taking the end without a moment's hesitation into her mouth. She rubbed him slowly up and down as she sucked him, opening her legs wider, unknowingly allowing Lisa a perfect view of her open sex-lips as she delved into them with her other hand.

Lisa pulled and prodded at her own clitoris, her panties becoming sodden as she watched the superbly erotic scene unfold before her.

John was now naked. His body was even more heavily tanned than that of his colleague, a thin strip of white skin where his swimming trunks had protected his modesty betraying his real colouring. He too was fully erect; his stalk, slightly larger than that of his friend, was looming up from a thick bush of dark pubic hair.

He knelt between Janet's wide-open legs and took her hand away from her pussy, replacing it first with his own. As Lisa watched, he rubbed the obviously wet lips with his thumb before leaning forward and pressing his mouth against her, running his tongue deftly over her clitoris. The angle was perfect; Lisa could see everything, and it made her even more frustrated as she watched John expertly flicking his tongue over Janet's sex, causing her friend to writhe her hips on the bed, her moans of ecstasy muffled by the large penis she was busily sucking on.

5

With a sudden squeal she came, her legs gripping tightly against John's ears whilst his head bobbed up and down as he licked furiously at her. She took her mouth from Peter and shouted out, 'Oh, yes, oh yes, that's it!', gripping John's head with her free hand and pulling his face harder against her mound.

Lisa could see John's tight, puckered anus, his bottom pushed upwards as he nibbled greedily between Janet's legs, draining her juices into his hungry mouth. She wanted to reach out and stroke the firm, strong buttocks, and to let her tongue slide gently between them, but all she could do was watch and dream as her friend enjoyed the undivided attentions of these two, gorgeous men.

She rubbed herself furiously as she watched John position himself ready to impale Janet on his long, thick stalk, whilst Peter squatted over her face so that she could lick his balls and bum and rub his hardness with both hands. John pushed forward and Lisa's view was perfect as her friend's wet sex-lips accepted the thick intrusion; the full length slid slowly inside her in one movement. He held still for a moment, then began to pump steadily into her, Janet licking and suckling on Peter's hanging scrotum, taking one, then the other of his testicles into her mouth, and drawing in her cheeks to suck on the offered prize. She pushed them in and out of her mouth with the end of her tongue and licked greedily around them, behind the wrinkled sack and onto his anus, stiffening the end of her tongue in an apparent effort to penetrate the tight sphincter.

John started pumping into her mercilessly now, holding her long legs aloft by gripping them tightly around the ankles. The thrusting of his backside became a blur to Lisa's eager gaze. She had to bite on the finger of her free hand to stop herself crying out as Janet came again, biting hard into Peter's buttock and sobbing uncontrollably. How Lisa wanted to experience such excruciatingly delightful sensations! Lonely orgasms were never like this.

After a moment Janet relaxed, and the two men changed

places. John's sex seemed larger than ever now, the whole stem purple with lust, pointing almost vertically as he moved round to present it to Janet's mouth. She turned onto her hands and knees, offering her perfect bottom to Peter's attentions. He knelt at her feet and pressed his face against her soft bum, his tongue lapping between the pink globes whilst John knelt on the bed and guided himself into her willing mouth. Lisa took her hand from her soaking pussy and sucked on the fingers, knowing that this was the taste that her friend was savouring now, the warm wetness of her own sex-juices.

Peter took his face from the luxury of Janet's bottom and directed his stiff sex at her waiting opening; the lips wide as a result of their extreme arousal. He slid slowly but easily into her and started to pump quickly, his buttocks stiffening with each forward thrust. Janet gobbled heavily on her other lover's stiffness, one hand supporting her weight, the other fondling his heavy balls, a fingertip probing his tight anus. The two men were literally using the beautiful woman sandwiched between them, sating their lust on her gorgeous body as they humped into her.

Peter pulled his hardness from her body and lay on his back, holding his cock erect with his hand, and whispering something into Janet's ear that Lisa couldn't hear. Janet squatted over him, allowing him to enter her again, and held herself still with just a couple of inches of him inside her. John got off the bed and moved round to kneel behind her and, wetting his finger liberally with his spit inserted it into her tight anus. She breathed deeply as he worked it steadily in and out, replacing it with two, then three fingers, as though preparing her. She sighed as it seemed to become easier, until he withdrew his fingers from her and took hold of his long, thick erection. Lisa gasped quietly as she watched him aim the monster at the tiny, puckered hole, Peter's stalk still embedded inside her pussy.

'He'll never get it in there,' thought Lisa, but she was wrong. Janet gritted her teeth as her tight little hole opened under the pressure of the stiff intruder, and the thick, bulbous end entered her, making her groan with pleasure. Peter remained still as his friend penetrated deeper and deeper into her bottom, until John's thick pubic hair was pressed against the softness of her buttocks.

'Oh, yes!' sighed Janet. 'Give it to me there! I love that so much!'

Lisa went back to rubbing herself wildly, knowing she was nearing orgasm. The two men now began to pump simultaneously into Janet's holes; the sight of the two thick erections thrusting in and out of her friend made Lisa shake with lust. They started to hammer into her furiously, obviously getting close to coming themselves, whilst Janet screamed out obscenities, her head rolling from side to side.

John suddenly roared and Lisa knew he was shooting sperm up her friend's bottom as he thrust wildly into her, almost forcing her off his colleague beneath them. Peter shouted out something unintelligible and pushed his hips high from the bed. He held his throbbing stiffness deep inside Janet as he came, his fingernails digging into the sides of the bed, his arched back supporting the weight of both Janet and his exhausted colleague.

Lisa couldn't stop herself. She bit into the back of her hand as she rubbed madly at her clitoris, her own orgasm tearing through her young body with a violence she'd never known before. Incredibly, she managed not to make a sound to alert the collapsing lovers of her presence, but tasted instead her blood and felt the pain of the bite on her hand as her frustrated lust subsided.

Once she had recovered her composure, she carefully closed the bedroom door and crept out of the flat, heading sadly for the high street to find a cab; the wetness of her panties now feeling uncomfortably cold between her legs in the late-night air.

Lisa sat staring blankly at the flickering TV screen. With the sound turned off, its light was the only illumination in her small, dingy room. She was almost crying with the

8

frustration of what had happened earlier that evening, wishing it could have been her lying on that bed and being humped senseless by two hunky men.

She knew that her friend hadn't meant to upset her, of course, and that she had seemed genuinely concerned that Lisa had spent yet another evening alone. Nevertheless, it was a fact that Janet always seemed to be in the company of men who were either rich or handsome or both, and she always went to bed with them! The girl was positively insatiable!

Lisa mused that, given the chance, she would act in the same way; there wasn't a man alive who would be safe from her. She looked unhappily at her reflection in the large mirror by her bedside. Even in the soft, subdued light from the television she looked awful, and there was nothing short of major plastic surgery and a complete body transplant that would change things.

She slipped off her panties and lay back on her bed, her dress rucked up to her waist. She let her hand fall between her legs and onto her hairy mound, her fingertips finding her bud immediately. She started to rub herself gently, her mind wandering with thoughts of beautiful studs waiting in line to give her a good seeing-to; their naked, oiled bodies perfect in every way, their erections long and thick.

'Life can be a real shit, sometimes, can't it?'

The voice was darkly male, and came from the shadows behind the TV set. Lisa sat up, startled. 'Who's there?' she called, her voice shaking with terror.

'Don't worry, my dear,' said the voice, 'I won't hurt you.' Lisa reached over and switched on her bedside lamp, the weak bulb casting a dim light across the room. A small, rather malevolent-looking old man was seated on the floor in a corner.

'W-what do you want?' She could feel her heart thumping hard against her chest as she forced herself to breathe steadily.

The old man rose and approached her slowly. Lisa sat back defensively against the headboard of her bed, tucking

9

her legs under her body. 'Don't you come near me, I'll call for the Police!'

The old man smiled evilly and carried on walking towards her, his short body slightly stooped with age. She reached out and grabbed the receiver of her phone and began to dial with difficulty, her hands trembling. Her visitor stopped and raised his hand, clicking his fingers as he did so. The telephone was snatched immediately from her grip as though by some unseen hand, and remained motionless, suspended in mid-air. Lisa stared at the floating object, her terror increasing with every second.

'Relax, my dear,' the old man said, sitting on the end of her bed, 'I said I won't hurt you. I'm here to help you.'

'What do you mean?' said Lisa, her mind racing. 'How did you get in here? I know I locked the door.' She looked again at the telephone receiver as it hung ridiculously in the air. 'How do you do that?'

He smiled and motioned with his hand at the phone, which drifted gently back to its place on the table. 'I can do just about anything I want, Lisa.'

'How do you know my name?'

'I know everything about you, Lisa. That's why I'm here.'

'What do you mean?'

'You are sad and unhappy, dear Lisa. I can help you.'

'How?' Lisa was beginning to stop trembling, soothed by the man's calming tone.

'What would you want, more than anything else in the world, Lisa?'

'I don't know what you mean.'

'You want to be beautiful, like your friend Janet. To have all the men you desire, just like her. Am I not right?'

Lisa pouted miserably. 'What if you are? There's not much I can do, is there?'

He chuckled, a strange, guttural sound coming from the back of his throat. 'I can make you beautiful, Lisa.'

'Don't talk rubbish!' she said, beginning to get angry. She wanted to throw this silly old fool out, not listen to his insults.

'I tell you, I can make you gorgeous. Trust me.'

Lisa looked at the old man's face; his dark eyes twinkled at her in mock amusement. There was something convincing in his manner, and she desperately wanted it to be true that he could do something. After all, he could make a telephone fly!

'How could you do it?' she said, weakly.

The old man smiled and patted her gently on the knee. She suddenly realised that her skirt was still rucked up and that her visitor could see everything she'd got, although she didn't think that even this repulsive old man would be remotely interested in what she had to offer. She covered herself up nevertheless, wishing to maintain some dignity.

'You must tell me what you would like to look like,' he said, 'then I will calm you into a deep sleep. When you awake you will have your dream made true.'

Lisa snorted. 'Oh yes,' she said, in a sarcastic tone, 'you mean you'll put me under hypnosis or something, then probably rape and rob me. I'm not stupid, you know.'

The old man held out both his hands and clicked his fingers again. Immediately, Lisa was naked, spread-eagled on the bed, totally unable to move. 'If I wanted to rape you I would have done so. Now do you believe me?'

Lisa nodded in total submission and he clicked his fingers again, allowing the movement to return to her body. She lay still without bothering to cover herself. Rather than feeling any fear, she felt quaintly ashamed of the way her body looked to this stranger. 'I *would* like to be beautiful, I really would,' she said in a quiet, half-pleading voice.

The old man smiled as kindly as his evil face would allow, and ran his hand gently up her inner thigh. His touch was soothing, calming. Lisa relaxed and closed her eyes, waiting for him to touch her between her legs.

Instead he moved his hand onto her fat stomach, then over her small breasts, examining her in an almost clinical way. 'Let's talk about how you would like to look,' he said, with the tone of a doctor to a nervous patient.

11

'I want to be tall, blonde, with a perfect figure and a beautiful face. I want to be so lovely that no man will be able to resist me. I want them to gasp when they see me walking down the street, like they do for Janet.'

'Very well, Lisa. You shall have your wish. Now, sleep . . . sleep.'

Lisa woke slowly from the deepest sleep she'd ever experienced, as the morning sun shone harshly through the window of her small room. Gradually, as she became more and more conscious, she began to remember the strange events of the previous evening and her eyes snapped open. It had been an incredible dream.

She sat up slowly, swinging her legs out of the bed as she fought desperately to wake fully. She stretched her arms between her legs as she sat up, shaking her head and yawning.

'How do you feel, my dear?' The old man was sitting in his corner again, and looking just as evil despite the bright daylight that filled the room. Lisa jumped with shock. 'No, my lovely, it wasn't a dream. I was here last night. Why don't you take a look in the mirror?'

Lisa did as he asked, turning quickly to the large mirror over her dressing table. She gasped with both surprise and joy at the reflection that met her gaze. Gone was the short, fat, freckly frump; instead she saw a devastatingly beautiful, blonde girl with a face so utterly gorgeous she almost cried; still recognisably her own face, but somehow sculpted as though the old man had taken the original clay that formed her features and moulded it into this perfect vision of loveliness.

Lisa touched her cheeks gently with her fingertips, as though afraid that she would spoil the illusion. She watched in disbelief as the reflected beauty did the same. Her hands trembled as she felt her thick, pouting lips that looked as though they were made to be kissed, and she ran her fingers down to her body. Her breasts, once tiny, were now huge: the size of melons and just as firm with long, dark nipples that jutted slightly upwards, almost arrogantly.

She stood up, feeling the soft touch of her long, blonde hair against her back, which almost reached her bottom. She ran her hands over the narrow waist and flat, firm stomach and onto her slim hips. Turning sideways, she looked with pleasure at the perfect curves of her buttocks and the long, long sensuous legs that completed this picture of sheer perfection in womanhood.

Turning back to face the mirror, she ran her hand over her sex, now only sparsely covered with a down of almost white-blonde hair. The lips were much larger and more prominent than before, and were already damp with the lust she was feeling for herself. She started involuntarily to fondle her clitoris, feeling it grow under her touch to over twice the size she was accustomed to, like a tiny penis.

The old man rushed from his corner and pulled her hand away. 'You won't need to do that anymore, Lisa,' he said, almost revealing panic in his voice. 'Now, is there anything you would like me to change, or improve?'

Lisa looked back at her reflection. At first, she could think of nothing, but then, standing sideways said, 'My breasts . . . could they be just a little bigger? I've always wanted big ones . . . mine were so very small . . .'

'They're already over forty inches, you know.'

Lisa looked at him imploringly. 'Please, just a couple more inches.' The old man shrugged and cupped her breasts with his hands. Lisa shivered as he stroked them, seemingly drawing them out with his touch.

After a moment he stood back and let her examine herself in the mirror. Sure enough, the huge globes had grown even larger, but still as erect and firm as before. Lisa smiled happily, and looked down at her bottom. 'Now, my behind,' she said, giggling with elated pleasure, 'I want it to be bigger; not fat, you understand, I want it to stick out the way it does on some black girls . . . they've always got such incredible bums!'

Once again the stranger touched her, this time running

13

his hands sensuously over her buttocks. As he moulded their shape she felt her sex getting wetter and wetter, and the feelings of lust begin to make her shake. Even watching Janet's escapade the night before hadn't made her feel so randy; she wanted this ugly old man to go so that she could sit in front of the mirror and bring herself off whilst looking at her new, gorgeous reality.

He stepped back, allowing Lisa once again to check over his handiwork. Her bottom now thrust back in an incredibly sexy way, arching to a delicious curve between her legs as though begging for male attention.

'There are a couple of things you must know.' The old man spoke in a serious tone, sitting down on the edge of her bed.

'Here it comes,' she thought to herself, 'I knew there'd be a catch!'

She sat next to her benefactor, totally unashamed of her nudity. Already she was feeling confident, ready for anything he might throw at her.

'Firstly, you must never divulge the secret of your new-found beauty to anybody, no matter what the circumstances.' Lisa shrugged nonchalantly. Nobody would believe such an incredible story anyway.

'Next,' he continued, 'you are now a very beautiful woman. Just occasionally, I may call upon you to use that beauty in some way, to give pleasure to people I may wish to influence.'

He looked into her eyes seriously. 'These will be very rare demands, but I ask you to comply as a sort of payment for what I have done for you. I assure you that you will never be asked to do anything unpleasant. Do you agree?'

Lisa nodded, against her better judgement. She knew she might be letting herself in for something unusual, or even criminal, but she was so happy with her new looks that she would have agreed to anything.

'Two more things,' the old man said, standing, 'you must never, I repeat *never* masturbate. You may only

14

receive sexual relief from another person, although it may be of either sex. Nor must you *ever* refuse the advances of any person, provided they do not wish you harm. If you break either of these rules you will return to your original, plain state. Do you agree?'

'Yes, I agree,' said Lisa, 'but why?'

'Never mind. You will not find it hard to accept these conditions, anyway. You will be insatiable; at first you will want and will experience all forms of sex, unable to satisfy your lust completely. Soon, this urgency will wear off, but you will still need sex at least daily. You will also discover that you have a special talent, one sexual technique or desire that you will be able to perfect, whilst never losing the enjoyment of all the many variations of pleasure.'

'Talent?'

'I have decided that oral sex will be your gift. You will quickly develop the skills to please both men and women with your mouth and tongue, so much so that they will beg you for more. Does this suit you?'

Lisa nodded absently, glancing again at her wonderful reflection in the mirror. He could have demanded anything of her, so entranced was she with her new beauty.

'That brings me to the final condition. You are a virgin; I know because I checked whilst you were asleep. I am to take your virginity.'

Lisa cringed, then smiled. The man was quite disgusting to look at but, incredibly, she didn't feel in any way repulsed. She *wanted* this scruffy old man to take her, to screw her rigid. She needed sex so badly, she would have had it with anybody and, after all, she did owe him an awful lot.

She smiled again weakly and lay back on her bed with her legs wide open, watching nervously as he started to remove his tatty clothing. He threw his jacket to one side, quickly followed by his shirt, revealing an extremely hairy upper body. He tore his boots off without undoing the laces, obviously desperate to sate his lust on this lovely youngster, then pulled down his baggy trousers and whatever underwear he wore in one movement, so that he now stood before her, naked but for his socks.

Lisa gasped. His penis was fully erect, curving upwards from between his hairy legs; it was far longer and thicker than anything she'd ever seen or imagined. 'Oh, my God, it's far too big!' she cried, meaning every word. It was easily a foot in length, and as thick as her forearm.

The old man took her hand and made her hold his stiff phallus, her fingers unable to meet around its firm girth. 'You'll be glad of its size when I have taken you,' he said. 'I am going to teach you how to fuck, how to please a man, so that you will truly be one of my Angels. Now, lick me!'

Lisa leant her head forward, wondering what he meant by his 'Angels', her small hand still holding onto his stiff stalk, her mouth anxious to taste a man for the first time. Her long hair fell forward, brushing against his thighs as she pressed her thick lips against the huge, bulbous end. She kissed it wetly, letting one hand begin to rub his stem up and down almost automatically, cupping his large balls with the other. She drew her face back and looked closely at the hard erection, knowing that it would soon be inside her and, despite its incredible size, she knew that she wanted it badly.

She felt the stem throb against the palm of her hand and watched, fascinated as a small blob of white pre-come oozed from the large slit set in the angry, purple head. She leant forward and pushed her tongue into the slimy fluid, running it over her upper lip, tasting sperm for the first time in her life. She found the slightly salty taste pleasant, the texture sensuous.

Lisa opened her mouth as wide as she could and took his hardness between her pouting lips, feeling it press firmly against her tongue. Drawing her cheeks in and out, she sucked on the monster, forcing saliva over it to ease its movement as he involuntarily started to move it in and out of her lovely mouth.

Lisa pulled her head back, letting the thick end of his tool leave the warm wetness of her mouth. A trail of spit joined her lips to the object of her lust, like the strand of a spider's web covered in dew. She pushed out her tongue and licked along the side of his length, tracing a line down one side to his balls, then back up the other side to the tip again, lapping greedily at the huge stalk. Somehow, she knew exactly what to do and how to please this man with her mouth; it was as though she was receiving silent instructions. The old man had kept his promise; this was her gift.

He lay back on the bed, and Lisa held his sex vertically as she now squatted over his face. Lying on top of his body, she knew that he would be staring directly between her legs, whilst she continued to gaze in adoration at his superb length. She took it into her mouth again, trying to swallow more of his hugeness. She felt his hands groping obscenely at her buttocks, his fingertips probing her virgin lips roughly.

He dug his fingernails into her tender flesh and pulled her bottom down towards his face, pressing his mouth firmly against her sopping wetness. She squealed as his expert tongue worked on her, licking furiously at the puffy lips and erect clitoris.

Lisa rubbed his stiff cock heavily with both hands. As he sucked greedily at her sex, she felt her first ever orgasm with a man building up within her loins. Her vision blurred and her skin seemed to become tender as, with a loud cry, she came, grinding her bottom into his face. As he continued to lap at her, she licked and kissed his hardness, the ecstatic sensations tearing through her young body.

It was over so quickly, but it had been so very good.

After a moment's recovery she climbed off him, kneeling by the side of his small, hairy body, still clutching his tremendous erection in her tiny hand.

'Sit on it.'

His tone was insistent . . . this was it, her virginity was about to be lost.

Without a word the lust-crazed teenager positioned herself over his lower body, facing him without seeing his ugliness. She squatted on her heels as he pointed his mighty phallus at her waiting hole. She lowered herself down slowly, until she felt the spongy tip touching her aching sex-lips. She paused a moment, then lowered herself a little more, letting about an inch or so inside her. She could feel the hard intruder touching the thin tissue of her maidenhead and she worried that it may hurt. She knew, however, that there was no going back now.

Before she could do anything more, he suddenly thrust upwards, driving over half of his immense length into her eager warmth. She shouted out with the sharp pain, but quickly relaxed as her body accepted his invasion. She slowly began to move her hips up and down, letting more and more of him enter her tight, wet pussy.

He let her do all the movements; obviously content to watch as this devastatingly gorgeous girl sated herself on him, her rhythm becoming faster and faster as she got used to his size. Soon she was taking every inch with long, easy strokes, teasing him out, almost to the very tip, them ramming her bottom down hard on his pelvis; his length disappeared easily within the heavenly wetness of her hot, young body.

'You're a natural, my dear,' he said, breathing heavily, 'a natural.'

She looked at herself in the mirror, unconcerned that her sex-partner was repulsive, delighting in the sight of her newly acquired loveliness being impaled in such an erotic way. She raised her bottom in the air so that just the tip of his penis was inside her, and revelled in the sight of the immense length of the shaft between them. Then she sat down again slowly, once again happily accommodating the superb stalk.

The old man gripped her thighs and raised her, pulling out of her wet sheath, and lay her on her side, so that she faced away from him and towards the mirror. Holding the ankle of her upper leg he raised it into the air, pushing himself back into her pussy from behind, until his groin pressed against her soft bum. He started to take charge now, his thrusting steady and controlled, the position allowing maximum contact between his stiffness and her erect clitoris. She could now see her entire body reflected in the mirror, and watch herself being impaled in every detail: his wonderful phallus, covered in the wetness of her juices, was slithering in and out of her body like a big, pink eel; his gnarled hands were pawing roughly at her massive breasts.

She matched his movements with her own, pushing back her lovely bottom against his crotch as he shafted her relentlessly, feeling her second orgasm building up inside her. He must have sensed what was happening to her because his pumping became more urgent, his full length banging in and out of her with each hard thrust. She arched her back and groaned loudly as the climax tore through her, and to her joy felt him throbbing within her as he pumped his sperm deep into her young body.

Her climax seemed to go on for ages, the ecstasy of the moment taking her higher than any drug could have done. He was gripping her breasts hard, pinching the nipples and holding every inch of himself inside her as his final throbs sent the last of his warm juices into her womb.

Suddenly she shouted out again as, incredibly, a second wave of pleasure hit her, making her cry out with the sheer exhilaration of the sensation of a multiple orgasm. She pressed her backside hard against him, forcing him onto his back and lying on top of his puny body, pinning him down until the feelings within her body subsided.

His quickly softening penis slid from her and almost immediately she began to feel the results of his lust begin to slip from her. She climbed quickly from her ancient lover and scurried to the bathroom.

As she cleaned herself up, she looked into the mirror of the medicine cabinet and smiled happily at the beautiful, if flushed, face that stared back at her. 'Well, Lisa,' she thought, 'you've finally lost your cherry . . . and, by God you've got a lot to catch up on!'

Still naked, she returned into her sitting room. The old

man was gone; the only proof of the event being the ruffled blankets on the bed, and the slight stain of virgin's blood on the sheet. She felt a slight twinge between her legs as she remembered the sharp pain she had felt when he first entered her innocent body, and then how quickly it had subsided as the lust within her had taken over and allowed her to accommodate his huge phallus.

Already, she was feeling randy again, needing sex. Her hand drifted towards the tender mound between her legs, until she recalled the old man's instructions: no masturbation, on pain of losing her newly acquired beauty.

Reluctantly, she pulled her hand away and decided to dress. It was then that it occurred to her that her old clothes hadn't a chance of fitting her new, sensational body. She was now five foot eight, over seven inches taller than her old self, and her figure couldn't be compared in any way.

Lisa opened the sliding door to her large wardrobe and gasped as she looked inside. Gone were the smock-like, bulge-hiding floral dresses and chunky pullovers it had been her curse to wear in the past. In their places were rows and rows of fine, designer clothes in sensuous materials, thin cottons, silks and leathers. She ran her hands over the expensive items, savouring the touch of garment after garment. Pulling a small, white dress from the rail, she held it against her naked body and looked into the wardrobe mirror. The thin silk was almost completely see-through. As she examined other items of clothing, she realised that, apart from being of very high quality, they were all extremely sexy, both revealing and erotic.

Like an excited child, Lisa opened her underwear drawer expectantly. To her delight her heavy, white pants and bra sets had been replaced by all manner of flimsy garments: tiny panties, stockings, suspenders and teddies. In another drawer she found an array of basques and shiny PVC and leather underwear and, in another, various types of sex-toys: dildos, vibrators and all manner of erotic attachments.

She ran her hand lovingly over one of the dildos; a long, black phallus as big as the real one she'd accommodated just moments before. She wanted to grab it and ram it deep inside her soaking pussy to relieve the frustration that was becoming unbearable, but knew that she couldn't, that it would be against the rules. She shut the drawer quickly, and closed the wardrobe doors.

She looked again at the face reflected in the dressing-table mirror. Sheer sexuality seemed to ooze out of every pore, and her eyes shone with lust. Lisa looked closer at her eyes realising that, apart from her voice, this was the one part of her that hadn't changed in any way. Curiously, she felt quite pleased; the old man had actually not been able to improve on part of her, even if it was only her eyes.

The doorbell rang. Lisa grabbed hold of a small, diaphanous nightie that had miraculously appeared at the foot of her bed and slipped it over her nakedness. 'Who is it?' she called through the locked door.

'It's Jim, the caretaker,' said a familiar voice, 'I've come to tell you about the lift.'

Lisa opened the door wide. Jim looked casually at her, then did a quick double-take. 'Oh, sorry,' he said, his eyes darting as he feasted on the lovely girl before him, 'I was expecting the other girl.'

'I'm her cousin,' Lisa said, surprised at her own quickness of thought, 'she's gone abroad for a while.'

'Oh, right.' Jim was staring at her breasts, gulping visibly. Totally unused to having this type of effect on a man, Lisa was loving every minute of his attentions.

'Do you want to come in?' she said brazenly, opening the door wider and stepping to one side. He walked into the room almost zombie-like and sat on the edge of the bed, without taking his eyes off her for a moment. As she followed him she glanced again at the mirror and saw that the nightie was virtually useless as far as preserving her modesty was concerned; the sheer fabric revealed every contour of her superb body. Even the thin wisps of blonde hair between her legs could clearly be seen, as the direction of his gaze soon confirmed. She smiled and sat next to him on the bed, resting a hand softly on his thigh.

'Would you like a drink, or something?' she said, her face inches away from his.

'Yes, er I mean, no,' he stuttered, 'I just came to tell you that the lift might be out of order occasionally today.'

'You don't have to rush off, do you?' she said, squeezing his leg, 'I could do with a little company.' She looked straight into his eyes and pouted her lips gently. He was a handsome chap, possibly in his late twenties, square-jawed with short, fair hair. He wore a white, one-piece overall which buttoned up the front, although it was open almost to his waist, revealing the smooth, muscular and hairless chest of a man who obviously worked out regularly. Lisa had often lusted after him when she'd seen him working around the apartment block, but without a hope of ever getting anywhere with him. Now it was going to be different.

'I'll be OK for a little while, but then I really have to get on with my work.'

Lisa smiled and put her arm around his strong shoulders, kissing him lightly on the cheek. He turned and looked into her eyes again, and their lips met. They kissed gently at first, then she forced her tongue into his mouth and he responded immediately, their lips parting as their tongues playfully darted around each other.

Lisa ran her hand up his thigh and cupped his genitals, squeezing them quite hard. That was the only signal he needed. He started to tear at the buttons of his overall as she slipped the nightie over her head and lay back on her bed. Jim stood up and stepped out of his denim work-clothes, pulling off his boots and socks at the same time. Now naked, he approached her, his erection jutting firmly out in front of him, waving about obscenely as he moved. Lisa opened her legs wide, parting her wet sex-lips with the fingertips of both hands. 'Fuck me,' she said, 'just fuck me.'

22

There was no finesse in the way that Jim almost leapt on the gorgeous teenager who was offering herself to him; no foreplay; and that was just how she wanted it. His thick penis found its target immediately, sliding in to the hilt with one easy thrust. Lisa groaned with the pleasure of it, her hands grasping at his muscular buttocks, her nails digging into the hard flesh. 'That's it, Jim,' she sobbed, 'that's just what I want; really give it to me hard!'

'Christ, you're a wild one!' he said, pumping heavily in and out of her receptive body. Lisa responded by thrusting her hips furiously back at his, taking his full length each time, mewing ecstatically with each thrust. Her finger found his tight anus as she wriggled it inside, forcing it in and out in time with the screwing she was getting. 'Oh baby, yeh!' he cried, his rhythm increasing wildly as he took both of them towards orgasm.

'That's it . . . more . . . harder . . . that's it!' shouted Lisa, as she felt herself coming. 'That's it . . . more, give me all you've got!'

Her orgasm ripped through her body like a tornado, tearing her senses apart, sending her mind into an oblivion of sheer pleasure. Jim roared as he climaxed, the rate of his pumping increasing dramatically as he shot his sperm deep into Lisa's wriggling form. With each throb of his hardness he groaned loudly, until gradually his pleasure subsided and he fell heavily onto the gorgeous girl beneath him.

After a short while he stood up and dressed, albeit rather shakily. 'I'd better get back to work now,' he said, smiling weakly.

'Bye, Jim,' said Lisa, waving from her reclining position on the bed. She watched him leave, then hurried to the bathroom to clean herself up yet again.

She stood and looked at her reflection in the long mirror next to the bath, savouring the sight of the overwhelmingly beautiful creature that met her gaze: her ruffled hair; her mountainous breasts bearing slight red marks where her two lovers had pawed at her; her pussy lips large and wide open, glistening with her lust.

'If it's gonna be like this every day,' she thought, 'I'm gonna have one hell of a time!'

Chapter Two

Janet walked into the block of flats where her friend lived, with some trepidation. She felt really bad about the way she had treated Lisa the previous night, but knew she simply couldn't help herself. John and Peter had been absolutely gorgeous, and certainly knew how to give a girl a good time in bed. The three of them had spent the whole night together, sating their lust in as many varied ways as their collective imaginations allowed. They'd drifted off into sleep as the first light of dawn approached, and Janet had woken a couple of hours later to find John pumping into her yet again whilst Peter lay exhausted on the floor.

After another hour-long bout of sex she managed to get rid of her two lovers, and decided to call on Lisa to apologise. In a way, she desperately wished that she could get her friend to do something about herself, to slim down at least; but then she thought that, in all honesty, it wouldn't make much difference.

She did know another way, but also knew that she could never tell her, even if she thought that she might be believed . . .

Janet pressed the call button of the lift and waited. She watched the indicators as the elevator moved with agonising slowness to the ground floor, and the heavy doors groaned as they reluctantly opened. She stepped into the brightly-lit area and pressed the button to Lisa's floor. The lift shuddered into motion, moved upwards about three or four feet, then stopped with a hydraulic sigh.

Janet immediately started to perspire, despite the fact

that, as usual, she was wearing very little. A skin-tight, black lycra dress, cut just below her crotch was all that covered her modesty. Black, high-heeled shoes completed the outfit. Nevertheless, she felt the heat of terror, trapped as she was inside this coffin-like room. She pressed all the buttons in a panic, but the lift refused to budge.

She noticed a button on the other wall marked 'ALARM' and, breathing a sigh of relief, pressed it. There was no sound, no reassuring bell or buzzer. Janet began to shake, her fears becoming irrational. She shouted out, 'Help, help!' banging her fists against the metallic sides of the enclosure, but there was no response. It was mid-morning and most of the occupants of the flats would be at work; it was unlikely that anybody would discover her plight until lunchtime at best.

It was her greatest fear, to be trapped like this; the stuff of nightmares. She began to think that it was some sort of retribution, a punishment for the sinful way she conducted her life, at least where sex was concerned.

Just as she was thinking of declaring a solemn, if unlikely oath of celibacy there was a loud noise from above her head. She looked up and saw that a small aperture in the roof of the lift was being opened from above and realised that help was at hand.

The metal trap-door was opened wide and the smiling, distinctly handsome face of Jim, the block caretaker, peeped through like a ray of sunshine on a miserable day.

'Hi,' he said, cheerily, 'you OK?'

'No, I'm not,' said Janet, her angry tone concealing her trembling, 'what's wrong with this thing?'

'I've been trying to fix it all morning, no good though. I've had to call for the lift company ... they should be along in about an hour.'

'An hour!' exclaimed Janet. 'Can't you get me out?'

'I could if you could climb up the shaft, but I wouldn't recommend it; I nearly killed myself coming down to see to you!' He swung his legs into the narrow opening and gradually lowered himself down into the lift. Janet watched with great interest as she noticed the way his white boiler-suit became pulled tight under his crotch, the outline of his genitals clearly visible. She wanted to reach out and stroke them, her fears quickly forgotten.

Jim dropped the last couple of feet onto the carpeted floor, his knees buckling slightly as he lost his balance, causing him to grab hold of Janet round the waist to steady himself. She held his strong arms as he steadied himself and didn't mind at all that he didn't let go; if anything, he held her slim waist even tighter.

'I'll keep you company, if you like,' he said, smiling broadly, his face inches away from hers.

'How are we going to pass away the time?' said Janet, in a suggestive tone, her tongue running over her upper lip invitingly.

'Oh, I'm sure we'll think of something,' he said, pulling her slim body against his so she could feel his hardening sex against her mound. The rough material of his denim suit and her thin dress were now all that separated them. He moved his face towards hers and she closed her eyes and parted her lips to receive his kiss. As their mouths touched her tongue darted forward, meeting with his as she wrapped her arms around his broad shoulders. She moved her hips from side to side as they kissed, rubbing her crotch against his large bulge, letting him know in no uncertain terms that she wanted sex.

Jim ran his big hands down to her bottom, fondling the small, firm globes roughly, causing her to press her body even harder against his. He caught the hem of her short dress with his fingers and pulled it up to her waist. Returning his hands to her now naked bum, he ran the tips of his fingers between her soft buttocks, pushing underneath them to feel the wetness of her aching pussy.

'We've something in common,' he said, drawing his face from the passion of her wet kisses, 'neither of us wear knickers.'

Janet started to unbutton his overall. 'Ooh, that's nice,' she said, her voice husky with lust, 'let's have a look.' She undid enough buttons on his overall to allow him to shake the garment free, watching him pull it off his feet as she deftly removed her dress over her head.

She mewed quietly with pleasure as she viewed Jim's muscular, smooth physique; his only body hair was that between his legs from which his thick erection jutted angrily, the end weeping with lust for this beautiful, horny young girl.

His eyes leered over her nakedness in the same way, taking in the wonderful sight of the slim, erotic shape of the girl he was about to have, his manhood throbbing involuntarily in expectation.

Janet knelt at his feet, took his stiffness in her small grasp and began to rub it up and down quickly. 'Steady, love,' he said, biting his lip, 'you'll have me coming if you keep that up!'

Janet slowed her pumping and kissed the bulbous end lightly. 'Ooh, that'll never do; not until I've had you inside me.'

She parted her lips and took it into her mouth, expertly moving her position until she swallowed the full length. She drew her mouth back, drawing in her cheeks so that every inch of his hardness was touched until she held just the tip between her lips. She then took the whole lot back into her mouth, making gulping motions with the back of her throat as she sucked him down.

After a few minutes of this Jim pulled her head from his sex and, holding her tenderly under the arms, raised her from her knees until they were again face to face. Janet smiled knowingly, raising her leg high so that it slid around his waist, her heel resting against his firm buttocks. She caught hold of him around his neck with both of her arms and, using his body as leverage, raised her other leg to the same position. Jim caught hold of her bum with one hand to give her extra support whilst he took hold of his penis and aimed it at her wide-open sex.

As soon as she felt the thick end of his stalk touch her between the legs she lowered herself onto him, taking the hard length into her tight, aching sheath. She nibbled at his neck and started to pump her body vigorously up and down on the welcome invader, her erect nipples rubbing sensuously against his hairless chest.

Jim now gripped her buttocks with both hands, pulling at them roughly as he matched her thrusting movements with his own. 'Oh, baby, this is definitely my lucky day!' he said through gritted teeth as he humped his second lovely conquest of the morning. Janet, not knowing of Lisa's session with Jim earlier, took the words as a compliment to her alone and began to increase the rhythm of her downward thrusts as she felt her orgasm building up inside her.

'Yes, baby, yeh, give it to me!' Jim shouted as he hammered back into her, pushing her against the cold metal wall of their temporary prison.

Janet was almost delirious with lust now. 'Fuck me, oh fuck me with your beautiful cock!' she yelled. 'Fill me up, fill me up!'

Suddenly, the lift shuddered into motion, heading upwards. 'Oh, shit!' exclaimed Jim. 'We must've shaken it loose.'

'Oh, please don't stop,' begged Janet, 'I'm coming, I'm coming!'

The lift carried on its relentless journey as the rutting couple banged away at each other, desperate to climax before it reached its destination. Janet tensed her body and came explosively, the sensation sending searing, electrical pulses down her legs as she ground her soaking sex against her lover. With a cry he let go and she felt the familiar throbbing as he pumped his sperm deep into her body, the thumping sending spasms of pleasure through her entire frame.

Almost immediately the lift stopped and the doors juddered open. Two elderly ladies stood in the hallway, their mouths open in shock at the sight of the naked couple joined together at the lower abdomen in post-coital bliss. Janet grinned sheepishly at the women, lowering her feet to the floor. The two lovers untwined themselves and hurriedly tried to dress, although Jim couldn't fasten the buttons of his overall due to his shaking hands.

Janet managed to pull her tight dress over her body and stepped out of the lift, smiling sweetly at the old ladies as they walked past her with disapproving looks on their faces. Jim remained in the lift, trying in vain to push his still half erect penis within the denim, whilst the two women pretended to ignore him.

As the doors to the lift closed, however, Janet swore she saw one of the old dears craftily squeeze Jim's thick, wet dick . . .

Janet trembled as she rang Lisa's doorbell. She was still shaking from the screwing she'd just experienced, but the reason for her visit, the need to apologise to her friend, was now foremost in her thoughts.

'Who is it?' Lisa's voice sounded much more cheerful than usual, coming from behind the locked door.

'It's Janet. I thought I'd better call and see you.'

She heard the sound of the door being unbolted. 'I hoped you would,' said Lisa, opening the door slowly, 'I really did.'

Janet made to walk into the room, then stopped dead in her tracks. Instead of her friend she found herself facing probably the loveliest girl she had ever seen; a tall, gorgeous blonde wearing skin-tight jeans and a flimsy T shirt, the latter garment being forced upwards obscenely by two of the biggest breasts she could have imagined, the long, thick nipples clearly outlined through the thin cotton.

'Oh, I'm sorry, I thought . . .' stumbled Janet, confused, 'where's Lisa?'

Even as she spoke the words, she knew. This *was* Lisa, her expression still shy and innocent, but looking so very different.

Her friend stood and smiled, her eyes sparkling with joy. Janet looked into her face, then the eyes, to quell any uncertainty. 'Lisa?' she said, staring into her face incredulously.

'Hello, Janet,' Lisa said, 'I've got something to tell you.' She beckoned for her to come in, and closed the door. Janet sat on the edge of the bed, transfixed by the sight of the beautiful woman before her. Lisa perched on a small dining chair, apparently unable to stop smiling. 'I don't know where to begin,' she said.

'You've met the old man, haven't you?' Janet knew she could speak the truth now, the rules no longer applied. Lisa looked astounded.

'You know about him? How?'

'How d'you think?'

'But you've always been so pretty. Why did you need him to come to you?'

Janet shrugged. 'Vanity, I suppose. You remember when I left school, and I went abroad with my parents? Well, I overdid it on continental food and wine, and got rather fat and incredibly spotty in a very short time; then I got depressed and virtually suicidal . . . anyway, that's when he appeared.'

'So he gave you your looks back?'

'More than that,' Janet was beginning to relax, having got over her original shock, 'he moulded my body as I wanted it, you know, slim and lithe, like those models in magazines.'

'I got him to make me look as I had always dreamed of being,' said Lisa, as she stood up, proudly displaying her superb body to her friend.

'He's done a good job. Mind you, he went a bit over the top with your tits, don't you think?'

'That was my fault. I've always wanted huge boobs.'

'And now you've certainly got 'em.' Janet stood up in front of Lisa and ran her hands gently over the mountainous curves of her firm breasts. Lisa shivered slightly under her sensuous touch, feeling her nipples becoming erect. 'Let me see you naked.'

Her friend obeyed, as though in a trance. She pulled her T-shirt over her head, smiling happily as Janet drew in her breath at the sight of her massive, unfettered breasts. Lisa

31

undid the top of her jeans, drawing the zip down carefully so as not to catch her pubic hair in its vicious teeth and peeled the stretch material from her legs.

Janet stripped and walked around her friend as she stood naked for her inspection. She casually ran her hands again over the large breasts, squeezing each hard nipple in turn, and licking her lips. She was still wet from her earlier screw, but she was getting randy again, wanting to possess this gorgeous, innocent teenager in ways she knew Lisa couldn't have experienced before.

'You really are lovely,' she said, running one hand gently across Lisa's firm, flat stomach and the other over her large, perfectly curved bottom.

'Am I, am I really?' said Lisa, in a little girl voice, the mock cuteness hardly matching her brazen nakedness.

'Yes, oh yes, and so *very* sexy!' Janet could feel her pussy becoming soaked, the plump lips thickening and opening as her lust took over her body. She felt Jim's sperm gradually oozing from her slit onto her thigh. Lisa noticed it too.

'Jesus, it sure doesn't take you long to get wet! No wonder you're always at it!'

Janet laughed, running her fingers through the juice and putting them to her mouth. 'It's not all me,' she said, licking her fingers, 'I had a quickie with your caretaker in the lift on the way up.'

Lisa smirked. 'Hmmm, you too, eh?'

Janet noticed her blush and smiled, knowingly. 'I see,' she said, 'he's had you, has he?'

Lisa nodded, proudly. 'Yes, this morning. It was great.'

'Not bad,' said Janet, with the tone of a highly experienced woman, 'what did you think of the old man?'

'Well, it's weird, you know. I mean, he's revolting to look at but I couldn't resist him.'

'He's got a great dick, hasn't he?'

'I'll say . . . of course, I suppose you've had him as well.'

'We all have, it's part of the contract.'

'All?'

'Oh, there are lots more like us,' said Janet, slipping her arms around her friend's waist and pressing their bodies together. 'I'll tell you more about them later.'

'What d'you mean, later?'

Janet kissed her friend lightly on the mouth. 'After we've had some fun. Remember, you're not allowed to resist anybody.' She kissed her again, letting her tongue play against the soft, pouting lips, sensing them begin to yield under the wet pressure.

'I don't want to resist you,' said Lisa, gently, 'I've always wanted you to make love to me.'

At first she stood still, then, as though a sudden wave of lust had hit her, she relaxed and wrapped her arms around Janet's shoulders, opening her mouth to admit her friend's darting tongue. Janet pushed hard against her and they fell heavily onto the bed, rolling over and over each other, giggling and kissing deeply, their hands roaming across firm young flesh, searching, discovering new delights. Lisa lay on her back and Janet spread-eagled herself on top of her, rubbing their soaking pussies against each other. She felt Lisa run her hands over her bottom, one finger finding her tight anus, still tender from the previous night's assault. The probing fingertip managed to gain admittance to the often invaded sphincter, causing her to grind herself even harder against the soft wetness beneath her.

'Jesus, that's nice,' exclaimed Janet. 'I love things up my bum.'

'I know you do,' laughed Lisa, 'I watched you last night.'

'I had a feeling you were watching us. You'll be doing things like that yourself soon,' said Janet, her tongue tracing its way over her friend's throat, between her breasts, heading ever downward to where Lisa desperately wanted it to go.

She licked playfully around her navel, then down, down to the edge of the wispy blonde hair between her legs, teasing her unmercifully. Lisa's hips started to buck and raise themselves from the bed, eager to have Janet's fluttering tongue make contact with her sex. 'Lick it, please lick it!' she groaned, forcing the other girl's head down with her hands. Janet chuckled and moved her body completely around, straddling her legs across Lisa's head. She lowered herself towards her friend's mouth, feeling her tongue begin to lap at her wet slit at precisely the same time as the tip of her own tongue found Lisa's large, erect clitoris. She drew the hard bud into her mouth, chewing on it gently with her lips, sucking it into her mouth and licking the end with her fluttering tongue.

Lisa copied her actions, anxious to please her loving teacher. The two girls lapped at each other for ages, soaking their faces with their juices, their hair wet with a mixture of sweat and sex-fluids.

Lisa came first, screaming out loud as she buried her face in the warmth of her friend's wetness, licking furiously in an apparent effort to bring Janet off with her. It took just a few seconds until both girls were writhing about on the bed, transported by the sheer pleasure and ecstasy they were experiencing, their faces buried in the soaked areas of their lust.

The friends who had now become lovers lay on their backs amidst the tangle of bedclothes, staring at the ceiling as they recovered from their efforts of the past, frantic moments. Outside, the constant hum of traffic and the occasional sound of a barking dog seemed to soothe them as they breathed deeply, exhausted, slowly coming down to earth.

'You were going to tell me about the others,' said Lisa, wearily.

'Oh yes, so I was,' said Janet, sitting up and wrapping a blanket around her shoulders. She paused a moment, her eyes glazing over, then flopped back down again on the bed. 'God, that was good!'

'Never mind that,' Lisa said, impatiently, 'what about the others?'

'There's five of us in our group; six if you join, which

I'm sure you will. We've all done the business with the old man and, like you the others are all gorgeous in different ways. The other thing we have in common is that we're all nymphomaniacs.'

'Nymphomaniacs? Are you sure?'

'That's the main catch with this arrangement, we can never get enough. Not that we're complaining; we're not like real nymphos, they can't have orgasms: we come easily and we love it. But you must have noticed that you are always randy?'

'God, you can say that again,' said Lisa, 'I've just come like mad, but I feel randy to do it all again; *and* I've been fucked twice this morning as well!'

'There you are then,' Janet said, stretching her arms above her head, 'you'll have no trouble fulfilling the condition about not refusing anybody, but it's an absolute bastard that you can't masturbate. What's your speciality, by the way?'

'Speciality?' Lisa propped herself up on one arm, stroking her lover's hair fondly.

'The old man gives us all an individual need or technique, so that we're all experts in different ways of sex.'

'Oh yes, I'm with you now,' said Lisa, 'he told me I'd be good at oral sex.'

Janet stroked herself between her legs suggestively. 'Well, you're certainly learning quickly!' Lisa laughed, kissing her friend on the forehead.

'What about you,' she said, 'what's your speciality?'

Janet smiled and turned over onto her hands and knees, sticking her lovely bottom out into the air. 'What do *you* think it is?'

'Your bum?'

'Got it in one,' said Janet, lying down again and taking Lisa in her arms. 'I adore anal sex; anything to do with bottoms. Loads of men like it, too. Not that I'm averse to anything else, of course.'

'Of course,' said Lisa, with amused sarcasm. 'How did you meet the others?'

'Well, after my session with the old man I went mad, screwing just about every bloke I could find and not caring who knew. My parents found out, of course, and they got this friend of theirs called Frank to chaperone me whenever they weren't around, to make sure I kept my knickers on.

'Needless to say, Frank fucked me on the first night, and every night for the rest of the time we were abroad. It turned out that he works for the old man, as a sort of agent, looking for girls like us who might need his unusual services.

'When we came back to England I met up again with Frank and he introduced me to the others. The group meets up about once a month, in various locations. Frank makes all the arrangements, and we always have a fucking good time.'

Lisa smiled at the thought of joining in the fun, but then her face took on a look of concern. 'What about these special jobs the old man said he would have for me? What does that mean?'

'Every now and then Frank will contact one or more of us to go and use our special talents on some businessman or politician, you know, that sort of thing.'

'You mean as a prostitute?'

'No, because we never accept any payment. No, it's fun, some of these guys are really inventive, and it's another way to get laid. I promise you, you'll be glad of it.'

'I must admit I could do with a good seeing to right now!'

Janet smiled and sat up, running her fingers through her short brown hair to tidy it up a bit. She looked lovingly at her friend, who still lay naked on the bed, her legs wide open, her wet sex-lips glinting in the strong sunlight. 'Tell you what,' she said, mischievously, 'you can help me out with a little job I've got on tonight.'

'Job?' said Lisa, turning over to lie on her stomach.

'Frank has asked me to deflower the son of a French politician. Apparently the lad is rather shy, unusual for a

36

Frenchman, and it's a present for his sixteenth birthday from his loving dad!'

Lisa grinned and swung her legs out of the bed. 'Oh, why the hell not,' she said, 'it's like an itch I can't scratch!'

Janet laughed and slapped the other girl's firm buttocks hard with the palm of her hand. 'I gotta go,' she said, grabbing her clothes and hurrying into the bathroom.

Lisa watched her go, still feeling somewhat bemused. Even the slap on the backside had given her a sort of sexual buzz.

Just what had the old man done to her?

The two girls arrived at the plush, seafront hotel in Brighton, the agreed venue for that afternoon's entertainment. Frank had made all the arrangements, although the receptionist was surprised to greet two girls instead of the one he had been led to expect. Nevertheless, showing the diplomacy and tact for which experienced hotel staff are renowned, he escorted them to a large suite of rooms on the first floor, and bade them wait for their young visitor.

Janet looked at her friend in admiration. The old man had certainly done a good job on her, that was for sure. Whilst still just recognisable as her friend of many years, her beauty was flawless, her body superbly sexual. Lisa was wearing a simple pair of tight, white jeans, the smoothness of which clearly indicated her lack of panties, and a black, basque-style top which did little to conceal her massive breasts which threatened to spill over their restraining cups at any moment. Even dressed so simply, she oozed eroticism and availability, whilst somehow maintaining an aura of youthful innocence.

Janet had chosen to dress more provocatively, selecting a black, lycra top which moulded itself over her apple-sized breasts, the long nipples clearly visible through the diaphanous material, and a short, black-leather skirt. The outfit was complemented by black stockings, suspender belt and high-heeled shoes. Due to the extreme shortness of the skirt, she'd decided, unusually, to wear panties and had selected a tiny pair, also in soft leather. The feeling of the cool material against her sex aroused her more and more with every movement she made.

Lisa was pacing around the room, obviously nervous. Janet smiled to herself, remembering the first time she had accommodated one of Frank's clients, and knowing how her friend must be feeling.

'Christ, I'm nervous!' said Lisa, her voice trembling slightly.

'I'm sure we'll have a great time,' said Janet, 'are you feeling randy?'

Lisa sighed loudly. 'What do *you* think!' I can't imagine a sixteen-year-old virgin boy is going to do much to satisfy me, either!'

'Don't worry, I'll sort you out if he leaves you high and dry.'

Lisa was still nervously impatient. 'Where is he? He'd better show up!'

'He should be here in a minute.'

Almost on cue, there came a faint knocking at the door. Janet walked over and opened it, revealing the slight figure of a dark, but fresh-faced young man, clearly the birthday boy.

'Allo, I am Simon Dubois,' he said, his accent subtle, almost unnoticeable, but very refined. 'My father told me to come to this room; he said you would have my birthday present for me.'

Janet took the young man by the hand and led him into the room, closing the door behind them. 'Come in, Simon,' she said, seductively, 'we *are* your birthday present!'

Simon looked both shocked and incredulous for a moment, then broke into a broad grin. 'I knew my father would do something like this! But two! He only gave my brother one girl on his sixteenth birthday. I am honoured!'

Drinks were poured and consumed, more to relax their guest than to calm their own nerves. Janet noticed that Lisa kept touching Simon lightly on the arm or leg as they chatted, clearly keen to get on with the business in hand.

She knew exactly how her poor friend must be feeling, remembering how she herself had behaved during those first few months after she had made the pact with the old man: the scores of lovers, each one only serving to increase her sexual needs.

Once the ice had been broken, the girls wasted no time. Lisa unfastened the narrow tie from Simon's neck, pulling it from his collar. Janet took off his shoes and socks, whilst the boy who was about to become a man just stood there, unsure what to do. Lisa now slowly unbuttoned his crisp, white shirt, revealing a completely hairless chest. He at last took the initiative and unfastened his cuffs, allowing Lisa to remove the shirt completely. Janet unbuckled his belt and unzipped his smart, grey trousers, before releasing the top button, allowing them to fall to his ankles. All he now wore was a pair of old-fashioned white briefs, bulging noticeably with his excitement. Lisa joined her friend kneeling at the front of the youngster, and together they took hold of the elastic waistband of his pants and gradually eased them down.

The girls smiled as his hardness sprang into view. He was bigger than either of them had supposed; a good seven inches which, against the slimness of his young body, looked vaguely out of proportion. The end glistened with pre-come ... he was obviously in a hell of a state and wasn't going to last long. Janet took hold of the incredibly hard stem and rubbed him slowly. 'That's a nice big one,' she said, gently. 'You're nearly there, aren't you?'

Simon said nothing. He could only gulp. Every nerve ending in his body seemed to be between his legs, responding to the delicate but firm caress from the beautiful girl at his feet. Janet cupped his small scrotum with one hand, a finger of the other spreading his juice over the end of his cock. 'I'm going to suck you now, Simon,' she said, slowly, 'and I want your sperm in my mouth. Then, when you've recovered and you get hard again, you're going to fuck us both, OK?'

'Yes, oh yes.' Simon was struggling now. He was so close

to coming, but no doubt wanted the promised suck. Janet
realised his predicament and quickly clamped her mouth
over his wet tool, making gentle sucking motions whilst
running her tongue round and round his shaft. Lisa moved
behind Simon and gently licked the soft, white skin of his
bum, tasting the clean sweat between the cheeks of his buttocks.

Simon groaned and started to make involuntary thrusting movements with his hips as he fucked Janet's face. He
throbbed within the tightness of her wet mouth, and she
felt the first spurt of his come hit the back of her throat.
She took as much of his rigid sex into her mouth as she
could, swallowing hard as the cream filled her mouth. He
was bent over her now, his hands on her shoulders as his
knees began to give under the strain of sheer pleasure. Lisa,
meanwhile pressed her face hard against his bum, her
tongue licking greedily at his hole.

He took it for as long as he could, then fell sideways to
the carpet, collapsing in genuine exhaustion. He lay back
and looked at the girls, who were sitting on the floor smiling at him. He obviously couldn't believe what was happening to him.

Janet got up and put some music on the hi-fi. 'Let's give
him a strip-show,' she said, beckoning to Lisa, 'come on.'

'You first.' Lisa watched as Janet began to gyrate obscenely to the music. The black top was removed first,
slowly peeled from her body like a second skin until it was
cast to one side on the floor. Janet danced around some
more, jiggling her breasts in front of Simon, whose sex was
already beginning to show signs of recovery. Lisa sat next
to him, and took the stiffening member in her hand as she
watched her friend's show. She rubbed it gently as Janet's
skirt slid down to her feet, and she stepped out of it.

She now wore just the black, leather panties, stockings
and suspender-belt. She fingered herself through the sensuous material of her knickers, partly for Simon but mainly
for her own pleasure.

'Can I keep my stockings on?' She wanted him to take

her in her stockings . . . she loved that. Simon nodded, now fully erect thanks to Lisa's expert manipulations. 'I'd better take these off though.' She made to pull her panties down, then walked over to the reclining young man. 'You do it,' she commanded. Simon reached up with both hands and caught hold of the black leather, pulling them down to her ankles in one, swift movement.

He stared for a moment at her wet sex, the lips open and ready, the dark hair hiding nothing. Then he reached gingerly forward with one hand and allowed the tip of his forefinger to touch the soft sex-flesh. Janet nearly came with this simple touch, she was so randy, and he was so innocent. He traced the line of her soaked slit, slipping two, three, then four fingers into her. Without allowing his probing to stop, she sat down next to him and took over the caress of his erection from Lisa, who stood up and started her own strip routine.

Janet watched with increasing lust as her friend ran her hands provocatively over her massive breasts; she fancied Lisa like mad, and she fully intended to taste her love-juices again. She wondered what Simon would make of that. He was transfixed by the sight of one, then the other breast appearing from the erotic encasing provided by the basque. The huge tits swung from side to side with the rhythm of the dance; Simon's stalk throbbed, and a small amount of sperm appeared at the end. Janet took it on her finger and, staring hard into his eyes placed it between his lips. He licked the offered finger and swallowed . . . he would have done anything for either of these sex-mad women.

Lisa meanwhile had kicked off her shoes and slowly peeled off the tight trousers before standing, nude before her two prospective lovers, her legs apart, her hands on her hips. Janet wondered at her friend's nakedness, still getting used to the sheer beauty of her incredible body. She knew what effect the sight was having on Simon; she felt it herself. She wanted to dive onto Lisa's loveliness, to bury her face in her pussy again, to lick and taste her

41

delicate flavour. She also knew that it was important to look after Simon first, to let him have the promised screw, before any other fun started.

Lisa walked over to where Simon sat and lifted one leg, putting it over his slim shoulder so that his face was just inches away from her wet slit. 'Lick it,' she said, moving her crotch forward.

Simon cautiously pushed out his tongue until it made contact with the slightly hairy, very wet lips. Finding the taste not unpleasant he started to lick gently, savouring the tang and exotic odour of a woman on heat. Janet went down on him again, sucking his stiff erection, careful not to bring him off this time.

Simon started to lick faster and faster, realising the effect he was having. Lisa was groaning, moving her hips back and forth, grinding her loveliness against his face. He had to pull away occasionally to take a breath, but each time thrust his tongue back into her with renewed vigour. 'Lick the top, lick the top,' said Lisa, directing his efforts to her clitoris, 'yes, that's it, that's it!' Simon had become an expert in an instant, his tongue flicking ever faster over the bud of her sex, causing her to squeal with pleasure.

Janet knew her friend was coming, and sat up to watch, still maintaining a grip on Simon's stiff member. Lisa gave out a long, low cry as she orgasmed into the virgin boy's mouth, holding onto his shoulders tightly, grinding her crotch into his wet face.

Lisa sat back on the carpet, sated for the moment. Janet lay on her back, her legs wide open. 'My turn, Simon!' The boy didn't need telling again. He dived between the inviting legs and planted his hungry mouth on the soaking wet target, licking at the soft folds before concentrating on her love-button, flicking his tongue up and down and side to side over the hard little bud.

Every now and then he would move his attentions down to nibble her loose sex-lips, sucking them into his mouth and slipping his tongue deep into her hole. She lifted her bottom from the floor, pushing her body up at him, willing him to devour her. Pulling her legs right back, she held her knees against her breasts, and thrilled as his tongue ran its wet trail over her anus, tickling the tight sphincter with the tip, before returning to her clitoris, knowing already that this was the way to bring her to orgasm. His tongue flicked and fluttered over her bud, not letting up for a moment.

Janet felt the unmistakable feelings of her come building up inside her body, starting as though deep inside her bum before pushing forward to centre on her sex; on the tender little button that controlled her lust. With a cry she let go, gripping his hair as he clamped his mouth over her entire pussy, sucking in the lips, the wetness, everything.

The two lovers fell apart, breathing heavily. Janet needed to rest for a minute, but only just a minute. Lisa looked hard at Simon, and at his stiff erection. He was ready for it now, and she wanted to be his first. She knelt on her hands and knees in front of him presenting her bottom towards his gaze. 'Fuck me, Simon,' she ordered, 'fuck me now!'

Simon knelt behind the woman who was to be his first lover and pointed his stiff length towards her. Lisa reached between her legs, took hold of it and guided it into her hot sex, thrilling as it slid in to the hilt in one, easy movement. Janet watched as Simon started clumsily to screw her friend, his pumping becoming immediately fast and urgent; a typical virgin male's first attempt. He came almost straight away, the thrusting of his hips becoming a blur, until he fell over onto Lisa's back, panting.

Lisa wriggled herself free of Simon's exhausted body, and sat next to Janet. The two girls looked in mock pity at their victim. 'We've got a lot to teach him, haven't we?' she said.

'Looks that way,' said Janet, 'but first, whilst he recovers, we'll give him a bit of a show!' She lay back and opened her legs again, signalling for her friend to join her.

At first Lisa paused, then smiled, licking her lips. She lay gently on top of Janet, pressing their soft, aroused bodies together, and kissed her mouth; their tongues meeting and

43

playfully darting around each other. Their hands stroked and explored each other's bodies, fondling breasts, buttocks, pussies, exciting each other to the point of no return.

Lisa now lay back on the floor, and Janet sat astride her face, her back to Simon. She lowered her sex onto the other girl's mouth, thrilling to the now expert technique of Lisa's tongue. She bent forward and paid the same compliment to the wet, red lips in front of her, licking hungrily at the tasty quim, swallowing and savouring the mixture of flavours as Simon watched, fascinated.

Janet raised her head from between Lisa's thighs. 'Fuck me, Simon, go on, do it now!'

He was there immediately, fully hard again, ready to impale the gorgeous orifice before him. He pushed straight into Janet, feeling the grip of her vaginal muscles close around his sensitive member, and the unmistakeable sensation of Lisa licking his balls as he humped her friend.

He started his fast thrusting again, as though trying to finish as quickly as possible.

'Slowly, slowly, I want it to last,' Janet cried out, 'take it nice and easy, sometimes fast, sometimes slow. If you feel yourself coming then stop until you lose the feeling. It's best when it goes on for ages. Anyway, Lisa's gonna want some more!'

'Definitely,' said Lisa, pausing from licking alternately between Simon's balls and Janet's sex. 'Lots more!'

Simon did as instructed, working in and out of Janet at varying pace, taking care to please her. Janet concentrated on Lisa's clitoris now, taking it gently between her teeth, applying slight pressure, licking the inflamed bud with the tip of her tongue at a ferocious rate. Lisa's hips started to buck up and down as her orgasm began to build inside her. Simon watched her movements and matched them involuntarily with his own. Lisa squealed once again as her orgasm ripped through her, the sensation apparently better than ever. She took Simon's balls into her mouth as she came, almost biting into the tender sack, remembering just in time that such action would probably not be appreciated.

Simon carried on driving hard into Janet as Lisa rested, his previous orgasms and the expert teaching he'd received helping him to last much longer. Janet was giving him all her attention now, pushing her bum back to meet each thrust, tensing the muscles within her vagina to afford him the best sensations. She still had the taste of Lisa in her mouth and this, combined with the incessant pumping she was receiving from behind, was bringing her back up to yet another climax. She let go with just a whimper this time, the orgasm not as violent as before, but satisfying none the less.

The three lovers lay apart for a short while. Simon sat on the floor, resting himself against a chair, whilst Janet and Lisa lay back on the floor, staring absently at the ceiling.

The sound of a police or ambulance siren echoed through the night outside the open window. Simon was sitting waiting, hard and erect, ready for whatever the girls asked of him. Lisa raised her head slightly from the carpet and opened her legs wide. She smiled at the sexy young man who looked like he belonged in a school classroom, instead of naked on the floor with two nymphos. He crawled over to her and positioned himself between her legs before letting himself slide effortlessly into her gorgeous, wet sex. Then, making long, slow thrusts, he would occasionally wriggle his bottom to cause a stirring movement inside her with his stiff stalk. She responded by using her inner-muscles to grip and release, grip and release; her sex acting like a suckling mouth.

After a little while, Lisa pulled away from Simon and guided him to lie on his back. She then climbed over his young body and sat down on him, feeling his sweet stiffness slide firmly inside her. 'Don't move,' she ordered, 'let me do everything.'

She started to ride him, slowly at first, gripping him tightly then letting the pace increase until she was riding him wildly, determined now to bring him to orgasm quickly. Her erotic movements became faster and faster with each stroke, her large breasts bouncing heavily. Still he refused to come; he had obviously decided he could go on forever if they wanted; that's what they had taught him, and now he would deliver.

Janet crawled over and sat astride Simon's face, lowering her well-used pussy onto his mouth. Immediately he started to lick swiftly, his tongue fluttering over her clitoris delicately, as though he'd been doing it for years. The two girls held on to each other as they rode their pupil, Lisa taking his full length with each thrust, Janet grinding her hot sex into his mouth. Their lips met, and the friends kissed deeply, fondling each other's backsides tenderly.

Janet slid a wet finger into Lisa's bottom, fingering her in time to the humping that Simon was giving her. She moved her own bum so that Simon could lick her anus, whilst Lisa reached down and fondled her clitoris. The constant rhythm of the game was at last having an effect on Simon, who was thrusting up to meet Lisa's downward hammering, his orgasm near. With a cry muffled by Janet's luscious buttocks he let go, as though hurting with exotic pain as his sperm shot up into Lisa.

The girls pushed Simon away almost immediately, self-ishly falling once more into their beloved sixty-nine position, licking greedily at each other's sex. They bucked and squealed, rolling over and over each other, grasping, feeling, tasting. Their orgasms were going to happen together, they both knew it, and they forced themselves to prolong the agony as long as possible.

Then it was just too much. Janet started to moan first, the sounds of her build-up setting Lisa off on the same route. Both girls cried out in unison as they came, suckling each other as though trying to drain the juices.

After a while, the only sound was the ticking of an antique clock on the bedside table, and the heavy breathing of three fully sated lovers.

Simon's lack of experience hadn't taught him what to say or do after a good sex-session, so he just sat and stared at the two beautiful girls who lay, still entwined in each other's arms, naked and sweat-covered on the carpet. Janet's black stockings were torn, and Simon was sure he could see a clear bite mark on Lisa's bum, though he didn't know if he or Janet had put it there.

Janet caught Simon's look and smiled. 'Did you enjoy that?' she asked. He nodded. She knew he would probably never have a better screw in his entire life, and felt proud that she had been one of his first lovers.

She also noticed that his young sex was beginning to harden again already. He wasn't done with these two beautiful nymphomaniacs yet.

The young girls of France had better watch their step in future, she thought wryly as she crawled over to begin again.

Chapter Three

Lisa walked slowly across the park opposite Janet's flat, enjoying the coolness of the early evening. The gentle breeze played against her young flesh through the thin material of her jeans and low-cut top. Around her people walked, jogged or played games; children laughed and ran in various, undetermined directions, and dogs sniffed at each other as dogs do. The sounds of summer pleasures filled her ears.

Simon had finally collapsed, exhausted after spending the entire afternoon screwing her and Janet. They had sent their virgin conquest off into the night to search for more girls like them on whom to practise his new-found talents.

Lisa marvelled at the way her life had changed overnight. Yesterday she had been a plain, unwanted virgin; today she was a beautiful, desirable girl who had already accommodated three wonderful male bodies, and it wasn't even dark yet! She found herself looking lustfully at all the men who passed her, willing them to talk to her, to proposition her. Men of all shapes and sizes, and for that matter ages; she fancied them all, and wanted them to make love to her.

Her session with Simon and Janet had been wonderful; she'd lost count of the number of orgasms she'd experienced that afternoon, but it still wasn't enough. No sooner had she walked out into the cool air than she found the now familiar stirrings beginning again between her legs, building up quickly into an unforgiving need.

Janet had told her that after a few days these incredibly

powerful sexual urges would calm down somewhat, and that she would be content with just one or two sessions each day. At the moment, however, she was like an animal on heat, desperate for lots and lots of good, hard screwing.

A couple of attractive young men wearing skimpy athlete's shorts ran past her, and she had to fight the urge to grab herself between the legs, to rub vigorously at her aching pussy. She knew that it wasn't allowed, but Lisa was desperate to ease the dreadful tension that increased with every step.

She began to shake and had to sit on a wooden parkbench to recover, her breathing stilted and shallow. She closed her eyes and tried to block out the image of the two men: their long, tanned legs, the firm buttocks and promising bulges in their tiny shorts.

'Are you all right, love?'

Lisa opened her eyes and focused with some difficulty on the newcomer who stood before her holding a large garden rake. He was a man in his early thirties, tall and strong-looking, his face bearing the stubble of days of abstinence from shaving. He was dressed simply in denim shorts and a small T-shirt. His skin was heavily tanned, probably from continuous working out of doors, and his scent of fresh sweat was sharp and distinctly male.

'Yes, I'm OK,' said Lisa, drinking in the sight of this handsome stud who had joined her on the bench. 'I came over a bit faint, but it's passed now.'

'D'you want a cup of tea? I've got a flask in the shed over by those trees.' He motioned towards a clump of greenery close by.

'That would be nice,' she said, rising unsteadily to her feet. He took her arm in his and they walked slowly across the grass, Lisa playing the invalid for all she was worth, leaning against his hard body and clutching his firmly-muscled arm with her small hands.

When they arrived at the shed the gardener fumbled in his pockets for his keys. Lisa sensed that he was nervous when she noticed his eyes darting occasionally to her

largely exposed breasts. His hands were shaking percep-
tibly as he unlocked the heavy, steel padlock and opened
the door, allowing her to walk into the dark, windowless
storeroom. He flicked on the light, and dusted off the
surface of the only chair, before helping her gently to sit
down.

He unscrewed a flask and poured some of the contents
into the cup, offering the steaming liquid to Lisa, which she
accepted gratefully. She had stopped shaking; her mind
was now on the seduction of this delightful park employee.
She sipped the sweet tea, then set the cup down on a nearby shelf.

'Thanks,' she said, 'that was nice. My name's Lisa;
what's yours?'

'Stan,' he said, a little nervously, 'I work here.'

Lisa giggled. 'You surprise me!' Stan blushed noticeably,
which she found very attractive. 'Do you work on your
own?'

'No, but Bill, my boss, is over the other side of the park.
He won't be back here for some time.'

Although much older than she was, Stan bore an incredible shyness, obviously unused to the attentions of a pretty
girl. Lisa wanted him badly, but was afraid that she might
scare him off if she was too pushy. She decided to let him
move at his own pace.

'Do you have a boyfriend, Lisa?'

'Nobody special,' she said, truthfully. 'I don't want to
get tied down yet.'

'Very wise. Have fun whilst you're young, eh?'

'Yes. I like having fun.' She looked into his eyes when
she said this, her expression betraying her lust. He
coughed, nervously. 'I bet you've had loads of girls in this
little shed, haven't you?' she said, with a cheeky grin.

'Not much hope of that,' he said, shrugging his powerful
shoulders. 'I wouldn't know what to say to get them in
here.'

'You got me in here.'

'Yes, I suppose I did.'

'I mean,' said Lisa, standing up in front of him, her face inches from his, 'for all I know, you could have brought me back here to have your evil way with me.' She ran her fingertip sensuously over the front of his T-shirt, tracing the outline of his firm pectoral muscles. She looked directly into his eyes, feeling an almost hypnotic power over this simple gardener, knowing that she was going to have him.

Suddenly he seemed to gain a new strength, as though a thought had snapped him out of her seductive grip. 'No, I'm sorry,' he stuttered, 'I can't; I'm a married man.'

Lisa was simultaneously consumed by lust and anger at this apparent rejection. She concentrated all her strength of will into her eyes, staring directly at him, insistent and determined.

Stan trembled, unable to speak clearly. 'I . . . I . . .' was all he could manage. Lisa smiled, and stepped back, her fingers going to the fastenings on the front of her thrusting basque, licking her lips seductively as she slowly revealed her massive breasts to his astounded gaze.

'You had better lock the door,' she said, throwing the basque onto the chair. Stan did as instructed, then turned to watch as Lisa began to unzip her tight, white jeans. She pulled them off slowly, turning her back to him and bending forward to give him a perfect view of her sensational bottom.

When she was naked she turned back to him and began to unfasten his shorts. She knelt down at his feet and pulled them and his underpants down, releasing his hard erection to her eager gaze. Without pausing, she took it into her mouth and sucked on it, running her tongue round and round the thick end, tasting his saltiness, savouring his scent.

She pulled her head back, releasing his stiffness from her mouth, and looked up at him, pouting innocently. 'Are you going to fuck me, Stan?'

He nodded, and raised her to her feet. Lisa turned her back to him again, and rested her hands on the rough wooden bench at the far end of the shed, pushing her bum out provocatively towards him. 'Go on then, Stan,' she said, aggressively, 'give it to me now!'

The gardener walked towards her as though in a trance. He was completely in her power, his stiff prick jutting forward. Lisa wondered at the power she'd been able to hold over him; the evil old man had given her more than just astounding beauty; she could actually *control* men, they were hers to do with as she pleased. How she would use that power! She would make up for the years of neglect, when men ignored her; now she would use and abuse them to her heart's content, to satisfy her perpetual cravings.

She sighed heavily as she felt Stan's hard stalk touch the wet, ready lips of her pussy, arching her back to make it even easier to take him inside her lovely body. He pushed the thick, bulbous head in and held still for a moment, gripping her by the waist. Carefully he pushed more and more of his length into her aching sheath, until she felt his groin pressed against the softness of her buttocks. He leant forward and reached under her to allow his big, rough hands to cup her pendulous breasts, holding them firmly whilst kissing the back of her neck.

She felt the thick hardness of his shaft slide easily out of her until just the tip remained, held between her soaking sex-lips. He pushed forward again slowly, his breathing heavy, his hands pawing at her superb body. Suddenly he cried out, 'Oh, my God, I can't stop it!' and began to hammer in and out of her, pumping his sperm deep inside her body, almost crying with the sensation.

Lisa pulled away from him angrily. 'You useless bastard!' she cried, 'I'm nowhere near!'

'I–I'm sorry, love,' Stan whimpered, 'I couldn't do anything about it. You're so gorgeous; those amazing tits, that fabulous arse; I just couldn't hold it back!'

Lisa pushed him back with a strength she'd never known before, forcing him to sit on the old chair. She raised one of her legs and put it over his shoulder, pressing her sex against his mouth and holding his head roughly by the hair. 'Lick it, and lick it good!' she commanded. 'You're gonna make me come!'

Stan did as he was ordered, his tongue lapping at her soaking hole, tasting the combined flavours of their lust. Lisa tightened her grip on his hair, twisting it around her fingers, grinding her mound against his mouth, seeing his face become soaked with their lust-juices. 'Faster, faster, lick my clit!'

He concentrated the fluttering, flicking of his tongue to the hard bud, gripping her buttocks with his rough hands, his fingernails digging into the soft flesh. Lisa was consumed by the power of the orgasm building up inside her, and by her domination of this strong man, revelling in the knowledge that she had total control of him.

Still holding his hair tightly with one hand, she let the other fall onto his back, scratching at his flesh viciously as her climax tore through her aching body, the roughness of his stubbled chin heightening the sensations that were exploding inside her young body. 'Oh yes! Oh yes! Oh yes!' she screamed, rubbing her tender pussy-flesh over his face, pulling his head between her legs, soaking his hair. The orgasm seemed to last for ages, and when it was over Lisa's knees buckled and she fell to the floor, shattered.

She knelt quietly for a minute or so, occasionally kissing his limp cock, as gradually she came back down to earth. Astonishingly, the come she'd just experienced had probably been the best yet, no doubt due to her urgent need for sexual release. She wondered how much pleasure she could take and whether it was good for her to enjoy it so much; to the point of exhaustion.

Stan didn't say a word as Lisa left the shed; he sat, looking dazed on the old chair, his hair matted and wet, apparently shocked and dumbfounded by the events of the previous few minutes. Lisa waved cutely as she closed the wooden door behind her, and blew him a kiss. Stan managed a weak smile.

Lisa walked slowly towards the block of flats where she

lived, her thoughts confused. She'd been amazed, even concerned at the measure of power that she'd held over the park gardener, and of the violence with which she forced him to satisfy her cravings. She'd been like a woman possessed as she'd driven herself to orgasm on his mouth, completely out of control, the need to sate her lust paramount.

Stan had been totally unable to resist her advances. True, he was a somewhat simple character, but she nevertheless felt that there was something within her, a force that no man could resist, and she wasn't sure she liked it. Perhaps there was more to the old man's deal than he had admitted.

She rounded the corner and crossed the street to the entrance to her building. She passed a large, grey and black limousine parked outside the door, wondering which of the impoverished tenants in the shabby block could possibly know anyone who owned such a vehicle. As she searched for her keys a tall, Germanic-looking man dressed in a smart chauffeur's uniform stepped out of the car and called to her.

'Lisa, Lisa Stevens?'

Lisa turned, and eyed the stranger suspiciously. 'Yes, what do you want?'

'I've been sent to collect you, miss.'

'Oh, have you, now,' she said, haughtily, 'and just who sent you?'

'Mr Frank, miss,' said the driver, walking towards her, his teeth gleaming white in a broad, dazzling smile, 'he said Miss Janet would have told you about him.'

'Oh, er yes,' said Lisa, a little nervous that she was about to meet the mysterious leader of the 'Lust Angels', 'I was just about to eat something.'

'Dinner will be prepared for you at the house, miss. You may wish to change, though.'

She took his none too subtle hint, smiled and went into the building, asking him to wait outside. There was something not quite right about the man, something intangible;

a sort of menace, even evil, that seemed to surround him in the same way she'd felt when she'd met the old man the previous evening.

She dressed carefully, selecting a long, black evening gown in chiffon which moulded itself perfectly around her smooth body. The sides of the dress split to the waist, revealing the flawless nakedness of her long legs and hips. She completed the outfit with a pair of spiked, high-heeled shoes and a small handbag, and viewed herself in the full-length mirror.

Lisa was still not used to her new looks, and gasped in sheer awe at the reflection, her heart bearing proudly as she remembered that she was looking at herself. The gown accentuated every curve of her tall frame: the fullness of her breasts, the slim waist, the erotic curves of her bottom. When she stood sideways she could see her naked flesh from her heel to her waist, and when she swung around quickly she caught a glimpse of her naked buttocks and the soft, blonde curls covering her sex. She would certainly impress this Frank person, that was for sure!

The chauffeur held the rear door of the sleek limousine open for her as she climbed in, then closed it gently as she sat on the sumptuous, white-leather upholstery. Whatever it was that he and the old man got up to, she thought, there was money in it, a lot of money.

The car moved off swiftly, its engine purring like a powerful cat. Lisa's mind was full of questions, but a screen between her and the driver precluded any conversation, so she sat back and watched the world pass by outside, wondering what she was letting herself in for.

The car headed out into the countryside. The journey took a little over an hour before the car finally slowed down and entered a thickly-gravelled drive that swept ahead of them between two giant, wrought-iron gates.

Lisa could just make out the shape of the large, old house as they drew up to the front door. The sun was now disappearing quickly behind the nearby hills and the scene before her was more than a little forbidding. Many of the windows were illuminated, but the house nevertheless appeared creepy to her. She began to wonder if she'd done the right thing in letting this stranger bring her here.

The front door opened slowly, the arched entrance framing the tall silhouette of a man, his back to the bright light within the hallway. Thoughts of Dracula in his castle, waiting for unsuspecting young girls filled Lisa's head as she peered through the window of the car.

There was a sudden click as the car door was opened, making her catch her breath with the shock. 'Are you all right, miss?' asked the chauffeur, as he held the door for her.

'Yes,' she replied, trying to regain her composure, 'you made me jump.'

'Mr Frank is waiting, miss.' The driver spoke without a hint of apology in his tone. Lisa took a deep breath, stepped out of the vehicle, and walked steadily towards her waiting host.

As she neared the man, his features gradually became visible in the dim light. Her eyes widened as she saw him: a face of infinite magnificence, strong, handsome and yet kind. His dark eyes seemed to have untold depths of expression; the smile that began to play across his sensuous mouth made her feel warm and welcome, her feelings of unease vanishing immediately.

'Welcome to my home, Lisa,' he said, his tone deep and soothing. 'I hope you had a comfortable journey?'

'Yes, thank you,' said Lisa, as he led her into the brightly lit hallway, 'your car is very comfortable.'

They walked into a large sitting room, the furniture antique and resplendent, the decorations sumptuous. He motioned for her to sit in a high-backed armchair and stood looking at her, his back to the unlit fire. 'My name is Frank. I believe our mutual friend, Janet, has told you about me?'

'Yes, she said you might be in touch. I didn't think it would be so soon.'

'Oh, I was anxious to have you join our little group as

soon as possible, once I'd heard about you. You are very special, you know.'

Lisa smiled, embarrassed. 'It's all been a bit of a shock, to say the least.'

'I'm sure that it has. Now you need help, instruction.'

Lisa couldn't understand. Instruction in what? 'I don't know what you mean,' she said.

'You already know that you are beautiful, and that men desire you. You may also have already discovered that you can control them, manipulate them to your will.'

'I–I think I know what you mean,' she said, remembering the episode with the park gardener.

'You will learn how to use these powers, for your own pleasure and,' he looked at her earnestly, 'for the benefit of the group.'

'How will I learn?'

'Through the group you will gain many opportunities to increase your experience of sex in all its many vagaries, to experiment, to enjoy and to give others pleasure.

'At the moment you will be going through a very lustful period, which you will need to satisfy with much sex. These cravings will tail off somewhat after a short while, although you will still be relatively insatiable, and it is my task to ensure your continued satisfaction.

'The group meets in three days time, at a colleague's residence in London. You will be sent an invitation. In the meantime, you may enjoy yourself in any way you wish.'

Lisa was about to speak when the sound of a gong echoed through the house. 'Dinner,' said Frank, motioning for her to follow him out of the room, 'come, we will eat, then make love.'

Lisa followed him quietly, not questioning his assumption. He led her into another room, even larger than the first, the centrepiece being a massive oak dining table, set for two. The chauffeur stood motionless to one side of the table, next to another, much older man dressed in the uniform of a butler, and a very young and pretty girl in the outfit of a maid.

The butler walked stiffly forward and pulled back a chair for Lisa to sit at the table. Frank stood waiting until the same courtesy was performed for him. A delicately flavoured vegetable soup was put before them, which Lisa ate gratefully, her hunger now almost ravenous.

The meal was delicious, and eaten in silence. Only when the brandies were served did Frank speak again. 'Was the meal to your liking?'

'Lovely,' she said, 'I was very hungry.'

Frank smiled. 'Good. Now, come here, my dear, I must satisfy your other hunger.'

Lisa rose and walked towards him, totally under the spell of her handsome host. She stood by his side, trembling as he ran his hand down her back and over her bottom, the thin material of her dress the only thing between her soft skin and his sensuous touch. His fingertips found her naked thigh and he pushed his hand under her gown, cupping her firm buttocks gently, his fingers fondling between them.

Lisa looked anxiously at the three motionless members of his staff, finding their faces impassive to the point of disinterest. Frank's probing fingers had now moved between her legs, his hand gripping her inner thigh at the top, his forefinger resting firmly against her damp sex. He slid his hand back up her body to the clasp at her shoulder, unfastening it expertly, allowing the gown to fall to the floor. She stood, proudly naked before him, enjoying the way his eyes devoured her luscious curves.

'All my ladies are beautiful,' he said, his voice husky with emotion, 'but you are superb. You will be well sought-after, I promise.'

Lisa smiled; although she wasn't quite sure what he meant, she took it as a compliment. She wanted him to sweep her up into his arms and carry her into his bedroom, to have his way with her, just like it happened in romantic novels. Instead, he sat down again, and started to unfasten his trousers.

He was going to do it here, in front of his staff! She looked at them uneasily, but they remained unmoved.

'Your first lesson is not to be worried about an audience,' said her host, obviously noting her concern. 'You must grow to love the performance, to show your techniques in front of others. Now, love me with your mouth. I am told that this is your speciality.'

Lisa knelt at his feet, and finished unzipping his trousers, reaching inside for his hardening tool. She pulled it out and gazed lovingly at it, long, thick and gnarled, its roughness perfect for stimulating her clitoris. She wanted him deep inside her sex, but knew that she must first obey him and give him the best sucking she could manage; she had to see if the old man's promise that she would become an expert at oral techniques was true.

She kissed the fat end of his erection with her pouted lips, then drew it in between them, running her tongue over the large slit. She held onto his thick stem with her hand, rubbing it gently up and down, feeling it harden dramatically, the size causing her jaw to ache.

She licked the end again, then planted kiss after kiss wetly up and down the long, hard stem, squeezing the base tightly with her hand. Her tongue took over, licking the side of the huge organ, soaking it with her saliva, making sure that every part of his thickness was administered to.

Kneeling between his legs, she let her tongue move down to his scrotum, tracing a line between the firm ovals to the patch of sensitive skin between them and his anus. She licked there delicately for a while, feeling his hips move slightly in response, his breathing heavy.

She took his plums into her mouth, first one, then both, sucking on them like a baby does a bottle, letting the tip of her tongue tease his hairy sack, before running her tongue back up the long length of his superb shaft, over the thick end again to the slit, the tip teasing it open slightly. Opening her mouth wide, she swallowed as much of him as she could, taking it to the back of her throat, wetting it with her cheeks and pulsating tongue. She moved her head up and down, gobbling him in and out, giving him as much sensation with her mouth as her instincts told her.

She decided to try something else. She'd read about it, now she knew she had to try it. The problem was, of course, that he was so big; still, if she could do it to him, she could do it to almost anybody!

Keeping his stiff phallus in her mouth she arched her body so that the back of her head rested against his stomach, her legs straight and wide apart, no doubt presenting a wonderful picture to the three servants. She pushed her face down on his tool, feeling the end touch her tonsils. She gagged slightly, but instead of pulling back she swallowed, trying to take his length down her throat. At first she choked, and had to pull her head back, taking him back to the roof of her mouth. She tried again, contracting her neck muscles, swallowing hard, pushing her face towards his balls.

She managed to adjust her position so that she could force a little air into her lungs, past the thick stem of his sex. Once she'd mastered this technique she relaxed, swallowing more and more until, to her delight her lips touched his pubic mound, and she knew she had every inch of his long, thick cock inside her mouth and throat.

She held still for a moment, then tried to move her head back and forth, but found that the rubbing of his tool against the back of her mouth made her feel sick. Instead, she learned that she must hold him fully down her throat and swallow continuously, the rippling effect of her muscles no doubt causing him the most incredible sensations. He groaned as she swallowed repeatedly, breathing loudly through her nose, her lips clamped firmly around the base of his penis.

Lisa kept this treatment up for what seemed like ages, learning more and more how to take his full length orally in comfort. Finally she drew his wet sex from her mouth, and raised her head, looking into his eyes triumphantly. Frank smiled warmly, waiting for her next move. It was clear that she had to make all the running, that this was some sort of test.

She rose and stood astride him, pushed his legs together

and lowered her lovely body down to the waiting shaft, eager to be impaled. She took a deep breath as she felt the large end of his sex touch her tenderly aroused pussy-lips, and sank down slowly on him, the hard length entering her like a hot knife into butter. She moved easily up and down, savouring the full length of the gnarled tool, its roughness exciting her quickly.

She glanced over at the three servants who still stood where they had been throughout the meal. The men showed no emotion, although the young girl was beginning to look flushed. Lisa looked back at Frank, his face fixed in the same warm smile, hardly a sign of lust anywhere in his expression. He was obviously used to plenty of screwing, but she desperately wanted to make an impression, to astound him with her sexual prowess.

She contracted and released her vaginal muscles as she drew herself up and down on his stalk, making sure that he could feel every part of her saturated sheath. He took her big breasts in his hands and kneaded them, muttering, 'Superb', and licking greedily at the long nipples, drawing one, and then the other between the tight lips of his mouth.

Lisa took this treatment for some time, then pulled herself reluctantly from him, his length falling heavily against his stomach. She turned her back on him and lowered herself again, sure that the sight of her perfect bottom was enough to excite any man. Once again, she felt the long stiffness enter her to the hilt, and she rode him hard, clutching his knees as she hammered her sex down on his.

Her orgasm was building up; she wanted him to come with her, to complete this perfect union. 'I'm coming, I'm coming,' she shouted, willing him to do the same. There was no sound, not even heavy breathing. She pounded up and down as hard as she could, her massive breasts bouncing wildly as her climax gripped her, sending electrical pulses down her legs to her feet, making her squeeze hard on the thick intruder within her body. She drew herself up, so that just the tip was inside her, and held still, until she screamed from the sheer excruciating pleasure of the final release. She let herself fall onto his lap, once more accepting his full, hard length inside, and tried to recover from the mind-blowing sensations that had just enthralled her.

Finally, Lisa slipped from his lap and sat, exhausted at his feet, staring disappointedly at the still erect penis. Immediately, the young maid walked forward and knelt beside her, matter-of-factly taking Frank's sex in her hand, licking it wetly and using a napkin to wipe it clean. Once her task was complete, he stuffed his now drooping phallus back into his trousers and zipped himself up, handing Lisa her gown.

'I rarely come,' he said, smiling kindly, 'I prefer to remain interested. Dress now, and Saul will drive you home, my little Lust Angel.'

Lisa felt a sense of pride, knowing that she had somehow passed the test; that she had been accepted. She wondered what other surprises the group had in store for her; there seemed so much to learn.

Lisa had been home for less than an hour when the phone rang. It was Janet. 'How did you get on with Frank?' her friend said, excitedly.

'Fine,' said Lisa, nonchalantly. 'He's very nice.'

'Are you in the group?' Janet sounded anxious.

'Yes,' said Lisa, proudly, 'he called me his little Lust Angel.'

'Oh, great! He fucked you, then; he wouldn't have fucked you if he wasn't going to let you in the group.'

'Well, I'm in. He's quite a guy.'

'You said it. Boy, have you got some fun coming up!'

'What sort of fun?'

'You'll see. Listen, come to my aerobics class tomorrow. It's run by one of the group, a girl called Sonia. You'll love her.'

'I don't think I've got the right sort of gear,' said Lisa, in truth wondering if her new body was fit as well as gorgeous. She had barely looked at an exercise bicycle and, despite the new perfection of her body the idea still held horrors for her.

'Don't worry, we'll sort something out for you. I'll meet you at the gym at eleven. Bye!' Janet hung up before Lisa could think of another excuse. Oh well, she thought, at least it will be something different.

Lisa stood outside the Fitness Centre, looking apprehensively at the entrance. She'd visited the club once before with Janet, when her friend was trying to get her to lose weight, but it had all been too much for her. She'd come out after less than ten minutes of warm-up, exhausted and still fat, swearing never to take any exercise again.

Perhaps it would be different this time, though. She certainly felt fit, ready for anything, and some of the antics she'd got up to when screwing her lovers of the previous day had required a considerable amount of suppleness. She walked through the door with renewed confidence, and headed for the bar.

Janet was sitting at a table waiting for her, next to a beautiful coloured girl whom Lisa assumed to be Sonia.

'Hi,' said Janet, standing to greet her friend, 'want a coffee?'

'Lovely,' said Lisa, staring almost rudely at the lovely African, 'you must be Sonia.'

The black girl smiled, her huge mouth showing two rows of gleaming white teeth, her thick lips wet and sensuous. Lisa felt an immediate need to possess this girl, to have her, right there and then. She began to shake visibly with lust, and sat down quickly in order to calm herself.

'I can see we're going to get on really well,' said Sonia, her voice deep and husky. Lisa smiled, and Janet returned with her coffee.

As Lisa took the first sips of the hot beverage, Sonia stood up, revealing her full height for the first time. She was easily six feet tall, with long, powerful legs, large hips and bottom, slim waist and remarkably huge breasts, bigger even in that area than Lisa. Clearly the old man had worked wonders when he moulded her.

'I've got a class,' said the big, voluptuous woman, 'you coming along?'

'I'll watch this time,' said Lisa, noticing Janet's smile, 'is that OK?'

'Sure, no problem. Finish your coffee and join me later.'

'See you in a minute, then,' said Lisa, her eyes betraying the lust she was feeling as she watched Sonia go off to the changing rooms.

'She sure is something, isn't she?' said Janet, her eyes twinkling, 'I'm sure you'll enjoy watching her perform her movements.'

'Aren't you coming to watch?'

'No, I think I'll stay here, if you don't mind. There's a chap by the bar I thought I might have a go at.'

The aerobics session was in full swing as Lisa arrived and sat at the back of the room. About twenty men and women of all ages were rhythmically stepping up and down onto small raised platforms in time to blaring disco music, Sonia's shouts of 'turn, step, higher, keep in time!' spurring them on. The sweat poured already from the victims; Sonia was really putting them through their paces, clearly with some pleasure on her part.

Lisa waved to the big, black girl who smiled in response, carrying on with the strutting movements which her class imitated as best they could. She was wearing a pink leotard but without tights, the tiny garment barely covering her Amazon form, straining with the force of her huge breasts. When she turned she revealed that the narrow sliver of material at the back disappeared between her large, firm buttocks, giving the impression that her bottom was naked. It was only when she bent forward that the tiny, pink strip could be seen just covering her anus and sex.

Lisa wondered if she was shaven; there was no sign of hair peeking from within the confines of the leotard at the crotch; and would she taste as good as Janet? She was getting randy now, shifting in her seat as the thoughts of lust for this beautiful African began to take hold of her.

Due to the extreme shortness of her skirt, Lisa had worn panties to the gym: a particularly tiny, lace affair, now thoroughly soaked and gradually slipping between the folds of her wet pussy. She wanted to whip them off and rush over to sit on Sonia's face, to feel the thick lips and long tongue work on her as she was sure they could.

It wasn't too long before the lesson was over, and the exhausted participants gratefully filed out to collapse in the changing rooms. Sonia joined Lisa on the bench, greeting her again with her permanent, dazzling smile. 'Hi,' she said, 'did you enjoy the show?'

'Yes, you're very good,' replied Lisa, taking in the gentle, musty smell of the sweating woman. 'I don't know where you get your energy!'

'Oh, I need a lot of that,' said Sonia, still grinning, 'I live with two very demanding lovers.'

'Two!' exclaimed Lisa, wondering if they were men or women, or both, for that matter, 'you lucky cow!'

'I suppose I am,' said Sonia, getting up to go to the showers. 'Perhaps you'd like to meet them . . . they'd love you!'

'Would they?' said Lisa, walking with her to the changing room. 'Why's that?'

'Black men love a bit of white pussy for a change.' The matter-of-fact way in which Sonia spoke quite startled Lisa, but it only served to heighten the sexual attractiveness that seemed to ooze from every pore of her body, like the droplets of sweat which created a sheen on the flawless, ebony skin. She knew now that Sonia liked men, very much so, it seemed, but that was no problem. She would be happy to watch her new friend getting seen to by her two lovers and, of course there was the likelihood that she would receive the same treatment herself.

'Sounds good to me,' she said, as they entered the changing room. 'Arrange it whenever you like.'

Sonia peeled off the little leotard and stood, totally naked in front of Lisa, who drank in the sight of her amazingly voluptuous body with a hunger which couldn't have gone unnoticed. Her breasts were massive, easily fifty inches. They jutted forward with a pert arrogance, supporting long, jet black nipples that Lisa ached to suck on. Her back was small, her waist narrow but her hips wide and, as Lisa had suspected, her sex was totally hairless, the puffy, black flesh looking as sexually attractive to her as any big cock. 'How about tonight?' she said, turning to retrieve her clothes from the small sports-bag on the bench.

Lisa looked longingly at the large buttocks, wanting to run her tongue up and down the crack. 'OK,' she said, then sighed in desperation, 'Look, you must excuse me; I know it sounds silly, but I've just got to take my knickers off!'

The wetness between her legs was getting unbearable. She pulled the tiny, soaking lace panties from under her skirt and threw them on the bench. Sonia picked them up and sniffed at the material suggestively.

'Well,' she said, holding the lacy material to her lips, 'if this is the effect the mere thought of fucking with a couple of black blokes is having on you, we're in for a good time tonight!'

'I'm sure we are,' said Lisa, staring pointedly at Sonia's sex. 'A fucking good time!' The use of the obscenity seemed appropriate in the presence of the other girl's animal-like sexuality.

Sonia reached over and stroked her new friend's hair gently, then kissed her lightly on the lips. 'See you tonight, then.' The beautiful, tall negress walked slowly off to the showers, pausing to glance sexily over her shoulder before she disappeared round the corner. Lisa watched her go, shaking with lust and anticipation. There was going to be more than just sex with two men tonight . . .

Lisa rang the doorbell to Sonia's flat with excited nervousness. A male voice spoke over the intercom. 'Yes?'

'It's Lisa, I'm a friend of Sonia's.'

The voice sounded more friendly. 'Oh, yes, we're expecting you. Push the door.' She did as instructed and walked in to a long, dark hallway, hearing the sound of someone coming down from the floor above. It was Sonia.

'Hi!' The massive, gleaming smile that greeted Lisa put

her instantly at her ease. 'You found it OK, then?' Sonia was wearing a pair of tight, denim shorts, a large, floppy T-shirt and a pair of white trainers. Lisa still wore the short, pleated skirt and white blouse that she'd worn at the gym, although she'd not bothered to put her underwear back on in anticipation of the evening to come.

Sonia led the way upstairs, her bottom jutting provocatively in the tiny shorts. Lisa could feel herself creaming already. They entered the lounge of the flat: a small, tidy room, comfortably furnished with brightly coloured fabrics and rugs. Two young, black men stood up to welcome her. Sonia walked over and stood between them, her arms around their waists. 'This is Sam and this is Tyne. They're my lovers.' She said the last phrase with some pride; the two men just smiled.

Sam was shorter than Sonia, about five foot ten, but very broad, a strong, muscular torso emphasised by the tight T-shirt he wore. He was completely bald, in current fashion, with pronounced African features. Tyne was quite different; he reminded Lisa of a young Sidney Poitier, his face refined, intelligent and very sexy, his physique slim and tall.

Lisa was made to feel welcome, and the four indulged in small-talk for a while, nibbling on a light salad that had been prepared for the visit. After a time, however, the conversation became less stilted and more and more suggestive as the copious amount of wine they consumed began to have its effect. She was sitting on the floor, facing the two men who watched intently as she crossed and uncrossed her legs, ensuring that they caught the occasional glimpse of her naked sex.

Sonia, also sitting on the floor stretched her arms above her head. 'God, it's hot in here,' she said, 'you don't mind, do you?' With that she took hold of the hem of her T-shirt and pulled the garment over her head, revealing her big, naked breasts. The two men smiled, Sam casually stroking the bulge at the front of his jeans. Now that the initiative had been taken, Lisa felt ready to join in. After all, they all knew why she was there; it wasn't as though they had to play any games.

'I think I'll join you,' she said, unbuttoning her blouse at the front. The men watched in silence as she removed the crisp, white covering from her breasts, arching her back and pushing them forward to their lustful gaze. She couldn't hope to compete with Sonia in size, of course, but they were still quite something, and Sam and Tyne were definitely impressed.

Sonia sat at Sam's feet, stroking his thigh and the ever growing bulse as they watched Lisa unhook the little skirt. She pulled it off quickly, now naked save for long, white socks and trainers. She sat back, faced the three Africans and opened her legs wide, rubbing her fingers suggestively over the wet slit. Sonia removed her shorts and joined her on the floor, taking the hand away from her glistening sex and replacing it with her own. Her caress was gentle, the fingers playing expertly with the bud causing the blonde's juices to flow, readying her for the pleasures to come.

Lisa put her hand between Sonia's widely splayed legs, feeling the softness of the hairless pussy, its wetness matched only by her own. For a moment the men were forgotten as the women prepared each other for fucking, expertly masturbating their engorged cunts with darting, probing fingers.

The men obviously decided that they wanted some of this. Both began to strip, their powerful, black bodies exposed quickly to Lisa's eager gaze. They clearly worked out, though in different ways; whilst Sam was hugely muscular, Tyne was slim and athletic, the contrast between them being ideal in her eyes.

Having stripped completely they sat back on the sofa, their erections jutting upwards, resting against their stomachs. Sam's was the smaller of the two, about six inches in length but very thick, with a large, bulbous head. Tyne's was a good two inches longer but not quite as fat; the combination of the two was going to give Lisa the satisfaction that she craved. She tore herself from the heavenly mutual masturbation session with Sonia and crawled over to the two men, kneeling at their feet.

She looked both innocently and excitedly into the dark, brown eyes of the handsome men, and took a stiff tool in each hand, gently rubbing them up and down. They hardened simultaneously with her touch, Sam's throbbing a couple of times, producing a short stream of sperm from the wide slit. Lisa bent forward and licked the come into her mouth, swallowing provocatively. She then moved her mouth to Tyne, taking as much of his slim length as she could, gulping hard, making her throat muscles simulate the movements of an excited vagina. He too throbbed, and she tasted the saltiness of his pre-come as she flicked her tongue round and round his hardness.

She moved her attentions back to Sam, opening her mouth wide to admit the huge head of his stubby erection. It was too fat to allow the playful circling of her tongue, so instead she made urgent sucking motions, wetting him with her saliva, taking him to the back of her throat.

Her face was buried in the mustiness of his pubic hair when she felt the warm wetness of Sonia's tongue against her bottom. At first it slid over her buttocks, tracing a trail from one side to the other, leaving its wet mark as it travelled. Then it slid up and round to the top of her crack, before slowly and agonisingly making its way between the soft, sensuous cheeks to her tight little hole. Here it paused, licking up and down wetly over her anus, causing the most unimaginable feelings in her lust-racked body. For a moment Lisa paused in her sucking, enjoying the feelings that Sonia was giving her, pushing her bottom out to allow the tongue more access to her hole.

Sonia soon seemed to settle in her task, happy to lick and probe orally into the other girl's anus. Lisa carried on enjoying the wet caress, and returned her concentrations to the two black erections in her hands. She took her mouth from Sam and began to rub both of them at the same rate, whilst Sonia lapped at her backside. She slid her tongue over Tyne's length, teasing his hardness with the very tip, at once tickling him and exciting him, bringing him dangerously close to orgasm. She licked around his balls, tightly held in their sack, and pushed his legs open so that she could lick under his scrotum, wanting to taste his hole, but his position on the sofa precluded that. Perhaps later.

She licked wetly over his balls again, taking them into her mouth together, running her tongue round and round them, sucking gently on the tender plums. She pushed them out of her mouth, then drew then in again, licking all the time, tracing a line with the tip of her tongue around the sack, then licked between the testicles and up along the vein of his shaft to the end, delicately teasing it with her expert tongue.

Sonia was licking around her anus now, no longer concentrating on the little hole, teasing her in the same way as she'd been teasing Tyne. Lisa forced her bum out more, desperate to have her female lover's tongue back on its target again, but Sonia held back, still sliding her tongue over the pert cheeks, occasionally allowing just the tip to pass quickly over the sphincter.

Lisa felt she would cry out. She hadn't realised how much sexual sensitivity there was in this area of her body; it yearned as wildly for attention as her hot, wet sex. She swallowed most of Tyne's length, contracting her cheeks and drawing back her tongue to afford him as much pleasure as she could give.

His response was immediate. He cried out, 'Oh, shit, here I go!' his throbbing lust filling Lisa's mouth, his back arched, his face contorted with a wild expression. At the same time, Sonia pressed her large mouth firmly against Lisa's bum, the tongue lapping greedily once again at her anus. Lisa felt she would die, the pleasure was so great. She took her mouth from Tyne's wilting manhood and transferred it to Sam's stiff erection, bobbing her head up and down, sucking greedily on his lovely, black meat.

She felt Sonia part the cheeks of her bottom with her thumbs, pulling open the entrance to her virgin hole. She almost bit into Sam's thick erection as she felt the long, wet tongue enter her, pushing what seemed to be inches within her tightness, before sliding slowly back, and almost out. It slid back in, then out; in, out, in, out, her anus being expertly tongue-fucked. She could never in her wildest fantasies have imagined the feelings that were tearing her apart ... she knew she was coming, coming without the slightest touch to her sex. She arched her back, offering her bum completely to her lover, marvelling at the length of the tongue impaled inside her, the thick, black lips pressed leech-like against her buttocks.

She sucked hard and fast on Sam's thickness, cradling and squeezing his balls with one hand whilst clawing at his chest-hair with the other. Her cry was muffled by his tool as she came, the painful pleasure of the orgasm causing her to lift her knees from the floor, her body for a moment suspended between the penis and the tongue.

Lisa fell heavily back to the floor, releasing Sam's penis from her panting mouth. Sonia sat back and smiled hugely at her, suggestively licking her lips. There was nothing to be said; they all knew that this had been her first experience of a tongue like Sonia's, as long as a man's stalk, and far more devastating in its effect.

Sam still hadn't come; Lisa couldn't do anything for him for a moment, she was too dazed from the gut-wrenching orgasm she'd just experienced, so she sat back and watched as the big man took Sonia's head in his hands and brought her face to his sex. She opened her huge mouth and took him inside in one movement, clamping her thick lips over the root, drawing her cheeks in and out as she gobbled. Sam's backside began to thrust quickly in time to the sucking he was getting, and it was only seconds before, with an almighty roar, he came in his girlfriend's mouth, pumping heavily as she swallowed all he could give.

The four lovers lay entwined on the floor for some time, recovering their senses, preparing for the sex that was to come. Lisa lay with her head in Sonia's lap, licking sleepily over the fleshy lips of her friend's pussy, occasionally flicking

71

her tongue over the hard bud of her clitoris. Sonia slid her tongue round and round Tyne's newly hard dick, soaking it with saliva, whilst Tyne kissed and suckled on Lisa's labia lips. Sam concentrated on her bum; the combined sensuousness of the two erotic kisses caused her mind to drift into a soothing calmness.

Sam moved away from the others slightly and lay on his back, holding his short, thick dick erect. 'Come on, darling,' he said, 'it's about time I got myself fucked by a white girl!'

Lisa pulled herself almost reluctantly from the warm pillow of Sonia's crotch and squatted over Sam on her heels, allowing him to point his erection at his target. She lowered herself a little, just enough to let the end touch the warm wetness. He moved it back and forth, letting the thick, bulbous end tease the outer lips open, without pushing in. She lowered herself a little more, but still Sam teased her, rubbing the end of his penis against her clitoris, then sliding it along the full length of her slit. She couldn't stand it. With a sudden move she sat down hard on him, taking his length fully inside her. Although not overly long, the thickness of the tool stretched her, filling her completely. She started to move up and down frantically, her raw clitoris rubbing along his stiffness with each downward thrust. At the same time Sam began to meet her movements with hard, upward movements, hammering so hard into her she almost fell from his body. She gripped firmly onto his hips, her fingernails digging into the sides of his backside, as she tried to drive her black stud into the carpet.

She felt a wetness at her anus again. At first, she thought Sonia was about to re-start her tongue love, but realised that the wetness was not spit but cream of some sort. Tyne was spreading the clear, sticky fluid over her bum, massaging it between her buttocks, especially on her hole. He pushed a wet finger inside her hole, easing it in and out, lubricating, preparing. Lisa slowed down her thrusting motions on Sam, enjoying the probing of Tyne's fingers.

72

She watched as he spread a liberal amount of cream on his hard, long cock, and she knew. She'd never been buggered, and now she was going to get it, at the same time as being impaled on the stiff stalk of another man!

Tyne positioned himself behind Lisa's delightful bum and pointed his penis at the tiny sphincter he was about to deflower. Lisa watched as he pressed the greased knob-end against her, pushing hard at the resisting entrance. Suddenly she felt it relax, allowing him to push two, then three inches inside her. He applied more cream to his length, moving the tool gently in and out, her anus taking more and more with each push. She knew he could feel Sam's thick dick through the thin membrane now; she knew he could feel its hardness, the ridges and veins, and that Sam would be experiencing the same sensations.

The two men started to pump into their conquest in unison, filling Lisa's body with each forward thrust. She felt complete, totally full of hard cock, wanting it to go on for ever.

After a short while the men changed their movements; they were obviously well rehearsed in this type of screwing. As one pushed in the other withdrew, so stirring up the feelings within Lisa to a point of frenzy; her thighs had no idea which way to respond. She held herself suspended at the crotch as they had her in any way they chose. She was totally at their mercy, they could do anything they wanted.

Sonia had been watching her colleague's buggery for a while, but had now apparently decided to join in the fun. She knelt in front of her, offering the large, black buttocks that Lisa had longed to kiss. She wasted no time, pressing her hungry mouth against the warmth of the delicious backside, running her tongue greedily over the tight hole and large, wet sex-lips. All the time the two men pumped in and out of Lisa's holes, screwing her solidly in a way she would never forget.

Sonia turned and squatted over Sam's face, and then leant back on her hands so that he could lick her bum whilst Lisa worked on her sex. She savoured the musty

73

flavour, bathing her face in the wetness of her female lover's pussy. She chewed hungrily at Sonia's big sex-lips, digging her tongue deep inside the velvet passage, burying her face against the hairless mound. When she finally came, her orgasm threatened to tear her apart; the build-up being so long and excruciatingly pleasurable that she felt she wouldn't be able to stand it.

She screamed and Sam let go inside her, pumping hard into her young body. Tyne still hammered into her bottom, but he wasn't finished yet. As Lisa's orgasm subsided and Sam's wilting manhood slipped from the confines of her soaking pussy, Tyne pulled swiftly from her bum and pushed her onto her back on the carpet. He forced open her legs and rammed his incredibly hard tool deep inside her sensitive sheath, humping her as hard as anything she'd experienced so far. There was no finesse, no technique; he just fucked her, as simple as that.

To her surprise Lisa found that the force of this onslaught awakened her clitoris yet again. As Tyne screwed her like an animal, her swollen bud took her sated body into yet another orgasm and she screamed, raising her bottom from the floor, and allowing Tyne to push his full length deep into her. He came with a loud shout. His thrusting was so fast it felt like an engine's piston pumping into her body, the pent-up sperm flooding inside her from his throbbing length.

Tyne collapsed over Lisa's exhausted body. They lay quietly until he had the strength to sit up, whilst she lay back, looking with real affection at her three lovers. Just for the moment she felt she couldn't take any more sex, no more cocks, fingers, tongues, whatever.

She wasn't allowed to rest for long. Sonia still hadn't had an orgasm, and she wasn't going to miss out. She reached behind a cushion and produced a huge, black dildo, far bigger than anything Lisa had imagined. Sonia smiled and brought it over to her, inviting her to inspect the monster. Lisa did so nervously, worried what her friend had in mind. It was well over a foot in length and as thick as a man's arm; there was no way she would be able to take it, even in her current, highly excited state.

She needn't have worried. Sonia kissed her lightly on the lips and spoke softly to her. 'I want you to put this on and fuck me; will you do it?'

Lisa nodded, wide eyed and curious, and Sonia showed her how to strap the mighty phallus to her body; the thin, leather thongs tied around her waist, between her buttocks and down the front of her crotch, holding the dildo erect.

Sonia lay on her back with her legs wide apart, holding them as far back as she could by grasping behind her knees. 'I want the lot, every inch,' she said, 'fuck me, and ignore me if I scream!'

Lisa knelt between the beautiful Amazon woman's legs, pushing the obscenely huge appendage to her gaping slit. As the enormous knob-end entered the receptive lips, Lisa sensed she could imagine what it must be like for a man: like having a giant clitoris rubbing against the soft folds of woman-flesh. She felt a strange, almost alien quivering feeling just inside her anus as she began to pump into her lover, experiencing a feeling of domination as the active partner in the coupling.

She'd managed to get about ten inches inside the darkness of Sonia's pussy by now, but there was still half as much again to go. Sonia pleaded with her to push all the way in, to hurt her if necessary, so desperately did she seem to want to be filled by this giant tool. They changed their positions slightly, and Lisa found that, by keeping most of the dildo inside her friend and pumping carefully, she was able to slide the last exposed length inch by inch inside the ravenous hole.

Their pubic mounds touched now, Lisa's downy hair tickling Sonia's shaven flesh. They ground their pussies together, sharing their wetness, Sonia totally impaled on the monster phallus. 'I'm going to come, you darling,' shouted Sonia, 'I'm going to come!' Lisa resumed the heavy pumping action that her own body constantly yearned for, drawing the tool out almost completely, then ramming it hard against the black girl's cervix, causing her to shout with the pleasure and the pain.

Suddenly Sonia arched her back and let out an almighty scream, so forceful that Lisa thought she might have seriously hurt her lover. The cry was of lust in orgasm: the violent release after incredible sex with two men and a girl. Sonia beat her fists hard on the floor, shaking her head from side to side, thrusting her hips upwards to meet Lisa's powerful humping.

Gradually, as her feelings subsided, Sonia relaxed, lying, sweat-covered on the carpet. Lisa slowly pulled the dildo out of its wet sheath and sat back, exhausted. She unstrapped the phallus and laid it to her side, then lay back against the sofa, panting. Sonia was out for the count, absolutely sated.

Lisa looked at Tyne and Sam, the sight of their shiny, black bodies causing familiar stirrings in her loins. She took a deep breath and gulped as she watched them crawl towards her, their erections once again hard and ready.

It was going to be a long night . . .

Chapter Four

'Good morning, Lisa! Come on, wake up: it's a lovely day!' Sonia's annoyingly cheerful voice snapped Lisa awake from her sleep of exhaustion, the bright light of day hurting her eyes. She was alone in the giant bed where she and her three lovers had ended up during their night of sexual excess, and was lying naked on top of the sheets.

'What time is it?' she said, sleepily, not really caring.

'Just past eleven. The boys went off to work hours ago. I thought you were never going to waken.'

'Well,' said Lisa, climbing unsteadily out of the bed, 'we didn't get a lot of sleep last night.'

'You'll get used to it,' said Sonia, chuckling, 'we all have to. Did you enjoy yourself?'

'Definitely. We must do it again, sometime.' Her eyes focused on her new friend, watching her busily preparing coffee. Sonia was wearing nothing but a tiny pair of white lace panties, her superb ebony body glistening in the sunlight. As she operated the handle of the coffee-grinder her massive breasts jiggled provocatively, causing familiar tremors of lust to course through Lisa's loins. 'You've got a fantastic body, Sonia.'

'So have you, Lisa. Sam and Tyne said that, apart from me of course, you were the best fuck they'd ever had.'

'Really?' Lisa was genuinely flattered, that two obviously experienced men had said such a complimentary thing about her.

'Sure. Mind you, that's all part of being a Lust Angel.

You'll find that sex comes naturally to you. You'll want to do things that you never knew existed.'

'I already have,' said Lisa, blushing slightly. 'The way you used your tongue . . . it's amazing!'

'The old man gave me a really long tongue; that's my speciality, along with domination. I really get off when I tie a bloke up and give him a good thrashing! You should try it some time.'

'Maybe I will, one day.'

'It was obvious what your special talent is,' said Sonia, grinning broadly, 'Sam and Tyne said they'd never known such a brilliant cock-sucker!'

'Thanks. It seems to come naturally to me, and I do love it.'

Lisa retrieved her skirt from the floor and pulled it on, joining Sonia at the table. The coffee percolator was beginning to bubble, promising impending refreshment to her parched throat. 'How long have you been a Lust Angel?' she said.

'Getting on for four years, I suppose. I'm nearly twenty-two now.'

'What did you look like, you know . . . before?'

'I was short and skinny.' Sonia laughed at the memory. 'The exact opposite of what I look like now!'

'Me too, I mean I was short but fat. It really is too good to be true, isn't it?'

'You might say that, although we have to work hard sometimes.'

'What d'you mean?'

Sonia looked serious for once. 'We are asked to be sort of unpaid escorts on occasion, for businessmen and politicians. Don't get me wrong, it's great fun; some of the things these blokes get up to surprise even me. I think Frank and the old man use us to gain some sort of power over them though, and I'm not so sure it's all above board. Still, that's not our problem, eh? As long as we get plenty of dick, why should we complain?'

Lisa smiled in agreement. Her new strength of will, her

ability to control men, this was all down to her ravishing good looks, nothing more. She excused herself and went to the bathroom.

Inside, she almost habitually caught a look at herself in the mirror. Despite the night she'd just experienced she still looked fantastic, albeit a little tired. She lifted her skirt, squatted over the toilet and began to pee.

Sonia walked in, smiling as usual. Lisa stopped her flow, unused to being disturbed in this way. Sonia grinned and reached down, touching her between the legs. The pee started to flow again, running copiously over the black girl's hand as she fondled Lisa's sex. Their mouths met, and they kissed passionately.

With a sudden, almost shocking urgency Lisa came, still urinating over her friend's hand, her cry muffled in the depths of their kiss. She flung her arms around Sonia's neck and gripped her tightly, until the sensations subsided, and she fell back heavily on the toilet seat.

Still grinning, Sonia rinsed her hands in the bathroom sink. 'Do you feel better for that?' she said.

'I didn't even think I needed it, but it was fantastic!' Lisa rose from the loo and turned on the shower. 'Don't we ever stop wanting it?'

'Nope. Listen, I gotta go now. Help yourself to coffee and something to eat, and lock up when you leave, won't you.'

'Yes, sure, er . . . thanks.'

'Don't mention it. See you at the party.'

'Party?' Lisa half remembered something that Frank had said.

'You'll get your instructions,' said Sonia, pulling on a pair of tight jeans and a sweater, 'they'll probably be waiting for you when you get home. Bye.'

'Bye.' Lisa watched her lovely friend hurriedly leave the flat, her thoughts confused but excited.

Lisa arrived back at her flat just after midday. As expected, a parcel was waiting mysteriously in her letter-box. She undid the parcel, bursting with curiosity, and carefully took out the flimsy, white garment, holding it in front of her. It looked like a very short dress, made of lightweight cotton, with a rather unusual halter-neck design. It was accompanied in the package by a slim rope-belt and a pair of sandals with particularly long leather straps. Also in the bundle was the note from Frank, which Sonia had told her to expect.

She'd been delighted when Sonia had reminded her about the party; Janet had told her of these almost legendary events, enviously listening as her friend recounted tales of wild orgies of Bacchanalian proportions and she'd longed to join in; now she was to have her chance. She was also delighted to learn that Janet and Sonia were to be there; she couldn't wait to see their lovely naked bodies again as they humped themselves crazy on some well-endowed studs.

She opened the envelope and took out the expensive notepaper inside. Apart from giving her the time and address details, Frank's instructions were short and to the point.

She was to wear the costume, covered only by a coat, and take a taxi to an address in nearby Brighton. There she would meet a professional photographer, who she must allow to take 'glamour' pictures of her in the costume, copies of which she must bring to the party as proof. She must do whatever the photographer asked of her, he being a well-known and somewhat temperamental character, and she mustn't upset him. After the photo-session she would be brought to the party in a car. The final instruction was not to discuss her challenge with any of the other girls, as everybody had their own tasks to perform.

It was already getting near the time to start her journey so, after calling for a cab she started to dress herself in the skimpy material. She pulled it over her head like a dress and smoothed it down over her naked body.

It resembled a short, Roman toga of the type worn by overly-developed slave-girls in old Hollywood epics. The halter design held one breast firmly in place, but the other was completely exposed. The garment's length was cut just below her naked sex, but there were no panties in the package, so clearly none must be worn.

Lisa was already feeling excited; the toga was extremely erotic, showing off her superb breasts to their utmost. She tied the rope tightly round her waist, which made her bust seem even bigger, then worked out how to lace up the sandals. The leather straps criss-crossed from the soles of the footwear all the way up the legs, ending about an inch below the hem of her toga, where she was able to secure the brown leather with small, brass buckles.

She heard the taxi draw up outside, and quickly slipped a coat over her exposed body, grabbed her purse and hurried out.

The drive to the photographer's took about half an hour, during which time Lisa considered the events to come. The party itself would be fun, of that she was sure. She would be among new friends, there would be lots of booze and sex, just what she needed. The photo-session though, that was a different matter. The challenge seemed rather tame, even dressed as she was. Perhaps there was more to it than she'd been told . . .

The studio was situated down a dimly-lit alley in the centre of the town. A plaque on the door proclaimed the business premises of Chas Roberts, Photographer and Media Consultant, so it looked genuine enough. She walked nervously into the building and up a long, narrow staircase to the first floor, where a second plaque indicated that she had found her destination. She knocked lightly on the door and entered.

Inside she found two young men, surrounded by the various accoutrements of their trade; cameras, lighting equipment, fabric screens and one of those open white umbrellas on a stand, the purpose of which escapes most people.

One of the men came over to greet her. He was tall and

slim, with long, dark hair pulled back into a pony-tail, and sporting a closely trimmed black beard. He smiled. 'Hi,' he said in a very friendly voice, 'you must be Lisa. I'm Chas and this is Mark.'

Mark waved from his seat, surrounded as he was by masses of photographs. He was much younger than Chas, no more than sixteen, of fair complexion and short, cropped hair. Lisa couldn't help wondering if these two were an 'item', so perfectly suited did they appear.

'Take your coat off and have a seat,' said Chas, indicating a small chair with the least rubbish on it, 'I'll get you a coffee.'

She nervously slipped her coat off, revealing her near-nakedness to the two strangers. Chas looked her over, appreciatively, Mark gazed at her with a fixed stare, his eyes clearly focused on her large, exposed breast. 'Lovely,' said Chas, pouring coffee from a steaming jug, 'just perfect.'

Lisa smiled, took the cup offered to her and sat down. Mark continued to stare for a moment, then went back to his work. After a short pause there was a knock at the door and two young men entered. They saw Lisa sitting there, but didn't seem in the least bit concerned by her semi-nudity.

They chatted with Chas, obviously old friends, sipping at the coffee he gave them. He introduced them to her as Tim and Donny, two male models who were going to be in some of the pictures with her. She began to wonder just how far she was expected to go; she wasn't sure that she was ready to pose for pornographic photographs, but then these two men were extremely handsome, young, and clean cut with flawless complexions. She wondered what their bodies were like under the baggy clothes they wore.

Chas seemed to catch her thoughts. 'Don't worry,' he said. 'Tim and Donny are professionals, like me. You're here to do glamour photos; I won't ask you to do anything you don't want to do.'

She felt reassured now, and relaxed against the high back of the chair, taking another sip of the coffee. Chas sent the two men into another room to change, and began to arrange lights around a Victorian-style sofa in front of a small camera set on a tripod. She'd somehow expected the camera to be one of the huge affairs she'd seen in the past, but soon realised that technology had moved on somewhat since her school photographs had been taken.

Chas motioned for her to take her place on the sofa. She sat, bolt upright, as he busied himself with the hot lights. Tim and Donny returned, wearing similar togas to her own, but with the advantage of dark-coloured briefs to shield their modesty, Lisa felt this a little unfair; her genitals were naked, only just hidden by the hem of her garment, so why were these beautiful young guys allowed to have pants on?

They sat on either side of her, whilst Chas finished his work with the lighting. He then walked to the camera and looked through the aperture. He motioned with his hand for them to move closer together. 'Now come on, you three, bunch up. You're supposed to like each other. Tim, put your arm around Lisa's waist, that's it. Lisa, you've got a lovely pair of tits – push them out!'

She obeyed, arching her back so her breasts jutted forward like pink melons, her nipples hard with her rising lust. She felt the familiar wetness begin to soak her sex, and hoped it wouldn't stain the expensive sofa material. 'Now, Donny, put your arm over her shoulder and cup the bare tit in your hand, that's right. Lisa, you rest one hand between each of the boy's legs, as high up as you dare!' He was teasing her, she knew, but she was beginning to enjoy the game. She rested her hands between the two sets of firmly muscled legs, the backs of her hands just touching the bulges in their pants.

Chas took a few snaps, then stood back from the camera. 'It's no good, boys, I can still see your pants. They'll have to come off – you don't mind, do you Lisa?'

'No, no, it's OK. I'm not wearing any.'

The two male models slipped out of their knickers, revealing their hardening erections to her eager gaze. They resumed the pose on either side of her, and she returned her hands to their bulges, this time feeling the smoothness of their nakedness against her fingers. She felt both stalks pushing against her hands as they hardened, whilst Chas carried on clicking away at the scene which was fast becoming pornographic.

He started to issue some directions. 'Tim, take your hand from her waist and rest it between her legs, that's it; now, keep it an inch or so from where I know you'd like to put it; she's not that kind of girl.'

Lisa smiled. She wanted to shout out, 'Oh, yes I am!' but resisted the temptation.

Tim rested his hand as instructed, agonizingly close to her sex. She wanted to grasp his arm, to pull his fingers against her; she wanted both of these gorgeous men, but didn't want to spoil the session, unsure how far Chas wanted her to go. More photos were taken, all the time Donny caressing her exposed breast casually, whilst Tim moved his thumb gently against her inner thigh, almost but not quite touching her sopping pussy.

Eventually, she decided she'd had enough of the teasing. She pushed her hips forward as though making herself comfortable, purposely looking away from Tim. His fingertip touched her wet, outer-lips, sending a terrific tremor of lustful feeling through her body. She had never felt such excitement from just the simple touch of a hand to her sex; she felt her juices flowing copiously, and knew he must be feeling them too.

He didn't remove his hand; instead he moved his finger slowly up and down against her vaginal lips, opening them to his touch. She widened her legs slightly and he slipped his thumb inside her, rubbing the knuckle against her erect bud. She turned her hand to hold his erection, feeling its full length with a long, slow movement of her wrist. He was big, certainly over seven inches, and very thick. She repeated the action with Donny, finding him equally hard with a slightly shorter stalk of similar girth.

Tim was massaging her wetness with all his fingers now,

making her grind her pubis against his hand as though wanting to swallow the whole arm inside her sex-racked body. She gripped the base of both of the firm, hard rods now and rubbed them steadily and simultaneously, knowing that her movements must be obvious to the photographer.

Chas carried on taking snap after snap, clearly enjoying the way things were progressing. He took the camera from the tripod and moved closer to the threesome, taking close-ups of their genitals from various angles.

'Now, Lisa,' he said, 'kneel on the sofa and hold Tim's dick with one hand . . . stick your bottom out towards Donny . . . lovely! Now, bend your head as though you are going to put Tim's cock into your mouth . . . that's perfect . . . now, Donny, kneel behind her and point your stiffy at her pussy; and keep your distance!'

Lisa held Tim's marvellous erection about half an inch from her open mouth. God, how she wanted to suck it! She knew she had another fine length just as close to her aching entrance – so near, yet so far! She was going mad with frustration. She felt she shouldn't make the first move, but knew also that these lads were professionals; they would do the photographer's bidding to the letter.

At length, she realised that once again she would have to take the initiative, albeit cautiously. She moved her head slightly closer to the large, bulbous knob-end before her, almost touching it with her lips. She stuck out her tongue slightly, the tip making contact with the slit, then pushed her tongue further forward, lapping around the thick, peach-shaped head, before moving her head sharply away a couple of inches, glancing nervously at Chas.

A thin line of male pre-come stuck to her lower lip, connecting it sensuously to the end of the hard cock. The strand glistened in the glare of the photographer's lights.

Chas was unconcerned; she could obviously do what she liked. She realised, at last, that she was there to do straight pornography, that the game had been to arouse her so that she would comply. She stripped off the toga, revealing her perfect, naked form to the two gorgeous men she was about to make love with, then reached behind her with her hand and clutched Donny's hardness. She guided the tip towards her aching pussy and took the full length inside her at one thrust. She then leant forward and took as much of Tim's member in her mouth as she could, and started to move both ends of her body erotically, backwards and forwards.

'Take it easy, Lisa,' said Chas, looking directly at her sex through the lens of his camera. 'You'll blur the photos. Just do as I say, and we'll get some smashing shots for you. There will be plenty of opportunities for hard fucking as we go along!'

Lisa held herself still reluctantly, wishing they were making a blue-video. Her two lovers positioned themselves so that just the tip of their superb erections disappeared into her, showing their full lengths to the camera.

'Perfect boys, now, fuck her slowly. I'm using quite a fast film, so it should be OK.' The men started to pump into the lovely girl sandwiched between them, the steady rhythm easing the pent-up agonies that had been tearing at her loins. She relaxed as the easy thrusting of Donny's tool in and out of her body began her build-up to the first of what she felt was going to be many orgasms. Tim's thick length felt good in her mouth, the end pressed against the roof of her mouth as she lapped her tongue hungrily around it, rubbing the exposed stem with both hands.

'Right, let's have some licking shots. Tim, lie on your back. Lisa, sit on his face and Donny, you stick your tongue into her arse.'

It all sounded rather clinical, but she did as instructed. She was far too high on sex to do otherwise. She lowered herself onto Tim's mouth, thrilling as his tongue lapped expertly around the wet lips of her sex. She bent right over his firm, perfect body and took him again into her mouth, arching her back to present her anus for Donny's oral attentions.

She caught her breath as she felt the wetness of his

tongue slithering over her small hole, prodding at it like a tiny penis. She remembered the ecstasy that she had felt when Sonia had pushed her long, wet tongue deep into her bum, and willed Donny to do the same. His tongue was nowhere near as long as her female lover's though, but he did manage to push the tip into her anus, moving it round and round, clearly enjoying the taste of her perfect bottom.

'Right, I want you to sit on Tim's cock, now.' Chas was still barking orders, but this time she objected.

'No, no!' she shouted. 'Not yet ... I'm coming!' With that she ground her nether-regions back at the two wet mouths that were pleasuring her and squealed as the flood of orgasm took hold of every sense in her body. She couldn't have stopped then; Chas would have had to have killed her first, but he just carried on clicking the camera incessantly, recording her release for posterity.

After a moment she relaxed, and obediently squatted over Tim's reclining form, taking his hard-on in her hand and guiding it to her wet slit. She sat down on his length, enjoying its size, and the way it throbbed slightly within her; the sensation electrifying her, readying her for more and more.

Donny knelt by the side of the rutting couple, facing the busy camera. Lisa took hold of his stiffness and brought it to her mouth, tasting her own sex-scent on his hard stalk as she gobbled him deeply. She rode up and down on the shaft that was impaling her, whilst never once letting the other marvellous erection leave her mouth. Donny thrust gently against her head, making love to her beautiful face, clearly impressed at the way she swallowed nearly all the length.

Lisa used all her recently learned expertise to please these two studs; both of them were no doubt used to screwing countless women in this way. She wanted them to remember; to remember the girl whose vaginal muscles gripped them tightly, undulating over their lengths, making them harder than they'd ever been before. She wanted them to talk about the way she used her mouth on their sex, the deep gobble that was her speciality. They'd look at the photos and want her again, of that she was sure.

She began to think of other people who might look at the snaps, hundreds, maybe thousands of men, their dicks in their frustrated hands, wanking at the sight of *her* getting fucked! The knowledge thrilled her, to say the least.

Suddenly, at Chas's signal, Donny took his penis from her mouth and moved behind her. She assumed he was going to enter her anus, but she was wrong. Tim pulled back so that just the tip of his erection was inside her wet lips, then she groaned with the pleasure of surprise as both of the thick lengths slid within her pussy, filling her beyond belief. They took her very slowly, both to make sure they stayed in the velvety sheath, and to afford Chas some splendid photographs.

The sensation of having two big erections inside her sex at the same time drove her wild. She could feel every part of them, every vein as they stretched her incredibly, pumping their full lengths with each synchronised thrust.

The humping got steadily faster, the men breathing heavily as they began to near their climaxes. Lisa could feel her own orgasm approaching quickly and gripped them tightly with her inner sex-muscles, arching her back and holding her arms above her head, her body totally supported by the two, hard tools.

'Oh, wow, that's fantastic!' she shouted, the feelings tearing at her sex, her bottom, her entire body. Her total consciousness now centred between her legs and on the amazing feeling as the two, thick pricks shot their seed deep into her ravaged hole. Both men pumped hard into her, gripping her bottom tightly with their fingers, the nails digging into her soft flesh, as their hips thrust and pounded against their willing victim.

When they were sated, when every drop of come had been drained from the three lovers they fell apart, Lisa lying across the strong body of Tim, their sweat mingling as they held each other.

'That was just wonderful,' said Chas, 'just perfect.'

She wondered if he'd been aroused, or was he so much a professional that he saw the copulating three-some merely as models posing? The thought intrigued her. He hadn't touched her in any way during the session, and there had been no sign of an erection in his tight jeans. Even if he was gay he would have surely responded to the sight of the two naked studs who had serviced her, but there was nothing.

The same could not be said for Mark, the young assistant who was now busily switching off lights and unplugging equipment. The crotch of his jeans bulged quite ridiculously, obviously concealing a hard-on of not insubstantial proportions. Lisa sat open-legged on the sofa watching him work, her two lovers having departed to another room to shower and dress. Chas had gone into a dark-room to develop the prints for her to take to the party, leaving his assistant alone with his new-found pornstar.

She smiled as she watched Mark work, seeing him glance surreptitiously at her, his eyes darting from her huge, heaving breasts to the wet, engorged lips of her well-serviced pussy. She knew he wanted her and, for that matter, that she wanted him. She marvelled at her own capacity for sex; as promised, she was becoming totally insatiable!

'Did you enjoy the show, Mark?' she said.

'Yes, yes, it was very good.'

'I bet you get to fuck all the models, don't you?'

'Er, no, I mean, I only started this week. You're the first I've seen like this.'

'Come here, Mark,' she ordered. He walked awkwardly over to her, his jean-front visibly straining under the pressure of his erection. She felt it really must be hurting him, restricted as it was. She rubbed the palm of her hand over the mountainous bulge, licking her lips. He started to breath heavily, his hand shaking noticeably. 'Relax, Mark,' she said, softly, 'you must relax.' She held the top button of his jeans with one hand and slowly unzipped him with the other, her face inches away. She pulled both his jeans and pants down over his slim thighs, gradually baring his pubic region. His erection was slowly revealed, the length pulled downwards by the movement of his pants.

Lisa pressed her mouth against the hair at the base of his hardness as she continued to remove the clothing, and licked slowly down the length of the back of his tool as it's proportions were uncovered. Finally the straining rod was released from the tight material, springing up against her mouth, pushing hard at her face. She took hold of the root, squeezing hard with her grip, watching fascinated as the bulbous end thickened even more, growing almost purple in colour. His sex was noticeably large, about an inch longer than Tim's, and considerably fatter, contrasting to his small physique and narrow, boyish hips.

She licked at the slit, already wet with his own excitement, and managed to take the large end into her mouth. She drew in her cheeks and bobbed her head back and forth, her tongue playfully licking around the end of the big tool, knowing that he would never have a better sensation than the one he was experiencing now.

She realised from the movements of his hips and the groaning noises he was making that he wasn't going to be able to hold back for long, so she withdrew him from her suckling mouth and lay back on the sofa, opening her legs wide and raising them into the air, one hand fingering herself between her legs.

'Fuck me, Mark, fuck me now!'

He almost leapt onto the body that was offered so erotically to him, plunging his full length into her. Immediately, he started on rapid strokes, thumping hard on her at an amazingly fast rate, grunting and pumping at this beautiful woman for all he was worth. Lisa cried out in delight as their pubic mounds thrashed heavily together, digging her fingernails into his small, tight bum. This was a perfect way to end the session, she'd had enough teasing, titillation and foreplay. The sheer violence of this inexperienced fucking-machine suited her mood perfectly.

'That's it, Mark, ram deep into me! Give it to me hard,

I need you to fuck me senseless! God, it feels bigger than when I had those two dicks inside me!'

His pumping became even faster, Lisa's body vibrating with the speed of the thrusts. His moment was near. 'I want you to come over me ... pull it out when you're ready!' Mark obeyed almost immediately, his withdrawal from her coinciding with Chas's return to the studio. He watched, transfixed as his young assistant's huge tool shot spurt after spurt over the lovely girl's body, the stream coating her hair, face and breasts with white, sticky fluid. She reached up and took the throbbing monster in her hand, teasing out the last drop of come, bending forward to lick it from the end of his still hard manhood.

There was the sound of a camera clicking, followed by the buzz of an automatic film-winder. 'Well, Mark,' said Chas, 'it looks like I've discovered *two* new models today!'

Janet was woken by the sound of her doorbell ringing. Sleepily, she struggled out of the warmth of her bed, and staggered naked to the door. 'Who is it?' she called, through the thick panelled woodwork.

'Post,' came the curt reply, 'parcel delivery.' Realising her naked state just in time, Janet grabbed hold of a coat lying near her on a chair and, holding the thick garment in front of her voluptuous charms, unbolted and opened the door. 'Morning, love,' said the postman in a sickeningly cheery tone, 'get you out of bed, did I?'

'Yes.' She took hold of the parcel and wrote something resembling her signature on the document offered to her by the delivery-man. To do this, she had to hold the coat against her breasts with one arm, which proved difficult. The postman just smiled, his eyes watching her lecherously.

It was only when she closed the door that she realised her body had been on display to his eager gaze from the waist down. 'Oh, bugger!' she said to herself, throwing the coat back onto the chair. Actually, she'd taken quite a fancy to this chap in the past and felt that this accidental nudity might have broken the ice. Maybe next time she'd invite him in . . .

The parcel was quite large and soft. Janet opened the envelope that was attached to it and read. It was from Frank. She'd been expecting him to call her as he'd invited her to the party in London that evening, and she didn't even have the address. The note gave her all the necessary information.

The party was to be held in a private house near King's Cross; a valuable client of his wanting to meet Janet and other colleagues of Frank's. He'd invited all the Lust Angels including Lisa, to her delight, and the party was to be fancy-dress. Her costume was in the parcel. Similar packages had been sent to the other girls, together with some special 'instructions'. This was typical of Frank; he always did something to liven up the party, to get the girls in the right frame of mind before they even arrived.

Janet was instructed to wear the costume and take the train to London, her challenge being to get herself laid on the journey. In common with the other girls, she would be required to relate her adventure to the party-goers during the evening. She tore open the parcel nervously. Inside was what appeared to be a rather ordinary set of clothes, dark in colour and of fairly rough material.

It was only when she started examining the items that she realised she was holding a school uniform of the type worn by hapless girls who attended posh, private establishments in the forties and fifties. Janet gulped. She had a sixty-mile train journey and a ride on the London Underground to look foward to wearing this gear. Getting laid wasn't going to be much of a challenge.

After taking a shower, Janet returned to the room and decided to try the costume on. Frank had missed nothing. First, she put on a pair of black, seamed stockings and lacy suspender-belt, then a tiny pair of leather panties, also black. Not really school issue, she thought, but he knew she enjoyed the feel of the soft material against her sex. The back was little wider than string, disappearing between her pert buttocks. She now put on the crisp, white blouse, buttoning the sleeves and the front up to her neck. In one of the breast-pockets she noticed a pack of condoms, the label clearly visible through the thin material. Janet smiled to herself. Talk about a pervert's dream!

Next she pulled on a navy-blue pleated mini-kilt, observing with little surprise that the hem only just covered the tops of her stockings. Finally, she dressed in a tie, regulation blazer and black, low-heeled shoes. The finishing touch was a small satchel, which she hung loosely about her shoulders.

She looked into her mirror, amused by the image that met her. The costume was definitely over the top; no schoolgirl would risk going out dressed in such an erotic way, that was for sure. But she had to accept that she looked good; her fresh, innocent complexion enabling her to be taken for someone a number of years younger, so she certainly looked the part!

The blazer and the skirt ended at the same place, just below her crotch. The striped tie lay almost suggestively between her firm, round breasts, one nipple visible through the cotton, the other hidden by the blatantly placed pack of rubbers. She turned sideways, quickly. The flick of the kilt revealed the darkness of her stocking-tops and a glimpse of white thigh. She turned her back on the mirror and bent forward, looking over her shoulder. Everything showed, including the thin strip of black leather disappearing between her buttocks.

She phoned Lisa in the hope of getting her to travel up with her, to give her some sort of support, but learned that other arrangements had been made for her friend and she had been sworn to secrecy. Frank had thought of everything. Janet was going to have to face the journey alone; she felt she'd be lucky to get to the party, dressed as she was and, if this was what she had to put up with, what on earth were the other girls wearing?

Lisa had said nothing and hadn't appeared nervous, but then she had changed a lot since her transformation; she was a horny little cow now, probably willing to do anything Frank asked of her.

The taxi arrived to take Janet to the station. She walked slowly to the car, her blazer done up at the front, the sight of her nevertheless causing the elderly driver to stare, open-mouthed. She sat in the front passenger seat, her legs pressed tightly together. She was amazed how nervous she felt; Frank was a bastard; he'd pay for this!

The cab arrived quickly at the station. Janet offered a note in payment, but the driver brushed it aside. 'Have it on me, darling,' said the old man, 'you've made my day. I'll be thinking of you when I'm in the bath, tonight!'

'Dirty old sod,' thought Janet, as she hurried to the platform to catch the London train. The ticket-collector whistled after her; a couple of young lads blew kisses. She was beginning to feel rather sexy.

She took her place in one of the comfortable, first-class compartments that the ticket Frank had thoughtfully provided allowed. She sat by the window, alone in the six-seated area, hoping, in a way, that no one would join her. Being a late afternoon train to London it was very quiet, unlike its journey back from the city, when every corner would be crammed with hordes of released commuters. It was quite possible that she was the only person in the carriage.

The train began to pull away. Janet was still alone, and was now beginning to worry that she would be unable to fulfil Frank's challenge. It was very important to her that she did what was asked, that she got herself laid on the train; Frank would be both surprised and disappointed if she failed in this simple task.

Suddenly, the door slid noisily open, and a distinguished-looking, middle-aged chap dressed in a smart suit entered, breathing quite heavily. 'Didn't think I was going to make it!' he said, throwing his briefcase onto the luggage-rack. He sat down hard on the seat opposite Janet, and only then did he seem to notice her. His breathing

94

stopped short for a moment, and he gulped visibly. She smiled to herself . . . he was impressed.

She opened her blazer and sat back. His eyes fell immediately to her chest, no doubt taking in the sight of her nipple and the pack of contraceptives showing clearly through the material. Then he looked at her legs. She opened them slightly, all the time pretending to look absently through the window, but in fact seeing his reflection in the glass. He could see the tops of her stockings now, and perhaps even the black vee of her panties.

He coughed. 'Going all the way?' She giggled, girlishly. She had an act to put on. 'I'm sorry, that's an old joke. You're a very attractive young lady, you know.'

'Thank you, sir,' said Janet, as innocently as she could. She knew she'd got him; now she had to take care she didn't scare him off.

'You don't often see schoolgirls dressed in full uniform. They tend to wear jeans and ugly, so-called trendy clothes. It's a shame, though, because a girl in a school uniform can look very sexy.'

Janet feigned surprise. 'Oh, really? Do you think I look sexy?'

'Very.'

'Oh, gosh, I don't know what to say!' The businessman smiled, kindly. There was a trace of sweat on his upper lip.

'Now, come on, young lady, you *know* you look sexy. I'm sure your school doesn't insist you wear your skirts so short, for a start.' She smiled, looking down shyly. 'And I can't imagine any school making the girls wear stockings instead of tights these days.'

'I hate tights,' said Janet, truthfully, 'stockings make me feel, well, nice.'

'You mean randy.'

'Yes, I suppose I do.'

'Do you like sex?'

'What d'you mean?' Janet's acting ability surprised even her. She was getting very wet between the legs; she just wanted this man to screw her, but she had to play the game.

'I can see the condoms in your pocket . . . you obviously like to be well prepared.'

'Oh, I see. Well, yes, I do like sex . . . very much.'

'Is there one special boyfriend?'

'No, I like lots of boys . . . and men.'

'Do you go with older men?' He was shaking visibly now, the sweat on his lip becoming more and more pronounced.

'If I like them.'

'Do you like me?'

She took a long look at him, for what must have been an age to the man. Then she smiled seductively, opening her legs a little more.

'I think you're really nice,' she said.

'May I sit next to you?' he said, standing up. She just smiled. The man pulled down the blinds against the partition to the corridor. 'There's no lock, but I don't think we'll be disturbed. The train doesn't stop until we get to London.' He sat next to her and slipped his arm around her shoulders. 'You really are a sexy little thing,' he said, hugging her tightly. 'How old are you?' Janet thought for a second.

'Seventeen,' she lied, suppressing the desire to lisp, thinking that would be a little over the top. She felt a slight tinge of disgust for this man, nearly three times the supposed age of the girl he was intending to have sex with, but then thought, what the hell: she was enjoying the game. It also had to be said that he was very good-looking: the powerful, executive type, which she found most arousing.

He put a slightly trembling hand on her knee and let it slide up her stocking-covered limb, his fingers soon touching the bare flesh at the top of her leg. She turned her face to his and they kissed. Janet used all her expertise; the little-girl act was over; there was fucking to be done. He seemed a little taken aback by the passion with which she kissed him, her tongue delving deep into his mouth.

'You certainly know how to kiss a guy!'

'Thank you,' she said, pressing her mouth against his once more. His fingers now touched the leather of her panties, and he started to roughly massage her sex. She groaned, feeling the wetness begin to flood as her pent-up frustrations and excitement took over. He ran his fingers up and down her slit, tracing the shape of her, until she pulled her mouth away from his.

'Take them off, take them off!' she commanded. He knelt in front of her, in order to obey. He pushed both his hands up her tiny skirt and clasped hold of the sides of the little panties. She raised her bottom from the seat and he pulled them down, over her stockings, and her school shoes. She sat back with her legs wide open, her heels on the seat, playing suggestively with the lips of her fully aroused sex. He watched for a moment, enjoying the view, then moved forward, burying his head in her crotch.

She caught her breath as she felt his tongue slide around her pussy-lips, teasing and stimulating her. She put her legs over his shoulders, pulling him closer with her strong thigh muscles. He responded by tucking his hands under her bum and lifting her slightly, allowing his tongue to drive deeper inside her.

He suckled wetly at his prize, for a while concentrating his licking to the outer lips, taking the fleshy folds in his mouth, drawing them in and out. Then his tongue found her bud and he fluttered it rapidly over the hardening button, bringing her closer and closer to orgasm. She was groaning loudly now, digging her heels into his back, certain she was hurting him.

He didn't stop; the more she groaned the more he lapped, tasting her sweet mustiness as she thrust her mound into his face.

He lifted her up a little more, adjusting his own position slightly, and began to lick cautiously at her anus. Receiving no objection he started to lick hungrily, slithering the full length of his tongue over the tight hole. He teased her with the tip, pushing it in ever so slightly. She loved every moment of his attentions: her enjoyment of the pleasures of anal sex was a most perfect gift from the old man, and it was teaching her new feelings, new lusts every day.

His tongue went back to her pussy. She was so close to coming that he just needed to let the wetness of his mouth touch her clitoris and she orgasmed, biting her hand to stop herself screaming with the rampant pleasure of his expert licking, fearing that the cries of her release would bring unwelcome help from another part of the train. Her thighs bucked, as she raised her bottom from the seat, driving her sex into his loving mouth.

After a moment, he sat back and watched as she recovered. She didn't move from her position on the seat, her heels still on the edge, her chest heaving as she breathed heavily. She let the fingers of both hands stray down between her legs, pulling at the wet labia lips, three or four fingers pushing in and out of her silky sheath. He watched, mesmerised. She was ready for him. She wanted him, hard and pumping, right now. She opened her legs wide again, the wetness glistening in the late afternoon sunlight.

'Oh, fuck me, sir, please fuck me.'

'Turn round,' he said. 'I want to do it from behind.' She wondered if he was going to put it up her bottom; she didn't mind if he wanted to do that later, but first she wanted a straight, hard seeing-to in her aching pussy. She knelt on the carriage seat, and held on to the arm-rests, her face pressed against the white linen of the head-restraint. She arched her back and pushed her bottom out to him, willing him to take her.

'Give me one of your rubbers,' he said, 'I daren't get a little schoolgirl pregnant, eh?'

Janet was safe in that respect, another bonus of being a Lust Angel, but continued to play the game. She handed him the packet, without moving her position. It seemed to take an age as he fumbled with the rubber, but at last he grasped her backside with both hands and she felt the thick end of his penis touching her wet sex-lips.

She pushed her bottom out even more, almost forcing

98

him into her. She groaned hoarsely as she felt him push deep inside her, the slight roughness of the ribbed condom stimulating her clitoris which had quickly lost its post-orgasmic tenderness and began to respond to his long, slow thrusts. The train rocked crazily as it raced over some points, the sudden movements enhancing the steady thrusting of hard erection inside soft, wet pussy.

The train's pace slowed down considerably for a time and with it their love-making. The screwing became gentler and less urgent as he relaxed into a steady pace, as though determined to give this young woman the best time she'd ever had.

The train picked up speed and, as though linked in some inexplicable way, the man started to move faster and faster, obviously nearing his climax. Janet moved a hand to her bud, rubbing it hard to bring herself off with her lover. His pumping was becoming more urgent as he hammered into his conquest. What must be going through his mind, she thought, as he shagged this beautiful, uniform-clad nymphet.

He groaned and started to come. She clenched her thigh muscles to grip his throbbing tool inside her. He stopped thrusting and held himself still, letting his sperm fill the rubber, enjoying the full sensation of the moment, before driving hard again inside her until he was sated.

'Tickets please!' The door slid open suddenly and the ticket-collector entered the compartment. 'Tickets, ple . . . Oh, my word, what have we here?' He closed the door quickly, locking it with his special key.

'You're a bit old to be doing that to such a young woman, aren't you?'

The businessman fell back, his drooping manhood still clasped in rubber. 'Oh, come on, mate,' he said, 'look at her; I couldn't resist . . .'

'It's all right, sir,' said Janet, resuming her little school-girl act, 'I asked him to do it.'

The railman looked hard at her, his eyes savouring the sight of her naked bottom, the stockings, the wet, puffily aroused sex. 'Did you, now? So, you like a good fucking, do you?'

'Oh yes, sir, I love it!'

'I really should report you . . .' he started, reaching out his hand and stroking her gently on the buttocks.

'But you won't, will you?' she said, preparing herself for another session. His hand cupped her sex, the warm, wetness filling his palm. He seemed a little reluctant at first; he was obviously about to break some ludicrous British Rail rule, but his doubts were short lived.

He fondled her bottom with both hands, feeling every part of her deliciously pert buttocks. 'What an arse, what a beautiful arse,' he said, pushing a finger between her receptive sex-lips, drawing the wetness from her and across her anus, then dipping his finger in her again, and coating it with the natural lubrication. He pushed his finger gently and deliberately into her tight rear, all the way to the knuckle, before pulling it slowly out then pushing in again, setting up a steady, erotic rhythm.

He unzipped the blue, serge trousers of his uniform and pulled out his stiffness, pointing it immediately at her gaping sex, pushing himself into her to the hilt. She groaned, more from the shock of the sudden entry than the pleasure. His finger remained inside her bum as he humped into her hard and quickly, thrusting in and out in time to the clattering of the wheels over the points. He pushed a second finger into her bottom, and she began to feel the tightness relaxing at his insistent touch. 'Do you want it up there, baby?' he panted, not letting up for a minute from the steady, hard pumping he was giving her aching pussy.

'Yes, oh yes!' she cried, grabbing at her sex and frigging herself wildly. He pulled his thick tool from within her hot cunt and entered the tighter hole, pumping as steadily and violently as he had before until, with a grunt, it was over.

He held himself inside her backside as his throbbing erection sent its jism deep within her body whilst she desperately rubbed at her clitoris. There was a sudden rush of air and deafening noise as another train sped by in the opposite direction, timing perfectly with her release. She relaxed, sobbing with sheer pleasure and the railman eased his wilting manhood from her young body, zipped up his trousers and smoothed down his crumpled uniform.

He unlocked the sliding door and made to leave. 'You'd better tidy yourselves up,' he said, 'we're coming into Victoria.' With that, he was gone.

Janet blinked. Her other lover was making himself decent, taking up his briefcase, getting ready for his meeting, or whatever. They said their somewhat embarrassed goodbyes, and he left the compartment, ready to leave the train and scurry down the platform. She used the tissues that had been thoughtfully placed in her satchel to clean herself up, retrieved her panties from the floor and put them on. The train pulled slowly into the station . . .

Janet eyed the entrance to the Underground Station nervously. Normally, she would have taken a cab from the railway terminus to the party address, particularly dressed as she was, in such an erotic fashion. Frank's instructions had been specific, however. She must take the tube from Victoria to King's Cross, then, and only then could she take a taxi the remaining short distance.

Frank would have expected the situation she now found herself in. The famous London rush-hour was well under way and the trains would be packed with commuters. She would end up pressed against the bodies of crowds of strangers and who knows what would happen to an obviously randy little schoolgirl in such a situation!

She walked down the steps to the booking hall, obtained a ticket from one of the machines and headed for the escalators. Already, she could sense men's eyes burning into her, lusting after her, the feeling serving to lubricate even more so her already highly aroused sex. She fought her way onto the packed platform and waited, nervously.

She had to let two trains go before finding herself at the front of the platform and, when the third arrived, she was almost carried bodily by the surge of the commuters onto the train.

There was no chance of a seat, of course. She was forced to stand near the sliding doors, her face almost pressed against that of a middle-aged, balding business-man. He was only a little taller than herself, the slight height differences allowing their genital regions to be per-fectly in line. She soon realised that he was deliberately pressing his crotch against hers and she detected him hardening within the confines of his pin-striped trousers. At the same time she felt a hand move up the back of her tiny skirt, fondling her almost bare backside. It wasn't the man in front doing the feeling; she could see his arms. She wasn't able to turn to discover the identity of her clandestine lover whose persistent caresses were beginning to thrill her. The mystery as to the owner of the wander-ing hand only served to increase her feelings of erotic pleasure.

The excitement of the businessman in front of her was also now very obvious; his long and thick hard-on pressed against her mound. She decided to give him a bit of what he wanted; why not, she thought, he could then go home and wank himself silly or screw his ugly wife, whilst all the time thinking of the sexy girl on the underground train.

She pushed her lower body against his and moved gently side to side, rubbing her sex over his, staring into his eyes. He held her stare and matched her movements, the faint trace of a smile playing on his lips. All the time, the un-known person's hand fondled and squeezed her soft, pert buttocks, occasionally tracing the line of the leather panties pulled tight in the crack. She gazed at the man in front of her, licked her lips and pouted, then moved her hand from her side to between them, until her palm touched his erec-tion, which pointed straight up behind his zip-fly. She rub-bed gently and the man sighed, his eyes closing momentarily.

The train stopped suddenly and they pulled apart as people pushed and shoved against them in their efforts to gain entry to the already heaving compartment. The fondling hand had gone from her bum and Janet missed it, although she quickly found herself pushed back against the chap with the raging hard-on. It felt different this time, though. She moved her hand back to it and found, to her astonishment and delight that he had removed it from his trousers and she now held a large, naked tool in her grasp. At the same time, she felt the fingers exploring her buttocks again and knew her other friend had returned.

She rubbed the firm penis as best she could in the confined space, her own breathing becoming sharper as she became more and more aroused. She closed her eyes and licked her lips, letting him know that she was enjoying the situation.

She took her hand from him, noticing his look of disappointment and pushed up her short skirt, pulling the leather of her panties away from her crotch. With her other hand, she prodded at the wet sex-lips, shoving her fingers inside, getting herself ready. Still holding the material of her knickers to one side, she took hold of his thick erection again and bent it down gently towards her sex, letting the end touch her wetness.

Suddenly realising what was happening he pushed forward, his hardness sliding deep inside her. She closed her eyes and whispered, 'Yes!' in his ear and they started to pump heavily together. The fingers on the hand on her bottom now found their way inside her panties from behind, the owner no doubt assuming that his (or, for that matter her) attentions were causing the thrusting movements of the young girl's hips.

She opened her legs wider, both to accommodate more of the stalk screwing her and to allow better access from behind. She felt the fingers trace their way to the base of her vagina, knowing that they must now feel the erection pumping into her. The hand was still for a moment, then moved slowly back until a well-lubricated finger touched her anus. With expert ease it slid in, her recent experience with the ticket collector making sure of that, and she felt her bum being finger-fucked in time with the thrusting she was receiving from in front.

The doors slid open again as the train arrived at yet another stop, but this time neither of her lovers moved from her. The reason was obvious as far as the business-man was concerned. As the train moved off again, he groaned quietly and stopped his pumping, letting his sperm shoot deep inside the willing girl. She felt the finger stirring rapidly in her anus and had to bite her lip to avoid crying out as she came, the intensity of the feelings causing her to fall against the man in front of her, shaking visibly.

The train slowed to a stop again and Janet realised that it was her station. She pulled quickly away from her lovers and pushed her way out, glancing back to see the business-man hurriedly covering his exposed manhood with a copy of the *Evening Standard*.

Chapter Five

Lisa arrived at the address Frank had given her, feeling randy but very nervous. The house was a large, Regency-style building of the type common in central London. Usually they were divided into many small flats and apartments, but this one had retained its original purpose as a private house for a well-to-do family. Janet had told her that it was owned by a charming Welshman by the name of Glynn who was a business associate of Frank's, a very important man in the City.

It was Glynn who opened the door to her, welcoming her with a broad smile that straight away endeared her to his Gallic charms. The other immediately noticeable thing about him was the fact that he was stark naked.

Lisa returned his smile and, as he closed the door behind her she reached out and gripped his heavily-drooping penis and kissed him lightly on the lips, as though it were the normal, polite way to greet a stranger.

'Hi,' she said, 'you must be Glynn. I'm Lisa.' She stared pointedly at his erection, which was already beginning to stir within her firm grasp.

'Hello, Lisa,' said the gorgeous, naked man, 'I've heard a lot about you from Janet. I love your outfit.'

'Thanks,' she laughed, 'I love yours, too.'

Glynn led her into the main room. Inside there were about twenty people, although only a few of them were girls. Like Glynn, the men were all naked, a veritable feast to Lisa's sex-hungry eyes.

The half-dozen or so girls, however, were dressed in their

various costumes as decreed by Frank, all, no doubt having undergone a challenge similar to her own and with a consequent story to tell.

She found Janet seated between two young, heavily tanned studs on the floor and joined her.

'God, I thought *my* gear was sexy,' she said, admiring Janet's schoolgirl get-up. 'You didn't have to go out like that, did you?'

Janet nodded, casually stroking the firm erections of their silent companions. 'I never thought I'd get here alive!'

'Why, what happened?'

'I can't tell you, I mean Frank has said that all the girls will have to tell their stories, in full and graphic detail, to everybody here. We've been waiting for you to arrive so we could start.'

'Are the other girls the rest of the Lust Angels?' said Lisa, looking around the room.

'Yes,' said Janet, beginning to point them out. 'You know Sonia, of course.'

Lisa looked across the room and recognised the Amazon form of the beautiful African, dressed in an incredible costume of black leather and chains, her shaved pussy fully displayed. She had her arms around two fat, balding and middle-aged men, both of whom were busily sucking on her erect nipples, their fingers probing at the dampness of her sex. She smiled suggestively at Lisa, blowing her a kiss with her thick, pouting lips. 'Oh yes,' said Lisa, 'I know Sonia, all right!'

'Yes, I heard,' said Janet, smirking knowingly. 'Now, the little blonde in the corner who looks too young for sex; that's Kate. She's actually nineteen, but men never believe her, which seems to suit some of them.'

'Animals,' said Lisa, with disgust.

'The Chinese girl is Jan,' Janet continued, indicating a willowy oriental girl of striking beauty sitting with an almost serene expression in a corner, her apparent lack of emotion at odds with the fact that a young, black youth was hungrily lapping between her legs. Just occasionally her eyes closed, betraying her enjoyment of the young man's oral attentions.

'And the other girl is Rani,' continued Janet. Rani was probably the loveliest of all. An innocent looking, olive skinned Asian girl, she couldn't have been more than about eighteen but seemed somewhat older, improbably dressed as she was in a severe police-woman's uniform. She was sucking gently on the stiff erection of a long-haired youth whom Lisa recognised as a whiz-kid entrepreneur who had figured in the tabloid press recently, following a rather shady business deal which had apparently netted him millions. Clearly she was in very select company.

As though on cue, Frank stood up in the middle of the room. Lisa admired the strong body she'd recently enjoyed, his long phallus jutting in almost full erection from his groin.

Looking at it, she felt her juices flowing again; she wanted him, or was it that she just wanted sex? Perhaps that was it. She saw that Janet was looking at his dick as well and smiled to herself, knowing that he had accommodated them both and no doubt would do so many more times in the future.

Frank announced that the first story of recent experiences would be told by Janet. Reluctantly, she left the company of the two young men and sat, nervously, on a rather high bar-stool that had been placed in the centre of the room, and surveyed the erotic scene before her.

Virtually all the fifteen or so men were hard, and those lucky enough to sit next to a girl were having their erections fondled gently as the guests listened to her tale.

She told her story with the most lurid detail; her session with the two men on the train, the incident on the underground, the stranger's hand which had given her bum so much pleasure. Halfway through her tale she stopped to remove her panties, telling the applauding group truthfully that the leather was so wet that it had become most uncomfortable.

At the end of her story there was more applause and she

107

resumed her place with Lisa, convinced that her experiences would be hard to top.

Lisa was called to the stool next and introduced as a new Lust Angel, to rapturous applause. Janet sat back between the two men, allowing them to finger her wet sex nonchalantly as they listened in awe to the story of her friend's busy day.

After finishing her account, Lisa rejoined Janet and showed her the photographs that proved her story. Janet licked her lips, seemingly turned on as much by the sight of Lisa's lovely body as by the men in the pictures.

Frank stood and now called Jan to the centre of the room. She stood for a moment, allowing her audience to savour the sight of her lovely body in its revealing costume. Lisa found herself strangely envious of Jan's perfect, Eastern looks, her tall, slim body with its firm, apple-sized breasts, her incredibly long legs and her beautiful jet-black hair which cascaded almost to her waist. Her dark skin enhanced the rare brightness of steel-blue eyes; a most unusual but incredibly attractive combination, which shone with the lust of the moment, as she watched the men looking at her, wanting her.

She wore a skin-tight, white body-suit, which covered her from her neck to her ankles. Despite this, absolutely everything could be seen, the stretch material serving to enhance the erotic nakedness of her form. Like Sonia, she had shaven her sex, the pink lips engorged with sexual excitement showing clearly. Even the little, erect bud of her clitoris could be seen, and her dampness was making the material between her legs virtually transparent. The only other items she wore were, incongruously, a pair of weight-lifter's gloves and pink training shoes.

She sat down on the stool and began her story . . .

'My task was to go to Greg's Gym, a place quite near to where I usually work-out. It caters mainly for the really serious weight-lifters and body-builders, so doesn't appeal to me normally, although I've been there once or twice. I was to be dressed exactly as I am now, and work out in the gym at what was their busiest time.

'I was to pretend to be native Chinese, with very little command of the English language and, after the work-out I was to shower and dress in the men's changing room, as though I had made a mistake.

'Greg was expecting me and allowed me to get ready in his office, leaving me to it. I expect many of the girls here know him and what a randy sod he is, so you won't be surprised by what happened.

'I had stripped off completely and was about to dress in this gear when he returned, wearing just a pair of track-suit bottoms and a little T-shirt. Being nude, I objected to his walking in without knocking; not too much, of course, because he is pretty dishy. Anyway he ignored me and put his big arms around my waist and started to kiss and lick my tits. Then he started to fondle my bum with his hands, before falling to his knees and burying his face between my legs.

'I felt his tongue licking at me and knew there was no way I was going to stop him. Once a man gets his tongue into me there's not a thing I won't do for him. I leant my hands back on his desk and lifted my legs over his shoulders, driving my pussy into his mouth, making him lap and suckle at me.

'Most of you know that my "thing" is body-builders, that the mere sight of a well-oiled and heavily muscled body is enough to make me come and this was no exception. I screamed and nearly strangled him with my thighs as I orgasmed, feeling the roughness of his stubble rubbing against my tender sex-lips. He carried on licking me until he was sure I was finished, then pulled back, kissing and nibbling my thighs.

'After a moment or two, we stood up and kissed each other really passionately, our tongues wrestling with each other as we seemed to be trying to climb within each other's bodies. I slipped my hand inside his tracksuit and caught hold of his cock. It's not very long, but it's incredibly thick; somebody told me once that it's about seven inches in circumference, which is quite something.

'I thought about sucking him, but I was too desperate for the real thing. I sat back on the hard surface of his desk with my bum on the edge, lifting and holding my legs high and wide apart. I said "Fuck it, fuck it now . . . that's what you want!" and he dropped his pants and pushed his thick knob straight into me. He really stretched me, I can tell you. It's an amazing feeling, having one so fat pushed up you; it takes some getting used to.

'He screwed me hard for about ten minutes, not letting up the power of his thrusts for a moment, his mouth suckling and licking over my boobs. I was going mad . . . I just kept coming and coming; I think I had four or five orgasms before he climaxed, grunting like the animal he is.

'After a moment he got off me and told me to get ready for my work-out. I dressed in my gear and I remember looking into the mirror, thinking that I might just as well go in amongst these sweaty, macho men stark naked, for all the good the body-suit was.

'I was really nervous as I walked into the weight-room; there was about a dozen or so men in there and there was a sudden, scary silence as I entered . . . they just stopped whatever they were doing and watched me.

'I stood in front of one of the wall-mirrors and saw that my soaking pussy was completely visible, like it is now and it was quite obvious from the puffiness of the lips that I was very aroused. No wonder they ogled me!

'I walked over to one of the exercise bikes and climbed on. The saddle was rather too high for me, but I left it as it was, knowing that it would make my bum stick out even more, so that anyone behind me would be able to see the full shape of my bottom through the thin material.

'I cycled for about five minutes, by which time the men returned to their exercises, the novelty having worn off. I was a bit worried that I wasn't having the necessary effect; these types always seem more interested in their own bodies than anything else, so I decided to work-out in the middle of them.

'I selected two very light dumbbell weights and lay back on a bench that was free, my legs splayed on either side, my head back over the edge. I performed normal chest exercises, knowing that the men would be able to see and enjoy the sight of my little snatch, seeing every hairless detail through the wet material, whilst they thought I didn't know they were looking.

'After a little while I sat up quickly, looking some of them straight in the eye and smiling, letting them know that I knew, and that it was OK. It seemed that every one of them was bulging at the crotch, those wearing tight shorts showing everything they'd got. It was an amazingly erotic situation. I wanted them, they wanted me, but nobody knew how to make the first move.

'I carried on doing all sorts of weights exercises, making sure that I adopted positions and postures that were way over the top, pushing out my bum or opening my legs wide, giving them whatever view I thought they might desire. Some of them helped me with one or two of the lifting disciplines, though really they were just taking the opportunity to let their hands stray "accidentally" onto my body, brushing against my legs, bum and breasts.

'After about half an hour of this constant male attention and continual, lurid innuendos, I was absolutely screaming for sex, and I knew that the next move was up to me. I put on my best Oriental accent and said, "I go shower, now," and walked over to the door which was clearly marked "Gents Changing". I looked behind me as I opened the door and winked. They just stood there, open mouthed.

'There was nobody in the changing room when I entered . . . they'd all been watching my show. I was just about to strip when two of the body-builders came in and told me I was in the wrong room. I said, "No, I shower . . . you shower too?" and that was it. They were naked before I was, both sporting lovely big hard-ons. I looked at their erections and smiled, telling them that Chinese men didn't

111

have such nice big ones, then went into the shower, hearing other men coming through the door, obviously wanting to join in.

'The two naked men and I rubbed soap all over ourselves as we stood under the hot showers, then they decided I needed more soap, which they started to apply liberally all over my body. They seemed to think I needed an awful lot of soaping over my bottom, my breasts and between my legs.

'I rubbed my hands all over their huge, wet bodies, before concentrating on their nice, fat cocks. Other men had joined us, now; the shower room was heaving with muscular, sexually aroused men; I was in heaven.

'I reached out and grabbed one dick after another, some big, some small, all hard. Fingers of one, two and even three hands were pushed inside me; somebody else pushed a well-soaped thumb into my bum . . . I didn't know what was going to happen next.

'I bent over, keeping my legs straight and took a cock in each hand and another in my mouth. The one I was sucking shot into me almost as soon as my tongue touched him, and I swallowed the lot before letting his wilting tool go from my lips. He was replaced quickly by a well-endowed black stud, with plums the size of golf balls. I felt somebody slide into my aching pussy, and I was complete.

'The hot water continued to pour onto our bodies as I was fucked at both ends, rubbing the other two stalks furiously. Whoever was screwing me from behind came inside me and his place was quickly taken by someone else, someone with a much bigger piece of equipment that seemed to tear into me, ramming right up against my womb.

'I took a face-full of lovely, hot spunk from my black lover, whilst the bloke who was going at me from behind throbbed and pulsated inside me as deep as you can get. I was held still between them for a few seconds before I was allowed to stand up straight. The backs of my legs were already beginning to ache, but I knew I had hardly started.

'Then the men led me out into the changing room. One

112

of them lay on his back on a long, narrow bench, his erection held upright in his hand. I squatted over him and sat down on the hard monster, taking it to the hilt. Before I could start screwing, however, I sensed another knob prodding at my behind and, with a little effort, it slid into my bum.

'As the two men started to hump my nether regions, two more picked up my legs and started to rub their hard tools with the soles of my feet. A couple more guys stood in front of me, on either side of the bench, pointing their dicks at my face. I took hold of them and pulled the two of them together, managing to take both bulging ends into my mouth. Finally, I caught hold of two more hard-ons with my hands and I rubbed them as fast as I could.

'It was then that I worked out that I was having simultaneous sex with eight men ... it has to be a record! I couldn't stop coming, it happened again and again and I've never felt so full, or so satisified.

'As each man came, he was replaced by another ... as far as I know all of the twelve had me, I sucked every one, and I think most went up my bum. I have never had such fantastic sex in all my life, and I can heartily recommend it to all girls with cast-iron insides!

'Oh, and by the way ... Greg has made me a life member of his gym.'

The party-goers laughed and applauded as Jan left the 'stage', her face flushed with excitement, her nipples firmly erect and the crotch of her body-suit soaked with her juices. There was a short interval in the proceedings, as glasses were refilled and bladders emptied, then the group resumed their places to hear more.

Frank introduced Sonia. There was the sound of sharp intakes of breath from the men as she walked slowly over to the stool and sat on the damp leather seat, her legs wide apart, her naked, hairless pussy on view to everybody. She looked absolutely devastating; her big, black body clothed in even blacker leather held together with thick-linked lengths of chain. Round her neck, she wore a studded leather choker, a full three inches in width, attached by a long piece of chain which fell between her massive, exposed breasts to a shiny, black basque affair, which itself supported her huge breasts but didn't cover them in any way. This garment ended just above her bare sex, leaving two thin chains on either side to support the long, almost crotch-length leather stockings that fitted around her shapely legs like a second skin. The outfit was completed by very high-heeled, stiletto shoes, which had made the already tall beauty tower above everybody else in the group.

Lisa looked lustfully at the amazing, African vision before them. She began to remember every lovely detail of her session with Sonia and her two lovers, wanting to rush over and bury her face in the wet pussy that was displayed before her, to lick the musky juices, to swallow and suckle, to worship at this temple to womanhood. She rubbed hard at an erection that just happened to be in her hand, not taking her eyes for a moment off the wondrous sight of the black girl's body.

Sonia started to speak, looking around at her gently masturbating audience.

'My story doesn't involve lots of men; in fact there's just one, but I think you'll like what I have to tell you.

'Frank told me he had arranged for an insurance salesman to come round to my place, the idea being to sell me some sort of new mortgage or something similar. It didn't matter what, because I had other plans for him.

'When he arrived, I was quite impressed. He was really gorgeous; tall, fair haired and slim, with teeth that shone nearly as much as mine! I could see that he fancied me as well, that there wasn't just selling in his mind.

'I'd greeted him dressed quite ordinarily, listened to his waffle and offered him a drink of coffee. I'd been supplied with a mild drug that I was told would knock him out for about thirty minutes, which I slipped into his drink.

'He went out like a light. When I was sure he was totally

unconscious I heaved him over my shoulder, not a problem for me, as some of you guys already know and carried him into the bedroom. Everything was prepared there for what I had to do next.

'I lay him on the bed and stripped him completely. He had a lovely body; slim, but well formed, and his flaccid tool looked promising. I put him on his back and strapped his hands together above his head, tying them to another strap which was already fixed to the bed-head. I pushed his legs slightly apart, and tied each one to the posts at the bottom of the bed. Finally I took hold of a long piece of leather strapping at the centre of the divan and pulled it tight across his upper thighs, making it impossible for him to raise his bum from the bed.

'I then dressed as you see me now, the only thing missing being a small cat-o'-nine-tails whip of the softest leather. I waited for him to awake, my pussy getting wetter with every second.

'At last he came round and saw me standing there, rubbing the strands of the whip between the wet lips of my sex. At first he looked confused, then a little worried, until I smiled. He asked me what I was going to do.

'I told him I was going to do anything I damn well pleased and I started to stroke his lower body with the whip. I flicked it quite hard across his soft prick and when he realised, because of the softness of the leather that it hardly hurt at all he relaxed and began to harden. I carried on whipping him across his thighs, his stomach and his sex, watching his erection grow more and more with each stroke.

'When he was fully hard I realised that Frank had arranged this particular salesman for me knowing, as he does, what I like. It was obvious from the man's reaction that he liked to be dominated and that he'd realised he was in for a good session. It was also nice that he was hung like a horse, the sight of it making my throat go dry with lust.

'My instructions were to tease him unmercifully, to not let him have what he wanted until he begged for it and then

115

only under my terms. No doubt in the past he'd had lots of silly little girls whose knickers had rolled off by themselves at the sight of his monster dong; he was not going to have it his way so easily this time.

'I told him that first he was to give me an orgasm with his tongue. I squatted over his head, facing away from his body, clutching the headboard and lowered myself onto his mouth. He started to lap at me immediately.

'His head was the only part of his body that he could move and he used this limitation to its full advantage, aiming his tongue into me from every angle. After what seemed like ages of this wonderful treatment he settled down to flick the tip rapidly over my clit, which really made me shake. I felt my first orgasm building up and I tightened the muscles of my thighs and bum and pushed my pussy at his mouth, almost suffocating him as I felt that excruciating pleasure between my legs. He didn't let up for a second, lapping at my clit constantly until the sensitivity I finally felt made me pull away.

'I climbed off him and looked at the restrained, reclining figure on the bed. His cock-head was almost purple with lust; he wanted a fuck real bad, that was for sure. I lashed the whip across his hard-on, seeing it jump visibly, but with pleasure, not pain. I ran the full length of the strands against the thick lips of my pussy, then rolled them up and pushed them into my mouth, mixing saliva with my own juices. I took it out and whipped him again, the wetness of the thongs making the pain a little more acute. His dong throbbed and a short stream of sperm shot over his chest. He hadn't come, but he was high, and no mistake.

'I licked the glistening trail from his smooth skin, then kissed him fully on the mouth, sharing his taste. He responded with a deep, wet kiss, his tongue savouring the shared intimacy.

'I then decided to give him a bit of a show. Standing with one leg on the bed and one of the floor, I took the whip by the wrong end of the handle and pushed the hard, leather rod into my pussy. Its length was about the same

as the real-life monster that was waiting to impale me but
it slid in with only a little effort. He groaned as he watched
me fuck myself with the leather staff and begged me to let
him give me the real thing. I wanted him, oh God, I wanted
him, but the game was giving me much more than just a
screw alone could ever do.

'I drew the thick wand from my soaking pussy and put
the end to my bum, pushing it in as far as I could. His face
showed the pain of extreme lust as I screwed myself in the
rear; he wanted that as well. I could only get about six
inches inside me, the thickness was too much, but the feeling was wonderful. I came again, totally without touching
the naked man in my power, calling out all manner of filth
and obscenities.

'I pulled the whip-handle from my bottom and put it to
my mouth, tasting my scent with the tip of my tongue. I
then offered it to him. He licked the end at first, then
opened his mouth and took it in, his tool so hard that its
full length was raised from his stomach.

'He was obviously about to come and I wanted it. I
dived my head down quickly and took the huge end into
my mouth, taking as much of the thick shaft between my
lips as I could. His thighs were shaking. He couldn't move
them to thrust, so I had to do all the work. I gripped his
big erection with both hands, rubbing the hard flesh frantically, trying to make him come in my mouth. At the same
time I bobbed my head up and down, sucking in and out
about five or six inches, using my long tongue and the
thickness of my lips to their full effect.

'He roared and I felt the throbbing start, the powerful
ejaculation hitting the back of my throat, the amount of
fluid nearly making me choke. I knew I couldn't take my
mouth from him, I'd teased him far too much for that, so
I swallowed and swallowed, as more and more juice flowed
from his throbbing tool.

'Finally, he relaxed and I sat back, watching his once
superb manhood return to its ordinary, flaccid state. I
released him from his bonds and told him of Frank's

instructions; the reason why I had raped him with my mouth.

'We kissed and cuddled on the bed for a little while, until I saw that he was stiffening again, ready for the bonk we both deserved. I lay on my back and he got between my legs in a very ordinary position and pushed his wonderful prick into me. His size was perfect, filling me completely. I wanted a long, slow fuck and that's what we did. With each thrust he pulled out almost to the tip, then pushed slowly in to the hilt, making me feel every inch of his length, his erection becoming an almost integral part of my own body.

'My clit began to awaken again to the steady rhythm of his humping and I felt yet another orgasm beginning within my loins. I don't come anywhere near as easily as Jan, but when I do, I go crazy. I grabbed hold of his buttocks and started to make him increase the pace of his thrusting, my legs kicking high in the air. Now the tables were turned ... I was in his power, I wanted him to fuck me hard and he knew it. He didn't tease me, thank God, his steady shafting responding to the thrusting of my thighs, still making me feel the full length each time. I stuck a finger deep into his tight little bum and told him I was coming and that I wanted his sperm deep inside me.

'He pumped into me faster and faster, our bodies leaping up and down on the bed, the woodwork groaning with the pressure. He roared again, this time throbbing and beating within the very depths of my womb. I came with him, screaming loudly, tearing at his backside with my fingernails.

'We collapsed in a heap on the sweaty bed. We lay, looking at the ceiling, getting our breath back. Then he took my face in his hands and kissed me gently on the lips and asked me if I was still interested in buying insurance from him ...'

After the laughter had died down and Sonia had returned to her place it was agreed that, whilst the stories were good

118

the assembled company were now ready for some real screwing and that the remaining tales could be saved for later.

Lisa and Janet didn't need telling twice and almost attacked the two guys they were sitting with, leaping astride them and taking their hard erections into their aching pussies. There was nothing that they wouldn't do; all this sextalk had driven them mad with frustration; no man was safe tonight.

As they bounced rapidly up and down on their willing victims, they looked at each other and smiled. 'This is what it's all about,' said Lisa, 'I'd never imagined how good sex could be!'

'There's lots more to come, Lisa. Let's see if we can break some records of our own tonight!' Janet would have realised that wasn't going to be difficult. With so many more men than girls at the party, they were going to have their work cut out.

The guy Lisa was sitting on came very quickly, but she had no sooner clambered off his sated form than she was pushed onto her back by an even younger, devilishly handsome stud who had been watching her for some time, desperately anxious to get inside her. He tore the little toga from her body, leaving her naked except for the long-strapped sandals, and rammed his thick staff into her welcoming pussy, her legs wrapping themselves almost automatically around his lithe body.

Immediately, another chap straddled her face, lowering his balls to her mouth. She licked greedily at the offered prize, reaching up with one hand and rubbing his hardness.

Janet's partner came at last and she quickly pulled herself from his body, allowing his wilting manhood to flop onto his belly. She moved behind the chap who was servicing Lisa and started to run her tongue over his bum, causing him to slow his thrusting as he enjoyed the feel of the wet tip teasing his anus. She stuck out her own bum provocatively, inviting someone to take her. It was only seconds before she felt the familiar pressure of a thick erection pushing against her sex-lips as, once again a stranger took advantage of the girl in the school uniform.

Lisa spent the rest of the party crawling around the room, savouring the glut of male flesh, until she could take no more. She'd watched Janet take Frank and Glynn in the way she had experienced at the photographers, both inside her at the same time, the difference on this occasion being that Janet took another penis in her mouth until she swallowed everything offered to her hungry lips.

So the party continued into the night. Whilst Janet had just lain back and taken whatever was given to her, Lisa had crawled from man to man, determined to have every stud in the room.

It was agreed the following day that both girls had succeeded.

Lisa woke slowly, unsure of where she was. The bright light of morning hurt her eyes and her throat felt dry, her tongue rough. A vaguely sweaty scent hit her senses and her pillow felt soft and warm. As her vision cleared, she took in the sight before her and remembered.

A few inches from her face she saw a long, flaccid penis. She lay with her head on the owner's stomach, his steady breathing movements becoming apparent as she came round. She raised her head carefully and looked at him. A dark, extremely handsome young man of about twenty lay before her; she couldn't even recognise him, let alone recall whether he had made love to her. Then she realised that he must have; she and Janet had made a point of taking every cock in the room the night before; how many were there? Ten, twelve – maybe more?

She looked around the room. All about her lay naked men and girls, mostly sleeping off the efforts of the orgy, although not all were totally sated. At the far side of the room, the youthful-looking Kate was sucking greedily on the half-hard sex of a drowsy black youth, whilst being penetrated from the rear by the ever rampant erection of Glynn, their host. In another corner Jan was lying, apparently fast asleep, but nevertheless being steadily humped by another male guest.

Lisa stood up slowly, desperately wanting a glass of water. She hadn't a hangover; she'd hardly drunk anything at the party, being too busy satisfying her sexual cravings. Her sex and anus felt a little sore from the attention her poor body had received from the dozen or more men that had used and abused her over and over again throughout the night, but already the sight of all this naked flesh was causing randy feelings to stir within her loins.

She climbed over the supine form of Janet, who was lying on her back with her legs wide open, apparently offering herself in her sleep to anybody who might wish to take her. Lisa was tempted to plant a loving kiss on her friend's ravaged pussy, but resisted, the need for a drink being too strong.

In the kitchen she found Frank, stark naked, busily preparing coffee. 'Morning!' he said, cheerily.

'Morning.' Lisa's first utterance of the day was hoarse, almost too quiet to be heard.

'Want some coffee?' She nodded, sitting on a cold chair by a small, breakfast table. She looked at Frank's superb body, his long manhood which dangled heavily from his groin, his firm buttocks. She wondered just how many times he'd had her last night; he had incredible staying-power, moving from girl to girl, satisfying every one of them.

'What do you think of the Angels?' he said, pouring out some coffee.

'They're all lovely, very beautiful.'

'Just like you. I'm sure you'll fit in very well. Did you enjoy yourself last night?'

'It was wonderful. I can't wait for next time!'

Frank handed her a steaming mug of strong, black coffee, which she sipped gratefully. They chatted more, totally oblivious to their shared nudity, of the memory of the previous night's events and what the future might hold in store.

After a short while, Lisa felt the need to pee. She found the door to the bathroom and was just about to enter when she heard the sound of an electric razor being used. At first she thought of waiting, then decided that was ridiculous. Whoever was in there had probably been inside her mouth, pussy and bum at some time just a few hours previously, so he wasn't going to be shocked by the sight of her having a pee in front of him whilst he shaved. She knocked lightly on the door and entered the bright luxury of the tiled room.

Inside, instead of some naked stud she found Sonia, seated with legs wide open on the edge of the bath, carefully shaving her thick, black pussy lips. She appeared unaffected by Lisa's sudden entrance.

'Hi,' she said, her big smile seeming to brighten up the room even more, 'have a good time last night?'

'Brilliant! Listen, d'you mind if I take a pee?'

'Go right ahead,' said Sonia, returning to the task of smoothing away any rogue pubic hairs, 'don't mind me.'

Lisa watched fascinated as the other girl busied herself with the razor. 'Doesn't that hurt?'

'No, it's quite nice, really, a bit like a vibrator if you get it at the right angle. You ought to do it, most men go crazy for it ... they love to lick a shaven pussy, and it really makes a difference for the girl, as well.'

Lisa sat across the bidet, washing the remnants of the night's activities from her nether regions. 'I don't know if I could; I'd be nervous about cutting myself.'

'No, you can't cut yourself with this type of shaver. Look, tell you what, I'll do it for you. Dry yourself well with the towel, and put a bit of talc on your pubes, then I'll get to work!'

Lisa did as she was told, then lay on her back on the soft, bathroom carpet, her legs widely splayed. Sonia knelt between them and switched on the battery-operated razor. Using a special attachment which had been designed to trim men's sideburns she carefully removed the longer pubic hairs surrounding Lisa's dampening sex. This done, she took up the towel and dried the wet slit, before pressing the foil head lightly against her flesh.

Sonia was right; the vibrations of the machine sent tremors through Lisa's lower regions, the sensations causing her little bud to harden with lust. She breathed deeply, stiffening her thigh muscles and buttocks to increase the pleasure, lifting her bum slightly from the floor.

Sonia noticed her response and grinned, finishing her work quickly and expertly, then concentrating her attention to the top of her mound, using the shaver as a sex-toy, no doubt well aware of the effect it was having.

Lisa felt her juices begin to flow and began to moan softly, pushing her hips from the carpet towards her electronic lover. Sonia took care not to let the razor stray too near to her wet lips, for fear of snagging them on the vibrating foil. Sensing that her newly-shaven colleague was nearing orgasm, Sonia pressed the side of the shaver flat against Lisa's pussy, so that the whole of her sex was stimulated by the quivering instrument.

Lisa squealed as she came, holding her legs stiffly in the air, pressing both of her hands on top of that which held the razor. Her buttocks tensed on the floor, her head moved frantically from side to side as she experienced a shuddering, crotch-tearing come. The buzzing, the vibrating seemed to increase with her release, as though it automatically knew what she wanted. In reality it was Sonia's expert manipulation of the unit's variable speeds which brought her off so quickly and so violently.

As she relaxed, Sonia bent over and kissed her sex lovingly. 'Have a look at yourself in the mirror.' Lisa stood, somewhat shakily and caught her image in the full-length glass.

Her pubic mound looked odd, like when she'd been a child, the engorged lips betraying the fact that they belonged to a sexually aroused woman. 'What d'you think?' said Sonia, as she blew the hair from the cutting edge of the shaver.

'I love it . . . it looks really sexy!'

Sonia took her into her big arms and kissed her lightly on the mouth. 'It is, because *you* are.' She kissed her again, this time much more passionately, forcing her long tongue into her mouth. They pressed their bodies closely, crushing their massive breasts together and rubbing their wet, hairless mounds against each other. Lisa ran her hands over Sonia's smooth, ebony skin, feeling her long back and the mountainous, firm buttocks she had come to adore. Sonia did the same, her fingers clutching Lisa's delicious bum as she ground her sex against hers, forcing her to the floor.

They lay on the carpet, their legs and arms wrapped around each other, kissing and licking each other's mouths furiously. They rolled over and over on the soft carpet, completely lost in their passion for each other, their minds oblivious to anything but the all-consuming passion they held for each other.

Lisa forced the beautiful African onto her back then, with a quick movement, switched her own position so that she sat gently down on her lover's face, thrilling as the incredibly long tongue slithered its wet way into her, like a soft, darting prick. She pressed her own mouth hard against the hairless pussy in front of her, kissing it deeply. The lips were freshly washed, but still retained the sensuous, musky odour that was Sonia, and which increased with her mounting excitement. Lisa chewed at the thick, wet labia, taking care with the pressure of her bite not to hurt, knowing just how much force to use.

Sonia carried on licking Lisa, driving the full length of her amazing tongue in and out, sending the most wonderful spasms of pleasure across her body with each thrust. Lisa started to concentrate her oral expertise on the bright pink clitoris, which showed angrily from the near-black folds of love-flesh, and she lapped and fluttered the end of her tongue over her target.

The girls' thighs moved erotically in response to the other's erotic actions, both of them heading to fierce orgasms. When they came, they did so together; their cries of lust and ecstasy buried within the mounds of soft flesh; their bodies a single sex-entity; their groaning and moaning a lustful harmony.

They fell apart, panting, their faces soaked, their hair matted. Lisa sat momentarily with her back resting against the cold surface of the bath, before staggering to her feet and running the shower. When the water was the right temperature she stood under the refreshing spray, wondering to herself just how much more pleasure she could take. Sonia joined her in the shower, the two girls gently soaping each other's abused bodies, kissing occasionally, like young lovers. Then, after drying off they went out of the bathroom and joined Frank in the kitchen.

They sat drinking coffee, hardly speaking, worn out from over twelve hours of love-making. Other party-goers came and went, most taking gulps of the hot drink before dressing and leaving. Soon, just the six Lust Angels remained. They sat naked around the breakfast table with Frank and Glynn, reminiscing about the previous night's events and planning the next party.

Frank left the room and returned, carrying a bundle of brightly coloured clothing. They turned out to be simple cotton dresses, which Glynn had taken the trouble to provide assuming, wisely, that their costumes would be lost, or at least torn during the orgy. The garments were made of one-size stretch material, so the girls picked them at random and pulled the tight dresses over their naked forms.

The dresses were very short, particularly on the tall frames of Sonia and Jan, the hems only just preserving their modesty. Lisa picked one in white which, as she had half-expected, turned out to be virtually see-through, especially where it covered her thrusting breasts, the dark nipples clearly visible.

'I've ordered a mini-coach and driver to take you back to Sussex,' said Frank, 'he should be here in a moment.'

There was little time to finish dressing before the doorbell rang and the girls collected what little belongings they had and made to leave, each one kissing the two men with genuine passion and gratitude, thanking them for a superb party.

Lisa was the last to leave. She put her arms around the naked bodies of her hosts and kissed them in turn, stroking their backsides and giving them just one more squeeze to their ample cocks, before bidding them farewell.

Outside, she found her colleagues climbing up the steep steps into the small coach, assisted rather unnecessarily by the handsome, young driver. He seemed to be taking every opportunity to glance surreptitiously up their short dresses, getting many an eyeful of their fresh, young nakedness. Lisa pretended to slip as she got in, giving him just the excuse he needed to put his hand on her bottom, the tips of his fingers touching her bare skin. She smiled at him and blew a kiss, then took her seat next to Janet.

'Don't you ever get enough?' Her friend was smiling, herself trying desperately to catch the eye of the gorgeous driver.

'He's a bit of all right, isn't he?' said Lisa, ignoring her sarcasm and resisting the temptation to finger herself as she looked at the promising bulge in his tight jeans.

He took his place behind the wheel, and started the engine. 'Right, girls, Sussex here we come! If you want to stop on the way, just holler!' With that, the coach pulled into the heavy London traffic.

Sonia was sitting next to the driver, occasionally whispering in his ear, her hand rubbing up and down his left leg. Lisa knew she wasn't giving him directions, at least not to Sussex anyway.

Soon, they were speeding through the leafy countryside of the Home Counties and heading South; the driver had chosen a slower, quieter route, avoiding the normal hold-ups on the main roads. Sonia now had her head in his lap, her movements clearly indicating that she was giving him an expert blow-job. Lisa began to get wet between the legs as she remembered how the lovely girl had given her so much sexual pleasure, just an hour or so previously.

She watched as Sonia bobbed her head up and down

quickly. The vehicle began to increase in speed as the driver's attention was directed away from the road, and the coach swerved round corners dangerously. Suddenly he braked and pulled sharply over to the side of the road, and his passengers were nearly thrown from their seats. He slumped over Sonia for a moment, his breathing heavy, then sat back, sighing with relief as Sonia raised her head from his lap and looked back at the girls. She smiled and pushed her tongue out from between her blindingly white teeth, a large dollop of sperm oozing from the tip.

Lisa grinned to herself, whilst the driver looked back at his passengers in bemused astonishment, obviously wondering what was going to happen next.

He resumed the journey, much more slowly this time; he was still recovering from the shattering come he'd experienced within the gorgeous black girl's mouth. She started whispering to him again, this time possibly giving him genuine directions.

After a short while, the driver pulled off the road and drove across a mown field to the shelter of some trees, well away from the view of passing traffic. He stopped, and turned the engine off. For a moment, there was silence. Lisa wondered what was going to happen, although she had a feeling that whatever it was it would involve sex. She wasn't wrong.

Sonia stood up and deftly removed her skimpy dress. Standing naked in front of the driver, she put her hands on her hips and glared menacingly at him. 'Well, what are you waiting for?' she demanded.

The man didn't move, stunned by the sexuality of the moment. Sonia sighed with exasperation and pulled him roughly from his seat, forcing him to the floor. The others leapt from their seats and caught hold of the man as he struggled, admittedly half-heartedly, on the floor of the coach. Sonia pulled off his shoes and socks as Lisa and Jan tore feverishly at the fly-zip of his jeans.

Rani, Kate and Janet wrenched at his flimsy T-shirt, literally ripping it from his body, revealing his slim, hairy chest. His jeans were wrenched off and he was naked. His manhood lay half hard on his stomach, having just satisfied itself with Sonia's accommodating mouth, but he was already beginning to show signs of recovery in response to the mauling he was receiving.

'Let's have him outside!' said Sonia, pulling the hydraulic door open. The others tried to lift him up, but there wasn't the space between the seats of the coach to offer enough leverage. The driver struggled to his feet, his erection now fully hard, jutting directly in front of him.

'I can walk,' he said, pulling himself away from the grasping hands of the sex-crazed women, 'I can walk by myself.'

'That's more than you'll be able to do when we've finished with you!' somebody said.

Sonia pulled him to the grass, lying him on his back, and sat across his stomach, proudly displaying her superb body to him. The other girls stripped quickly, until he was completely surrounded by naked nymphets. 'There's six of us,' said Sonia, in a mock menacing tone, 'and we all want fucking. You'd better not let us down!'

'I'll do my best.'

Sonia moved up his body until she squatted over his face, his tongue eagerly greeting her wet sex. Lisa lay between his legs on her front and ran her tongue up and down the length of his stiffness. Jan and Kate, meanwhile, lay on either side of him, licking the sides of his tool which they held pointing firmly skywards. Rani put her head on the pillow of his stomach and lapped at the back of his cock, whilst Janet completed the picture by bending over the others and taking his thick, bulbous knob-end into her mouth.

Kate and Jan now suckled heavily on the long stem, their lips meeting round its thickness, occasionally touched by Rani's tongue. Lisa concentrated her attention on his balls, taking them into her mouth, running her tongue round and round the hard plums.

The driver endured this five-girl gobble for ages, and his

recently spent erection remained hard, ready for whatever they had in store for him. He continued to lap greedily at Sonia's wetness until, with a sudden and unexpected shout, she came, driving her powerful thighs into his face, causing him to fight her off in order to breathe. As Sonia rested, the other girls carried on licking and stroking their willing victim, caressing and feeling his lithe, young body; the tips of their tongues explored every part of him. One by one, they sat on his face, presenting themselves to him as if in homage to his flicking, fluttering tongue.

After he had tasted the juices of the sixth pussy, he sat up. 'I want a fuck!' he said, simply.

Janet knelt on all fours, pushing her bum out towards him, looking over her shoulder at him, her mouth pouting invitingly. He lost no time; kneeling behind the offered prize, he took hold of his wet hard-on and pushed it into her open honeypot, the lips closing on him like a sweet trap. He held her waist and screwed her slowly and steadily, no doubt savouring the tightness; the movement of her muscles within her pussy were giving him all the sensations he could ever want.

Lisa wriggled her body underneath her friend, so that her face was in line with the sexual organs of the rutting couple. She licked again at his balls, then at the stem of his penis as it moved in and out, in and out. She relished the sweet flavour and scent of Janet's sex, lapping and swallowing, her tongue moving back and forth one to the other.

She saw Sonia's face press against the man's backside, and watched in awe as her long tongue slid into his anus, hearing him groan with the sheer pleasure of the phenomenon. He continued to thrust into Janet with long, slow motions, as Sonia's tongue moved in and out of his bottom matching his pace, and Lisa let her mouth suckle at his balls, his thick stem and her friend's clitoris.

This treatment was too much for Janet. She came with a cry, and fell forward onto Lisa's body, burying her face in her friend's wet sex. They lay in their sixty-nine position for a while, kissing and licking at each other, whilst Rani assumed a similar position to that demonstrated by Janet, and the coach driver found himself plunging his staff deep within her, as Sonia continued to penetrate his bum deeply with her tongue.

As the morning wore on, he shared his body with them all; taking them on their knees, their backs or astride him, licking pussy, fingering clits, holding back his desperate need to ejaculate for over two hours.

At one time, he lay on his back, with Lisa impaled on his erection, Janet sitting on his mouth, Sonia and Rani astride his hands, and Jan and Kate using his feet as substitutes for his penis, taking as much of these limbs inside their soaked pussies as they could.

It ended for him when they knelt together side by side on the grass, presenting their bottoms to him in a line, as though for punishment or inspection. He licked them each in turn, tasting the differences and similarities of their sex-scents, until, starting on the left with Jan, he pushed his purple-headed stiffness into her and gave her about six thrusts, before withdrawing and moving along the line in exactly the same way; to Sonia, Kate, Rani, Janet, and finally Lisa.

He only just made it, plunging into Lisa's silky, wet sheath and pounding into her like never before, thrusting with incredible speed, just a dozen or so times until he shot his sperm inside her, raising his hands above his head and crying out with pleasure. Lisa used her sex-muscles to squeeze him to the last within her tightness, causing him to shudder as the ultimate sensitivity finally hit him.

He fell back and sat on the grass. The girls dressed almost nonchalantly, tidying their hair and chatting amongst themselves, as though he wasn't there.

After a while, the girls climbed back into the vehicle, and waited to be driven home. As it was, Sonia did the driving, leaving their exhausted lover on the back seat.

Chapter Six

Janet picked up her phone and dialled Lisa's number. Frank's instructions had been perfectly clear, as ever. She was to contact the other members of the group and arrange for them to go to Squire's, a gentlemen's club in the centre of London, known to be frequented by the rich and famous, politicians and diplomats; even royalty.

They were to meet with four men, described only as American businessmen, and were to use their charms to entertain them, and their hypnotic powers to relax their minds, so that Frank could discover information which might be useful to him and the old man.

The morality of what they were doing hardly troubled Janet; she enjoyed the sex too much to let anything stand in her way. Anyway, what difference did it make if a few businesses lost money because trade secrets were prised out of unsuspecting managers? They probably used similar techniques themselves.

'Hello?' Lisa answered the phone with her customary anonymity.

'Hi,' said Janet, brightly, 'it's me. Sort yourself out with a nice, sexy outfit and meet me and the girls at the station by six o'clock. It's party time again!'

'Great! Where are we going?'

'A posh club in London. I'll tell you all about it on the way. Kate and Rani are coming as well; it'll give you a chance to get to know them better.'

Lisa laughed. 'Since they've both licked me between the legs and I've done the same to them, I think I already know them quite well!'

'You know what I mean,' said Janet, 'see you later.' She put the phone down and opened her wardrobe, running her hands over the large choice of erotic and sensuous clothing. She wondered what would be best to wear to please four middle-aged Americans.

She selected a simple, red mini-dress, considering that whatever she wore would be removed quite quickly. She pulled on a tiny, red-leather G string and slipped the little dress over her shoulders, smoothing the thin fabric over her slim body. It was extremely short, the hem just covering her sex, and ideal for her purpose. Her outfit was completed by matching, high-heeled shoes and a short, leather jacket.

The doorbell rang, heralding the arrival of her taxi. Janet picked up her purse and rushed out of her flat, down the stairs to the front door. Opening it, she was pleased to see that her driver was one of her regulars, a pleasant chap who often ran her to the station when she was off on one of her jaunts. He was good-looking in his early forties, and always full of humour and friendly chat. He smiled broadly when he saw her, opening the rear door of his cab.

'Can't I sit in the front with you?' she said, seductively.

'As long as you keep your hands to yourself.'

'Ooh, I don't think I can promise you that,' she said, scrambling into the front passenger seat, noting with some satisfaction the way he leered between her legs which splayed apart as she sat down.

The driver sat behind the wheel and started the car. 'Station, is it?'

'Yes, but don't rush,' said Janet, crossing her legs slowly, 'the train isn't due for an hour.'

The car drove off into the heavy, late afternoon traffic. They'd only been moving for a couple of minutes when Janet decided to have a little bit of fun with the driver. Well, it *had* been a good six hours since her last bout of sex, after all!

She reached over and ran her hand softly along the inside of his thigh. Fortunately, the vehicle had automatic transmission, so gear changing wasn't going to become a problem. The driver glanced nervously at her, then looked back at the road. 'What are you up to, then?' he asked, half smiling.

'Oh, nothing,' said Janet, rubbing his thigh more firmly, 'I just feel fruity.'

'Go right ahead, girl,' he said, pushing his hips forward slightly on the seat, 'don't let me stop you.'

Janet ran her hand up to the front of his jeans, cupping the bulge of his sex. She smoothed her palm over the hardening mound, then reached over with her other hand to unclasp his belt. Deftly, she unzipped him and reached in for her prize.

He was wearing small, tight briefs which she had to pull out of the way to release his hard stalk, the thick end almost purple. She clutched the stiff cock firmly and began to rub it steadily up and down, all the time watching with some amusement the expression on his face as he endeavoured to concentrate on his driving.

She felt him throb in her grip, the resultant betrayal of his excitement trickling down the thick stem to her hand. She bent her head to his lap and took the end in her mouth, tasting him and savouring his warm wetness. She knelt on her seat, sticking her bottom in the air, no doubt giving passing drivers a delightful view, and got to work with her expert mouth, suckling at his engorged sex greedily, running her tongue round and round the shaft, sucking and swallowing, drawing it deep into her throat.

The car started to speed up dramatically, as the driver pressed down involuntarily on the accelerator. He thrust his hips upwards, pushing more of his cock into Janet's mouth, as the beautiful youngster gave him what was probably the best blow-job of his life. She squeezed his balls tightly as she sucked, as though trying to milk them of all their love-juices, her sharp fingernails digging into his tender flesh.

A siren sounded near them, a police-car flashing past.

'Oh bugger,' said the cab-driver, 'he wants me to pull over. Finish me off, quick!'

Janet increased the pace of her sucking, her head bobbing up and down, her hand rubbing furiously at the exposed stem of his cock until he groaned and she felt the familiar throbbing as he came into her mouth. Whilst this was happening, he somehow managed to pull the car to a stop and she drew her head back from his lap, allowing him to stuff his rapidly wilting manhood back into his jeans.

She sat up and smiled innocently at the policeman, licking a small trace of sperm from her upper lip, and swallowing it.

'You seem to be in a dreadful hurry, sir,' said the policeman, with customary sarcasm.

'Yes, sorry, officer,' struggled the cab driver, 'my mind was elsewhere. It won't happen again.'

'See that it doesn't.' The policeman winked at Janet, then walked back to his car. The cab-driver breathed a sigh of relief, in both senses of the word.

'I'd better get you to catch your train,' he said.

Janet only just caught the London train, quickly finding the rest of the girls in a booked compartment. After the customary welcoming pleasantries they settled down for the journey, their destination being just a little over an hour away.

Once she'd relaxed in the comfy seat, Janet looked at her friends, noting their different choices in clothing. Lisa was dressed in a simple, black evening dress, full-length but cut at one side to her waist. She didn't seem to be wearing any underwear, just a pair of black hold-up stockings, heavily seamed at the back, and black, shiny, high-heeled shoes. The dress clung to her body like a second skin, highlighting her lack of panties or bra, accenting the thrust of her breasts, the long nipples and her flat, firm stomach.

Kate wore a smart, white trouser-suit over her small, delicate frame, the jacket-front cut in a most revealing way,

134

and Rani was dressed in a simple, green mini-dress, similar in style to Janet's.

Rani had certainly come out of her shell of late, she mused. Although she still maintained the almost child-like coyness well known amongst young Asian women, her clothes were much more feminine and erotic than when she had first joined the group, and she had lost her initial shyness, proving at the recent orgy that she was one of the girls. Despite all that, she still exuded a totally virginal aura; her soft, brown eyes and delicate expression giving the impression that she had never as much as seen a man, let alone given herself sexually to one. Janet decided to ask about her challenge.

'What did Frank get you to do before the party the other night?' she asked. 'Tell us in the same detail as we had to.'

'OK, then,' said Rani, smiling, 'as long as Kate tells hers.'

'No problem,' said Kate, 'I've been busting to tell you all, anyway!'

Rani sat forward, seemingly happy to take centre-stage. 'If you remember, my costume was that of a woman police officer. Although I love dressing up for sex, my speciality is being tied up or restrained in some way, so I couldn't see how this challenge fitted in with my needs.

'Frank's note simply said that he'd arranged for me to pretend to give a speeding ticket to a mate of his, and end up fucking him in his car. Apparently this bloke has got a thing about uniforms.

'I don't know if you noticed, but the uniform I was wearing wasn't exactly regulation, the black skirt being remarkably short, showing my black stocking-tops when I walked. I think a real police-woman would get into a lot of trouble if she dressed like that. My underwear consisted of a pair of black french knickers and a tiny matching bra.

'I took a taxi to the place where this chap was supposed to be parked. I was to look for a Rolls-Royce; Frank had given me the number, so there wouldn't be any embarrassing mistakes. Sure enough, there was this big limousine parked just where it was supposed to be: a huge, black car with the kind of windows you can't see through from outside.

'I stood in front of it and pretended to write a ticket, looking really officious and convincing, I reckon. For a moment nothing happened and I was beginning to wonder if there was anyone in the car, when one of the back doors opened and this bloke climbed out. He was about forty-five or fifty, really distinguished looking, with silver grey hair at the temples . . . you know the type. I really go for older men, at least when they look like him, and I began to get really shaky, knowing that I was to have sex with him.

'He said, "Can I help you, miss?" and I mumbled something about illegal parking. He suggested that perhaps we could sort it out if we sat in the back of his car. I naturally said yes, though I'm pretty sure a real copper wouldn't have done so, and climbed inside the sumptuous car.

'I sat on the big, comfy seat and he sat next to me, closing the car door. He poured me a drink and told me how attractive I was and all that stuff, whilst casually putting his arm around my shoulders. I told him that I wasn't allowed to drink on duty and he asked me if I was permitted to fuck on duty. I said I didn't think there was anything in the rules about that. He pushed his lips against mine and kissed me, pushing his tongue inside my mouth, running it along the back of my teeth.

'I was his. My pussy was soaking already and I needed screwing there and then; there was no argument about it. He put his drink down and put his hand on my knee. I opened my legs, allowing him to push his hand up my skirt, over the tops of my stockings onto the bare flesh, his fingers tickling and teasing me. I wanted him to touch my sex but he wouldn't, moving his hand up and down the inside of my thigh until I was going mad with lust.

'Finally, I grabbed his wrist and pulled it towards me, so that his hand pressed between my legs. Maddeningly, he just held it there, not moving at all – I could have killed

136

him! He kept kissing me on the mouth beautifully, but I needed him to finger me.

'At long last he did, moving his fingertips lightly over the lips, which by now were absolutely sopping wet, and I responded by pushing my hips at him and moaning down his throat.

'He pushed me back on the seat, lifting one of my legs onto the back window-ledge, the other staying on the floor. He rucked up my skirt and pushed his hand up one leg of my french knickers, and started to fiddle with my wet pussy. I was ready for a screw now; I didn't need any more stimulation. He probably knew, because he bent forward and kissed me lightly on my mound, then sat back up and unzipped his trousers.

'He pulled out his cock; nothing special but hard, which was all that I wanted at that moment. I pulled one leg of my knickers to the side as he knelt on the floor between my legs and raised himself awkwardly on one leg, positioning himself so that he could get inside me. I took told of his dick and put it against my sex-lips and he pushed forward, sliding about half of it inside me. He held still for a moment, begging me not to move. His penis throbbed and I could feel the warm wetness as a jet of pre-come shot inside me; he was obviously high and needed to calm down before he could give me the seeing to that I wanted.

'He pushed the full length in and held still again. I felt another throb, then another and then he shouted, "Oh shit!" and started to hump me really fast, unable to stop himself coming.

'When he finished pumping inside me he pulled his soft cock out and sat back. He kept apologising, saying it had never happened before, you know, like all men do. I told him it didn't matter, but I was in a hell of a state and felt really pissed off.

'I started to climb out of the car when I heard this gruff voice, right behind me. 'Can I help you, officer?' I looked round and to my horror saw two real policemen, huge guys, towering over me. I've never seen such big blokes.

They asked me what the problem was and I tried to bluff it out, but they obviously knew I was a fraud and promptly arrested me for impersonating a police-officer! I couldn't believe my luck: here was I, supposed to be going to an orgy, and this happened. The annoying thing is, I know loads of coppers in that area, but these two were strangers; I just hoped I would recognise someone at the police-station who would vouch for me!

'They sat me in the back of a police-car and one of them sat next to me, whilst the other drove. I felt like a criminal, it was awful. As we drove, my skirt kept riding up above the tops of my stockings and I noticed that the officer sitting next to me was looking at my legs. I smiled at him, hoping that I might be able to screw my way out of this predicament, but he just looked away.

'After a while, I realised that we were driving out of town. We pulled down a narrow, country lane and stopped in a field. They told me to get out and I just stood there by the car, I was so confused. The chap who had been sitting next to me took out a pair of handcuffs and put them on me, tying both my wrists together. Despite my fear, as soon as he did that I started to feel incredibly randy; that's the effect such things have on me.

'The driver told me to put my hands on the car boot and to spread my legs wide, like in some American movie. I did as I was told, knowing the hem of my skirt would be above my knickers, showing everything I'd got.

'I nearly jumped out of my skin with what happened next. One of the policemen went behind me, as though he was going to search me, but instead ripped my french-knickers in half in one swift movement. Before I could move he'd knelt down behind me and pressed his face against my bum and his tongue started licking at my pussy, his strong hands holding my legs apart. I looked at the other officer. He stood at my side, his erection in his hand. It looked like I was going to get the fucking I was desperate for, but I didn't want to be raped, no matter how dishy these guys were.

'I struggled and swore, until one of them told me what was going on. Yes, you've guessed it – these two were Frank's mates as well; the whole thing had been a set up from the start.

'Once I knew the truth I relaxed. They introduced themselves as Pete and Phil, the latter being the driver, Pete the one with his face in my behind. He started to lick me properly now and I stuck my bum out for him, letting him get his tongue deep into my pussy. Phil pushed his stiffy towards me and I held it with both hands, still wearing the handcuffs and took it in my mouth. I sucked hard on him, digging my fingernails into his scrotum, really intending to hurt him, to get back at them. He seemed to like it, though.

'Pete stood up behind me and I heard his zip go. A moment later he was pushing at my sex with his thick knob-end. I was so turned on by the events of the afternoon that he slid in easily, the marvellous feeling of complete fulfilment as I accommodated these two lovely lengths making me want to cry with joy.

'They had me like this for a while, then changed places. They were both big men in every way, and they were giving me a really good time, getting me really high. Pete pulled out of my mouth and went to the car. He returned with a camera and a truncheon. It was pretty obvious what he'd got in mind, but I wasn't sure I wanted to believe it. I said something like, "you've got to be kidding!" but, in my heart I knew he wasn't.

'Phil pulled out of my pussy and took the truncheon from his mate. I braced myself, begging him not to hurt me. He promised he wouldn't, but the sight of the thing still worried me. It was about eighteen inches long, and as thick as my arm.

'I felt the cold, hard end of the truncheon pressing against my loose sex-lips and I was so aroused I knew I wouldn't be able to stop it going in. Sure enough it slid in, lubricated by some cream Phil was spreading on it – they had certainly come prepared! Inch by inch he eased the black monster into me, Pete taking photo after photo. I should have felt degraded; instead I felt randy, totally at their mercy and wanting more and more.

'Finally, they could get no more inside me and started to fuck me steadily with the thick wood. It felt amazing, helped by the liberal amount of cream that Phil kept squeezing all over it. Pete unlocked the handcuffs and guided my hand to the handle of the truncheon that was still embedded in my body. He told me to do it to myself, which I did, glad to be able to control the rate and depth of the thrusts.

'The two policemen stood in front of me, their erections hard and ready. I sucked one, then the other, going back and forth between them, determined now to bring them off, whilst all the time plunging the monster shaft in and out of myself. Phil came first, closely followed by Pete, who lost his lot down my throat. Incredibly, I came with them, my pussy being torn apart by the pleasure I was giving myself.

'Afterwards, they took me to the party and gave me a couple of Polaroids as a memento. Want to see?'

Rani's story had the right effect on the assembled company, preparing them for the busy night ahead. The photos proved her story; even Rani herself was astounded at just how much of the implement her body had accepted: little more than six inches protruded from her tiny, vulnerable pussy.

But now it was Kate's turn . . .

Kate sat forward on the carriage seat, a gleeful look on her face. She had clearly been looking forward to telling her tale.

'I had the most marvellous time,' she said, chattering like an excited schoolgirl, 'it was really brilliant! Frank has this knack of fitting the right task or game to each girl's personality, or gift, as the old man calls it, and he certainly managed that for me.

'I absolutely adore screwing with sportsmen. I just can't

get enough of their sweaty, athletic bodies. I only have to catch the smell of a steaming jock-strap to get turned on! I think I'm even worse now than I was when the old man changed me from the ugly little girl I used to be. I've been sacked from the last four jobs because I was caught at it, but I can't resist if such a man comes on to me, I've simply got to let him into my knickers and if I can get off with more than one man, all the better.

'Frank's challenge was simple. He'd arranged for me to act as club mascot for the local football team, which meant that I had to dress in sexy sports shorts and a little top and run out onto the field with the team before the start of the game, pose with them for the local paper, then stand on the sidelines cheering and supporting them. My main task, though, was to try and lay a couple of them either during or after the game. I would be in heaven!

'Like everybody else, Frank had provided me with the outfit I was to wear, which I put on before taking a cab to the ground. Needless to say, the shorts were so tight and cut so high that they were obscene, leaving little to the imagination. The tiny top he sent me only just covered my breasts, which aren't that big anyway and the amount of bare flesh I ended up showing made me glad I'd been using the sun-bed regularly of late.

'When I arrived at the football stadium I was taken to meet the manager, who said he was delighted with the way I looked and asked me to join him for drinks after the match. I got a pretty shrewd idea what he had in mind though, dirty old bugger!

'He took me down to the dressing rooms to meet the team, who were lining up ready to go out onto the pitch. They seemed to approve of me too, judging by the whistles and rude comments, and I found myself getting damp between the legs already as I looked at the dozen or so gorgeous men in front of me, wondering who I would end up having sex with.

'Somebody called for the team and we walked out of the dressing room and along a corridor to the start of the tunnel which leads to the pitch. I could hear the crowd cheering and I began to feel nervous, even though all I had to do was run out ahead of the lads, pose for a photo, then run back to the manager's seats. A signal was given and off I went. I'll never forget the weird feeling I got as I ran out into daylight, cheered by thousands of people; I felt like a superstar.

'There were loads of whistles and cat-calls as I ran into the centre of the field where the photographers stood waiting and I began to feel deliciously randy, knowing that I was appearing half naked in front of this huge crowd. The team followed me quickly and the pictures were taken, the newspaper photographers seemingly more interested in me than the team!

'I ran back to the edge of the pitch, to the sound of more cheering, then the game got started.

'I've always been keen on football, and watching the two teams of hunky guys running about so close to me was a real turn on. I don't understand the finer points of the game, I'm only interested in looking at the lovely, strong bodies of the players.

'I soon got caught up in the excitement of the game, however, and ended up running about and jumping up and down like a cheer-leader. It was great fun and, best of all, we won.

'As the lads ran off the pitch at the end of the game they kissed me in turn, panting and exhausted, their bodies sweating like crazy. My thoughts quickly went away from football and back to the much more interesting subject of fucking. The problem was, of course, how was I going to get laid? I couldn't just walk up to one of the players and drag him off somewhere for a screw. I just didn't know what to do.

'I chatted to the manager and a couple of hangers-on for a short while, then it was suggested that I might like to go and congratulate the team in the dressing room. Like a lamb to the slaughter I walked down the corridor to where I could hear the lads singing and laughing; looking back, I can't believe I was so naïve!

'I opened the door to the room where the noise was coming from and went in. I expected to see some of the players half dressed or even naked, showering and changing, but I was wrong. There were some showers, true, and a couple of the lads were using them. The majority, however, were splashing about in this huge square bath, sunken into the tiled floor, and acting the fool like a load of little boys. The soapy water came up to their waists when they stood, although some of them were sitting on the floor of the bath, soaking up the hot water.

'I stayed still for a moment, unsure of what to do or say. The room went very quiet when they noticed me there, then one of them patted the surface of the water and invited me to join them. The others soon joined in, asking me to scrub their backs and so on, and I thought, well . . . what the hell!

'I kicked off my sandals and simply ran towards the bath, leapt into the air and landed with a huge splash in the middle of about a dozen naked, wet men. We splashed about like idiots at first, then I was picked up bodily and thrown from player to player, getting myself soaked. My shorts and top were now completely see-through and totally useless and I was developing an incredible wetness between my legs that had nothing at all to do with the water.

'Somebody pulled my little top off and then my feet and legs were lifted and what seemed like twenty hands pulled and yanked at my shorts, until they too disappeared into the foaming water. Now naked, apart from a little pair of white socks, I felt completely at their mercy and as randy as hell. I was thrown again from man to man, but this time they caught me they all seemed to manage to grab me by the tits, bum or between my legs. I felt around in the murky water, touching thighs, buttocks and occasionally a nice fat dick waving about in the churning water. Surrounded by all this beautiful male-flesh, I was screaming inside for sex; I just wanted one of them to grab hold of me and ram his prick into me there and then and I didn't care how many of them watched.

143

'I carried on "accidentally" feeling between their legs, noticing that their erections were beginning to rise and that the game was becoming more serious. Suddenly I caught hold of one that was as hard as steel and a whopper. I just stood still in the water and held on to this monster, taking it with both hands, my eyes wide open.

'The lads stopped larking about with a remarkable suddenness, obviously realising what had happened, and moved back to give room. Someone said, "She's got hold of Jim, I hope she likes 'em big," or words to that effect.

'Jim stood to his full height. He was big in more ways than one, a good six and a half feet tall and broad with it. Because of his height, the water only came to his crotch and I could see his magnificent tool in all its splendour. I've seen loads of them in my time, but nothing to match this; superbly long and extremely thick and I wanted it bad.

'I started to move my hands up and down over the length, watching it get even bigger, the thick knob-end growing almost purple. I bent my head and kissed it, then opened my mouth and took it in, tasting its soapiness. I couldn't get much into my mouth because of its thickness and my tongue wasn't able to do its work, so I just held it there, whilst my hands rubbed up and down the long stem.

'He took himself from my mouth then lifted me in his powerful arms so my body pressed against his hairy chest. He kissed me heavily on the mouth, his tongue pushing against mine and I wrapped my legs around his waist. I could feel the end of his monster shaft tickling at my pussy and I wanted desperately to lower myself onto it, to impale my aching pussy on his beautiful sex, but he held me firmly, teasing me.

'I looked at the others; they were staring between my legs avidly, waiting for the moment of contact. Somebody shouted out, "Go on Jim, let her have it!" and Jim let go of me, allowing my body to fall, unimpeded onto his hard erection.

'I managed to take most of it inside me as I slid down and I remember howling with pleasure as it filled me, stretching me in a way that I have never experienced before. There was a cheer from the rest of the players as my buttocks touched his thighs and I took the full ten or eleven inches of hard dong up me. Because I'm such a small person they were obviously surprised that I took it all with such apparent ease.

'We were still for a moment, then I started to ride him, taking his hard length in and out, using every wonderful inch to satisfy the lust that had built up within me during the game. I really hammered my hips on the poor man and, despite his strength I nearly knocked him over into the water with my wild humping a couple of times. He didn't move at all, he didn't need to. It was *my* fuck; I was in charge. I didn't stop for a second, my bum becoming a blur to those who were watching. He didn't touch me in any way, my arms wrapped around his neck and his erection being our only point of contact, my legs now floating in the water on either side of his body.

'I screwed myself silly on this wonderful phallus, the water splashing against my bum each time I thrust down, feeling like gentle slaps from a wet hand. I felt myself coming and I started to howl again, completely forgetting the presence of the other men, even the man I was impaled upon. It was just me and this lovely cock.

'As I came I bit into the hairy chest in front of my face and felt him throbbing inside me, filling me. I rode him as hard as I could, the water splashing over the sides of the bath, taking everything he could give me. He shook his head from side to side, gritting his teeth as the pumping went on and on, until I could feel his thick stem begin to lose its incredible hardness. When he'd completely relaxed, he lifted me off and we separated, drifting apart into the water.

'He was finished, but I knew I had a lot more to do. Almost immediately somebody grabbed me from behind, wrapping his arms around my body, his hands all over me, feeling my tits and my still sensitive pussy. He pressed himself against me so that I could feel his hardness resting

145

between my buttocks. I reached back with one hand and took hold of his head, pulling his face to mine and kissing him passionately, whilst I rubbed my bum against his stem, feeling him thrust against me.

'Another couple of players now stood in front of me, their hands groping at my nakedness. I let my legs float up in the water, finding their crotches with my feet, caressing their hard erections with my toes, as three pairs of hands fondled my sex-crazed body. The guy behind me was really working on me now, prodding and rubbing at my sex, pushing as many fingers inside me as he could. I pressed my feet against the pubes of the other two and raised my body, pushing my bum out, feeling the end of his prick slide down between my buttocks until it touched my pussy lips. I guided him in with my free hand, sitting back on the stiff dong until its full length was inside me.

'I put my arms around the necks of the other two men and, using them for leverage by pushing my feet hard against them, I rode up and down swiftly on my lovely stallion. Once again it was me doing the screwing and I adored it. So it seemed did my lover. We fucked for less than two minutes before he grunted and let go deep inside me, whilst I stiffened my buttocks and gripped him tightly, holding him inside me as long as I could.

'When he finally managed to pull away his place was taken immediately by one of the other two guys. He lifted me up by my waist with one hand and steered his tool straight into me, pulling my body hard down on it so that he was fully inside me in one thrust. He gripped me tightly by my hips and rammed me hard up and down against his strong body, the buoyancy of the water causing the most amazing sensations as my legs floated apart. The chap in front of me saw his opportunity and positioned himself between my legs and pushed his sex towards mine. His colleagues held still for a moment, his stiffy almost out of me, and then both men pushed forward, their lengths sliding inside the loose wetness of my pussy at the same time.

'The two players pumped into me in complete harmony,

shagging me out of my mind. I let my body float in the water, supported only by these two cocks, my cunt being stretched beyond belief, but wonderfully so; no pain, just sheer pleasure. They fucked and fucked me, and I looked dreamily up at the ceiling, the lights above me going in and out of focus. I was on a high, far better than any drug could induce. Two more of the players stood, one on either side of us and I grabbed hold of their erections and pulled at them, feeling their stiffness increase in my hands.

'I was at the total mercy of these men, their needs and desires, their fingers, their tongues. They could do anything they wanted, yet they must have realised that *I* was in control, that they must please *me*, that I could take them all. I was so sexed up I kept screaming and howling, my orgasms following almost one after the other.

'The two guys screwing me came almost together and I was pulled from them roughly and then almost thrown through the water onto the waiting erection of yet another who went straight at me like an animal, coming quickly. I climbed from him and went over to a beautiful young stud, having him against the side of the bath, then another, bouncing up and down on him like I had with Jim.

'I just couldn't get enough; I wanted more and more. I was crazier than I had ever been, a total slave to sex. There were fourteen men in that room and even that number couldn't satisfy me. Each one of them had me in turn, some more than once, until they had nothing left to give. I felt extremely powerful, a tiny little blonde floating in a sea of naked men, in complete control of their lust and sexuality. As far as this particular game was concerned, I had won.'

Lisa felt quite taken aback by the coarse way that Kate told her story, the fresh, innocent look on the young girl's face seeming somehow out of place.

But she wasn't finished yet.

'They dried me off and gave me one of their football shirts to wear, my own stuff being soaked. The shirt covered me like a mini-dress, the hem finishing level with my bare sex. I picked up my shoes and walked stiffly out of the room, waving to my lovers on the way out, feeling quite amused at the way they just stared after me, obviously astounded at the staying-power of just one little girl.

'I went up to the manager's office, knocked on the door and walked in. He was sitting at his desk, talking intensely to two of the line officials. I apologised for interrupting them, but he told me to come in and sit down, making no attempt to hide the way he leered at my bare legs, no doubt getting the occasional glimpse of my hairy little pussy.

'He asked me if I'd enjoyed myself and I told him I had. I sat with my legs slightly apart, knowing that all three of them could see my nakedness. I still hadn't come down from my sexual high, I was as randy as hell and hoped that the bonking hadn't finished.

'The manager said something about it not being fair that the players should have all the fun and the two linesmen agreed. I smiled and walked over to face the boss over his desk, taking my shirt off as I moved. I bent over and leant my elbows on the big, wooden desk, resting my head in my hands. My legs were slightly apart and my bum was pushed out, giving the other two men a delightful view. I told him I agreed with him.

'He stood up, unzipped himself and pulled out his nice tool; not too small, not too big. I took it in my hand and rubbed it gently, before putting it to my lips. I kissed the thick end with the fullness of my lips, then opened my mouth and let him slide in. I ran my tongue round and round it, pumping my head back and forth, fucking him with my face. With one hand I rubbed his hard stem, the other cradling his balls, one of my fingers tickling his anus. He matched the movements of my head, his hips thrusting gently, his eyes closed.

'I heard the sounds of movement behind me; I didn't look back, knowing what to expect. The line officials were getting ready to take me. I nearly bit into the manager's dick when I felt the warm wetness of a tongue running over my bottom and then another, as both men licked and nibbled at my buttocks. One of them pushed the tip of his tongue into my anus, then slid down to my wet pussy, drinking the juices from me. I wondered if he knew just what else he might be swallowing, but it didn't seem to worry him.

'I carried on suckling on the manager, my pussy aching for more attention. They didn't disappoint me. I felt that wonderfully familiar feeling of a thick knob-end parting my soaking wet sex-lips as one of the men entered me. I gobbled greedily on the prick in my mouth as the steady rhythm started, feeling yet another orgasm building up inside me. I squealed, the noise muffled by the thick tool pressed against my tongue and lifted my legs up from the floor. The guy behind me thrust quickly into me and I heard him groan as he came, falling across my body and biting my shoulder.

'He pulled his drooping dick from me and allowed his mate to take over. He took me in a gentler, steadier way, but the result was the same. Despite his efforts to hold back he cried out and came, throbbing heavily against the tender flesh of my vagina.

'The boss suddenly pulled from my mouth and almost ran behind me, ramming into me before I had time to move. He thrust into me no more than half a dozen times before filling me with his seed, his fingernails digging hard into the soft, tender flesh of my poor little bum.

'The three of them collapsed back on the sofa, saying nothing. When he had caught his breath, the manager got up and retrieved a package from inside the desk and handed it to me. It contained the little skirt and top I was to wear to the party that evening, Frank having assumed that I would need a change of clothing. As I dressed in the clothes I thought to myself that there was still an awful lot of screwing to do that day and I began to wonder if I was up to it.

'As you may recall . . . I was.'

* * *

The girls arrived at Squire's Club in a large, black taxi, the door held open by a flunky wearing a top-hat and long dress-coat. They were led quickly through the grand hallway to the back of the club, their purpose in being there obvious to the experienced doorman. He knocked and opened a large, oak door and ushered the four teenagers in. Lisa looked around nervously. She'd heard of places like this; men's clubs where great decisions were made, the home of the ruling classes. She felt more than a little out of her depth.

Frank was waiting for them, sitting on a sumptuous leather chair, talking to a small group of rather ordinary-looking, middle-aged men. He introduced them politely and poured some brandy, urging the girls to make themselves comfortable.

The conversation during the early part of the evening was kept light; the girls were oozing sexuality, and utilising every opportunity to come on to the clients. The men were, in fact, very good company and Lisa found herself warming to them, looking forward to getting more physical later on. It was Frank, of course, who set the ball rolling.

'We'll have a game of truth or dare,' he said, picking up an empty brandy-bottle. 'Everyone sit on the floor in a circle, boy-girl, boy-girl.'

The group did as instructed, waiting expectantly for the fun to start. Frank spun the bottle on the carpet. It stopped, the neck pointing towards Janet. 'Right, Janet, you ask the question or set the dare to the person it stops at next. They are not allowed to lie, or refuse a dare. Go ahead.'

She spun the bottle gently, watching as it stopped at one of the men, a Californian businessman by the name of Dennis. 'Right, Dennis,' she said, 'kiss Kate on the left nipple.' Kate gave a childish giggle and opened the jacket of her trouser-suit, offering her bared breast to Dennis, who happily obliged. It was then his turn to spin the bottle. It pointed at Lisa.

'I've just got to know ... the truth, remember,' he said, licking his lips, 'just what size are those lovely tits?'

150

'Forty-three inches. What size is your cock?'

'Oh no,' interrupted Frank, 'it's not your turn, Lisa. You must spin the bottle.'

She did as instructed, seeing it stop at Kate.

'Kate,' said Lisa, licking her lips, 'kiss Rani fully on the mouth.' She wondered if she'd over-stepped the mark, but neither girl seemed to object. Kate leant over and held Rani's face in her hands, kissing her lips wetly. They pulled apart slightly, letting the others see their tongues licking playfully together, then they kissed again, this time wrapping their arms around each other. Frank told the two of them to separate after a moment, which they seemed to do reluctantly, their faces flushed with excitement. Rani spun the bottle, the direction of the neck now indicating the turn of Andrew, another guest. He shuffled uncomfortably, awaiting his challenge.

Rani thought for a moment, the delay prolonging Andrew's agony. Then she smiled. 'Take your clothes off, Andrew, everything.' He looked around nervously at first, seeing the others waiting for him to comply. He shrugged and stripped quickly, pausing before removing his boxer-shorts, then throwing them over to the opposite side of the room with abandon. He sat back on the floor, his long cock resting, half erect on his thigh and took hold of the bottle. With great precision, he managed to arrange the force of his spin so that it stopped back at Rani.

She smiled, knowing what he wanted. 'Go on, everything!' said Andrew and she stood up and proceeded to undress. She kicked off her shoes and rolled the tight mini-dress up her body and over her head, throwing it on top of his shorts. She now only wore a tiny, green G-string, covering her prominent, hairy mound, her olive-brown skin shining flawlessly.

She stepped over to Andrew, unhooking a little bow at the side, letting the lacy nothing fall away, revealing her sex to her tormentor. She held the G-string to his face, letting him sniff her scent, kissing him lightly on the head. He took the little garment and put it with his clothes, probably as a souvenir, and Rani sat back on the floor, her legs open, her sex wet with her excitement.

The game carried on in this vein for a while and soon all the participants were naked. The dares became progressively more obscene, as the players became more and more aroused. Lisa was the last to strip, smiling with delight as she noticed all five cocks firm and erect as she revealed her sumptuous form to the men's eager gaze.

The other two businessmen, Eric and William were particularly transfixed by the sight of her nakedness, hardly taking their eyes from her shaven cunt. She sat purposely, with her legs as wide open as she could comfortably manage, enjoying their leers. She was desperate for sex now and with five fine erections within her reach she knew she wouldn't have to wait much longer.

Frank prolonged the agony, however, announcing a ban on dares for a while, permitting only truths. This proved quite interesting for Lisa, who learned that Rani had one female and four male regular lovers, all in the police force, which explained why Frank had chosen that particular task for her to perform for the party. She also discovered that Kate and Janet had enjoyed a brief sexual affair a couple of years previously. Other bits of nonsense were revealed, until Frank at last agreed that dares were permitted again.

Andrew spun the bottle, watching it stop in front of Eric. The latter had been gazing at Lisa, rubbing gently on his manhood, his mind not really on the game. Andrew realised this, of course.

'Eric, I want you to stand up,' he said, slowly and deliberately, 'walk over to Lisa and stick that hard cock of yours right up her cunt.' He glanced apprehensively over to her, but she just smiled and lay back, running a finger over her wet slit, waiting for Eric to fulfil his task.

He wasted no time, kneeling between her wide open legs, pointing his erection at the pouting lips of her sex. She took hold of his hardness and pulled it towards her, pushing the end towards its target.

'Go on then, fuck me!' she commanded, gripping his thighs. He started to pump heavily into her and she knew he would come quickly.

He grunted and groaned, sliding his full length in and out, in and out, bringing her rapidly to the point of orgasm. She cried out as the feelings shattered her, digging her fingernails into his fleshy back. He shouted, 'I'm coming, I'm coming!' and pulled himself from within her wet sheath to kneel over her masturbating himself with his hand. The sperm shot across her body, over her breasts and face. He continued to rub himself furiously, then fell forward onto her, lightly moving his lower body over the wetness of her soft breasts. As he relaxed, Lisa raised her head and took his drooping manhood into her mouth, her hands squeezing and fondling his buttocks. She gobbled him hungrily, until the sensitivity of post-orgasm caused him to pull her away.

As far as Lisa was concerned, it appeared the time for games was over. Clearly, it was time now for some serious screwing to be done.

She crawled over to Andrew like a tiger on heat and grabbed his stiff erection, forcing it into her mouth. She suckled on his hardness, licking and lapping all around the stem, drawing her cheeks against the thick knob. She knelt with her backside in the air, a prize too perfect to be ignored. William pounced on her, pressing his face hard against her lovely bum, licking furiously at her open pussy and tight anus. He ran his tongue heavily up and down the crack of her behind, with the fervour of a man possessed, forcing her to arch her back and push her bottom out for more.

Finally he mounted her, pushing his not insubstantial length deep into her. She groaned, biting gently on Andrew's cock, opening her legs more as the steady fucking started. William knew what he was doing, twisting and wriggling his hips so that his tool explored every part of her, prodding in every direction, rubbing against her engorged clitoris. He was able to hold back, his rhythm

153

regular and controlled, the end of his stalk just touching the entrance to her womb as he thrust forward.

She felt herself building up to another come and knew from the tremors within her lower body that it was going to be a good one. Her sex-lips started to tingle, the feelings rushing down her legs to her knees, causing her to raise them up from the floor, allowing William even deeper access to her honeypot.

Her climax was shattering, making her cry out, losing Andrew's length from her mouth. Seeing her opportunity, Janet squatted over his body with her back to him and lowered herself onto his fat tool, her sex inches away from Lisa's mouth. Lisa took a moment to look around, William still pumping steadily into her. Frank was servicing Kate on the floor, whilst Rani was accommodating Dennis as he sat on one of the large chairs at the edge of the room. The room was alive with the sound of copulation, of sighing and groaning in pleasure, of cries of orgasm as the orgy continued.

Lisa felt William withdraw from her pussy, then gasped as his tongue touched her anus, wetting it profusely. His finger slid into the tightness, moving around to ease its entry. She returned her mouth to Andrew as her bum was finger-fucked, finding that his cock was now deep inside Janet's bottom. She licked over his balls, sucking them in and out of her wet lips, playing them between the softness of her tongue and the roof of her mouth. Janet pounded up and down on his shaft and Lisa felt she could scent her friend's sex perfume as she satisfied herself in her special way on their mutual lover.

She ran her tongue upwards, over Andrew's balls again, over Janet's neglected pussy, then firmly against her erect clitoris. She licked rapidly over the hard, red bud, hearing her friend sigh loudly with the pleasure.

William pulled his wet finger from Lisa's anus and she felt the thicker intrusion of his large knob-end as he pushed into her bum. She pushed back, accepting the full length quickly into her tight hole, her hand moving to her pussy, frigging herself busily. As he pumped into her she squeezed her buttocks as hard as she could, making the hole even tighter, feeling the full length of his hard rod within the secret confines of her lovely bottom.

Janet was obviously coming now, grinding her backside heavily against both Andrew's hardness and her pussy against Lisa's fluttering tongue. She screamed, her hands grasping her friend's head and crushing her mouth to her sex, as Andrew pumped quickly in and out of her bottom. Lisa's face was pressed so hard against Janet that she imagined she could feel the throbbing of the ejaculating prick inside her body, wanting to share the mutual climax of the lovers in front of her.

Now Lisa began to concentrate on the feelings she was experiencing as William moved in and out of her anus, understanding fully why Janet loved this type of sex. She made him stop, his tool still embedded deep inside her, and pushed back until he was sitting on his heels with her bum resting on his lap, her legs splayed wide apart. She then took over the movements, raising herself up and down, impaling herself on his long, thick erection, her pussy being pushed forwards and upwards with each thrust.

Dennis was watching this from his seat; Rani had joined Kate on the floor and was licking at her sex greedily whilst Frank screwed her from behind. The American shuffled over and knelt between Lisa's legs, targeting his hard shaft towards her open pussy-lips as she ground her bottom up and down on William's sex.

She held herself still and leant as far back as she could in order to allow Dennis to put his weapon inside her. He slid in awkwardly until his full length pressed against that of his colleague, their tools kept apart by the thinnest of tissue. They started to take her in unison, in what had become another of her favourite ways of copulating. She used her thigh and buttock muscles to grip both cocks as they humped her, fingering her clitoris with her own hand.

Suddenly, Frank was standing by her. She took hold of

155

his wonderful shaft and put it straight into her mouth, tasting the anal and vaginal scents of both Kate and Rani.

She sucked and rubbed his sex vigorously, sensing that the two men pumping into her nether regions were about to come. She wasn't wrong. They groaned loudly as they filled her, whilst she desperately tried to get Frank to do the same, using her mouth as expertly as she could. She clamped her full lips over his stem, the end pressing against the back of her throat, her tongue licking at it wildly. She felt him swell to an even greater thickness and, to her joy it throbbed within the confines of her mouth. She held still for a moment, wondering if she had broken some mysterious rule. Delightedly she sensed the throbbing again and she gobbled and sucked, taking every drop, proud that she had made him come at last.

She pulled her face away from Frank's groin and looked across the room. Andrew was sitting half-dazed, enjoying the show. Janet had joined Kate and Rani on the floor in a mutual cunt-licking session, so he looked rather lonely. Lisa pulled herself up, the two lengths within her body falling lazily from her, and she staggered over to Andrew, the only one of the four businessmen she hadn't had. It was hard to say whether he wanted it or not. He was half-erect, obviously having satisfied himself within Janet's tight little bum, but she was determined to have him, pulling and tugging at his sex, forcing it to hardness.

Once it was erect she sat down hard on his lap, taking the full length inside her warm wetness, wrapping her arms around his neck. She rode him for all she was worth, her backside bouncing up and down on his lap as she shagged him mercilessly. He licked at her tits as they bounced heavily against his face, then she swung them from side to side, slapping hard against his cheeks with their not inconsiderable weight.

She was coming again, another pussy-tearing, explosive climax. She screamed loudly, arching her back and stiffening her body as the flood of orgasmic sensations hit her. Totally unable to control herself, she bit into the shoulder of her lover, drawing blood. He was past caring though, their crotches grinding together, the thumping of his tool sending shudders to the back of her brain.

At last he relaxed, softening quickly inside her, and she lifted herself from his lap, his limp sex flopping wetly on his thigh. She lay on the floor, flat on her back, legs and arms akimbo. She watched lazily as Eric screwed the other three girls in turn, then closed her eyes and drifted off into sleep.

Chapter Seven

Lisa had just settled down into a nice, hot bath when the phone rang. Reluctantly, she clambered out of the heavily-scented water and rushed to pick up the receiver. It was Janet.

'Lisa? Hi, listen, we've got another little job to do for Frank.'

'Already?' said Lisa, with some surprise. 'I don't know if I could stand it; I'm still sore from last night!'

'Oh, you'll be all right. This one's a bit different, anyway. There's an Ambassador from some Eastern Bloc country in town, and Frank wants to get some information from him.'

'What sort of information?' Lisa was beginning to worry about the role of the Lust Angels; the sex was fine, but there seemed to be more to it than simple escort duties.

'Military stuff, I believe.'

'Military!' Lisa was astounded at her friend's naïvety. 'How the hell are we going to get that sort of information? We don't know one end of a gun from the other!'

'We don't need to. All we have to do is fuck him, then use our powers to make him susceptible to interrogation. Frank does the rest.'

'You've done this before, haven't you?'

'Loads of times,' said Janet, totally without concern in her voice, 'it's how we pay the old man for what he gave us.'

'I'm not so sure that it's worth it. I mean, business secrets are one thing, but defence secrets ... oh, Janet, are you sure you know what you're doing?'

'Trust me,' said her friend, breathlessly, 'anyway, we've got no choice.'

'What do you mean?'

'If we refuse a job, we lose our looks, it's as simple as that.'

'I couldn't bear that.'

'Me neither. Anyway, what harm can it do?'

'I suppose it'll be OK,' said Lisa, unconvinced.

'Great. Now, meet me at the entrance to the Grand Hotel at noon; and wear something really erotic. Frank says he's a kinky old bugger.'

Lisa put the phone down, frowning at her reflection in the nearby mirror. She was not at all happy about the way things were developing. Oh, true the sex was wonderful, but even last night she'd been aware that everything was not quite right.

She'd woken during the night to see Frank talking earnestly to one of the Americans, the latter apparently drunk or drugged. At the time she'd thought nothing of it, assuming the man was simply exhausted from the orgy and had quickly drifted off back to sleep, but after Janet's call she began to wonder just what was going on.

She looked again at her reflection; the perfect body, the beautiful face. She knew that she could never allow herself to return to the awful, fat little frump she'd been before. Her vanity still had control of her will and she had to go along with whatever was asked of her.

Lisa returned to her bath, slipping gratefully into the still hot water. The soothing warmth had the immediate effect of awakening the now all too familiar lusts within her young body, the insatiable need for sexual relief. She desperately wanted to finger herself, to give herself an orgasm as she wallowed in the luxury of the bath, but knew such indulgences were forbidden.

Instead, she quickly washed and stepped out of the water, dried herself and went back into the other room to find some appropriate underwear for the forthcoming events.

She decided to wear stockings, and selected a thin, lacy suspender belt and some sheer, black hosiery from her drawer. She carefully put these items on, smoothing the sensuous material of the stockings over her long legs, shivering as even this simple action tantalised her, increasing her feelings of lust.

She looked again into her full-length mirror, admiring the way her hairless pussy was framed by the erotic lingerie.

It was then that she saw him.

A small mirror on the dressing table, coupled with the view provided by the full length reflection in front of her showed the unmistakable image of a figure just outside the window. She drew a breath, feeling a little nervous, unsure whether to move or not. Who was he? What was he doing outside of her window?

Then she remembered. A neighbour on the next floor had mentioned that he was having a burglar alarm fitted that morning; the events of the past few days had made Lisa forget all about it. So, he was no mad rapist, waiting for the chance to leap into her room and have her.

Was that disappointment she felt? Lisa wasn't sure. All she knew was that, rapist or not, he was outside her window, definitely looking in and she was naked except for a pair of black stockings and a skimpy suspender belt.

It would have been normal for a lady caught unawares in such circumstances to rush into the bathroom and wait until the uninvited visitor had gone; but there was nothing normal these days about Lisa. She didn't mind what he saw, she wanted him to look, to enjoy, to lust after her body. She also knew he couldn't see the small mirror, so wouldn't be able to figure out that she was watching him.

She decided to give him a show, something he would never forget; the sight of a beautiful young girl masturbating. Janet had told her that, provided that she didn't actually make herself come and providing the object of self-stimulation was to seduce or entertain someone else it was acceptable under the old man's rules.

Lisa smoothed her hands over her large, firm breasts, throwing back her head and arching her back to push them out even further. She tweaked both nipples simultaneously, feeling them harden under her touch, glancing again at the mirror. He was looking hard, his mouth half open, his tongue occasionally licking his upper lip. He wasn't at all bad looking; in his late teens with a shock of blond, curly hair and dressed in white overalls.

He became more and more transfixed as she ran one hand down over her flat stomach to her sex, the other hand continuing its caress of her luscious breasts. Although she had her back to the window, she knew that he would be able to see everything reflected in the full-length mirror whilst feeling safe in the knowledge that the angle prevented her from seeing him.

She was wet; very, very wet. She felt so deliciously brazen. She rubbed the waiting bud with the tip of her middle finger, now running the other hand down to between her legs, her fingers pulling gently at the puffy lips, feeling the wetness against the palm of her hand. She pushed two fingers inside and started to fuck herself with them, still rubbing her clitoris with the fingers of the other hand, moaning softly, sitting back on the bed, her legs spread wide for her secret lover to see.

She positioned herself now so that the mirror was unnecessary: he would be looking straight at her sex as she fingered and probed, lying on her back on the bed. She pushed four fingers inside herself, moving them swiftly in and out. She wanted him to smash the window, to jump in and take her willing body in any way that pleased him. She wanted his mouth on her sex, then his cock deep inside her . . . God, what was he waiting for?

Suddenly there was a cry of 'Oh shit!' and a crash. Lisa sat up, scared that her clandestine voyeur had fallen and hurt himself, or worse. To her immediate relief she saw that he was still at her window, although he now had a look of terror on his face, rather than lust. She quickly realised that, thanks to his being entranced by her erotic demonstration, he'd lost concentration and with it his ladder, which had been the cause of the crash.

She also knew her ledge was narrow and that he wouldn't be able to hold on for long.

She rushed over and quickly raised the window and helped him into her room. 'Are you all right?' she asked, forgetting her near-nakedness for a moment. She held his arm with genuine concern.

'I'm sorry, I . . .' was all the stranger could say. He was staring at her now, gazing at her lovely body, savouring the view.

She pretended embarrassment, turning from him and grabbing a small item of clothing, holding it uselessly against her body, knowing she was hiding nothing. 'Oh, my God, I didn't realise . . . I'd better put something on!'

'Don't trouble on my account.'

Lisa smiled and kissed him lightly on the cheek. Then she looked deep into his eyes, willing him to take her. For a second he seemed to waver, but the intensity of her will began to work on him, the little resistance that he held fading with the increase in his lust.

Their mouths met, their tongues immediately darting, licking, tasting. He ran his hands down her naked back to her bottom, making her press her crotch against his. He felt hard through the rough material of the boiler-suit, its very coarseness thrilling her. She unbuttoned the garment slowly from the top as he moved his rough hands to her breasts, feeling their size, their firmness, running his thumbs over the hard nipples, teasing them to button-hard erection.

When she had unbuttoned his overall to the waist she pulled it off his shoulders, revealing a strong, naked torso. One more button and she was able to pull the boiler-suit to his ankles, leaving him wearing just a pair of brightly coloured boxer-shorts. Lisa pulled these down in one quick movement, thrilling at the sight of his long, thick penis as it sprang up to meet her admiring gaze. She took hold of the firm tool with both hands and kissed him lightly on the

162

lips. 'Who's a big boy, then?' she said, sultrily. He didn't answer, still obviously unable to believe his luck.

Lisa knelt down and took his hardness into her pouting mouth, running her tongue deftly around the thick, bulbous end, tasting the erotic flavour of his excited state. Then she took it from her wet mouth and licked up and down the full length, occasionally rubbing it quite vigorously with her free hand; her other fingers were busily engaged in fondling her own sex, bringing her almost to the point of orgasm.

She stood up slowly, kissing his hairy stomach and chest, licking his nipples and finally kissing him hard on the mouth, whilst at no time letting her hand leave his hard erection.

Finally, without a word, she pulled him by his cock to the bed. 'Lie down!' she commanded. He did as he was told, his face holding the expression of a schoolboy about to be caned. Lisa removed the rumpled clothes from around his feet, followed by the heavy, workman's boots and rather tatty socks. He just lay there as she took in the sight of his strong body, a little too hairy for her taste but nevertheless beautiful, his manhood large and ready.

She climbed astride him and took his sex in her hand, guiding it to her wet opening. The thick end found its target and he pushed upward a little as Lisa sat down on the superb length, taking every inch inside her in one, graceful movement. She remained still for a moment, then began to slowly move up and down, screwing herself on his lovely stiffness, taking full control. This seemed to suit the stranger, who lay with his hands clasped behind his head, watching this vision of beauty impaled upon his hard stalk.

Lisa started to move with more urgency now, tightening her vaginal muscles as she felt him slide in and out of her body, maintaining wet contact with every inch. His hips began to thrust involuntarily upwards in time to her movements, and his breathing became heavy. She didn't want a long session, she just wanted to drain this stranger, to feel him come inside her, and to bring them both to orgasm when *she* chose.

She was riding him quickly now, leaning forward so that her pendulous breasts swung against his face. His breathing became sharper, his hands grasped her thrusting bottom and the fingernails dug painlessly into her flesh. She revelled in the knowledge that he couldn't hold back any longer, that she had taken charge, that she had seduced and then fucked a man under her own terms and now brought him to orgasm at exactly the right time to suit her needs.

He groaned and started to thrust violently into her. She matched his movements, leaping up and down onto his body, ramming herself onto him as she felt the magical waves of her own orgasm approaching. With a cry she came, feeling at the same time the pumping of his sex as the sperm shot deep into her body. She bit him hard on the shoulder as her orgasm took hold of her, almost crying with the sheer pleasure and ecstasy of her release. Finally, she collapsed exhausted on him and they lay still.

'I really shouldn't have done that,' the stranger said, nervously, 'I only got married this month. I don't know what came over me. I didn't seem able to stop myself.'

Lisa smiled, kissing him on the tip of his nose. 'It'll be our little secret,' she said, reassuringly. This was how the power should be used, she thought to herself. To seduce unsuspecting or even unwilling hunks in order to satisfy her own carnal lust.

The young man dressed quickly and left by the front door, still looking bewildered. Lisa returned again to the bathroom, and used the hand-held shower head to rinse herself between the legs.

The force of the warm spray soon had an effect and she found herself directing it unconsciously on her erect clitoris. She closed her eyes and gritted her teeth, feeling that another orgasm was near.

'Put that down!' The suddenness of the shouted instruction caused her to drop the showerhead, allowing it to clatter into the empty bath. Lisa looked around her, terrified. At first she saw nothing, then she glanced into the small mirror on the bathroom cabinet. The evil features of the old man glared out at her.

She trembled visibly as the disembodied face broke into a heinous grin. 'You know the rules, my dear,' cackled the foul voice of her benefactor, 'this is your last warning. No self-stimulation!'

'I–I'm sorry, sir,' she stuttered, 'I wasn't thinking. I won't do it again.'

'See that you don't,' the old man barked, his image beginning to fade in the mirror, 'or you know what will happen.'

He was gone as quickly as he had appeared. Lisa sat down heavily on the edge of the bath and caught her breath. Her suspicions were gradually being confirmed; she was dealing with something that was very wrong, very powerful and she felt afraid.

Lisa arrived at the Grand Hotel on time, the taxi-cab pulling up outside the main entrance. Janet was standing by the doorway, wearing a thick, full-length fur coat, looking very elegant and totally in keeping with the expensive surroundings. She smiled and waved when she spotted Lisa, beckoning her to come inside the building.

They walked together into the plush bar and sat at a small secluded table by the window. Janet had already ordered drinks, which were delivered by a rather overly familiar waiter, who had obviously deduced the nature of their business. He stooped as he placed the glasses on the table, pointedly staring at the way Lisa's breasts forced her coat forward almost ludicrously.

'Can I get you ladies anything else; food, or perhaps some company?'

Janet glared at him. 'Fuck off,' she said quietly, through clenched teeth. The waiter bowed in mock subservience and returned to his place by the bar.

'That was a bit strong,' said Lisa, a little embarrassed.

'No, it wasn't,' Janet replied, still angry, 'he thinks we're hookers; common prostitutes.'

Lisa looked uncomfortable. 'Well, we . . .'

Janet caught her roughly by the elbow. 'No,' she hissed, 'we are *not*. We do this for our own pleasure, OK?'

Lisa nodded, pulling her arm from her friend's grip. She wondered if Janet was quite so sure that their role was as innocuous as she supposed.

There was a silent pause. Janet unbuttoned her coat, revealing a high-necked, full-length black evening gown. Lisa looked at her with some surprise.

'I thought you said we had to dress erotically?' she said, a little perplexed. Her own choice was such that she daren't unfasten her own coat in the hotel bar, for fear of being arrested.

'I did,' said Janet, with a grin, 'you wait till you see the back of it.'

Lisa smiled, happy that the conversation had turned light again. 'I can't even open my coat at all!'

'I can't wait,' said Janet, with genuine lust in her eyes.

'What happens now?' They were alone in the bar, except for the smarmy waiter.

'A car will be sent to collect us. It should be here at any moment.' Janet peered out of the window into the brightly lit street.

Lisa sipped her drink thoughtfully. Despite her misgivings she was looking forward to the night ahead, wondering what sort of deviations the Ambassador might indulge in. She also knew that she couldn't wait to show herself to him and to Janet for that matter, certain that her outfit would have the desired effect.

'I think that's them,' said Janet, looking at a large, black car that had drawn up outside the hotel entrance, 'yes, yes, there's Frank. Come on.'

The two girls quickly drained their glasses and headed back to the reception area. Frank was waiting for them, holding open the large, glass door to the hotel. He ushered them outside and opened the door to the car.

He was dressed in formal, evening attire, complete with black bow-tie, a sight that Lisa found most appealing. She smiled sweetly at him as he helped them into the back of the sleek limousine, willing him to join them and have sex with her, but to her surprise the powers she had learned to use so effectively in the past were lost on him, his handsome, rugged features showing little emotion other than a polite smile.

She sat on the large, white leather seat in the rear of the car next to Janet, her disappointment obvious as she watched Frank sit in the front, next to the driver.

'It doesn't work on him,' Janet whispered in her ear, 'you can only have Frank under his terms.'

'Pity.'

'Tell me about it. There are times when I could fuck him rigid. Still, don't worry, we should be there soon.'

Lisa looked longingly into her friend's eyes. 'I need a feel. Give me a feel, please.'

She was almost begging. 'You randy cow,' said Janet, pushing her hand between the folds of Lisa's coat, her fingertips making immediate contact with her friend's pussy, finding her already damp. Lisa sat back in the plush seat, her legs wide open as Janet expertly fondled her sex, dipping her fingers deep into the welcoming honeypot, her thumb rubbing swiftly against the hard clitoris.

Lisa began to moan, pushing her hips forward to meet the probing fingers. 'More, more, push more in,' she said, opening her legs even wider, lifting her bottom off the seat. Janet did as instructed, filling the eager pussy with her hand, the thick, wet lips gripping her wrist. 'Yes, that's it, more!' said Lisa, feeling her friend's fist deep inside her body, loving every second of the new sensation. Janet used her arm like a giant penis, pushing in and out of Lisa, faster and faster.

Lisa began to cry out in time with Janet's steady thrusting, knowing she was about to come. With a sudden, deafening scream she let go, one of her feet accidentally kicking the back of the front seats, knocking Frank forward with the force. He turned and scowled, but she was past caring. 'Oh, God, yes!' she cried, as the waves of extreme pleasure began to subside, 'that's the most amazing feeling!'

Janet smiled and kissed her friend lightly on the mouth, pulling her arm gently from between her legs. 'I hope the Ambassador's got a big dick, or you won't feel a thing after that treatment!'

Lisa struggled to compose herself. Frank turned to face them again. 'Right, ladies,' he said, 'we're here. Sort yourselves out.' His tone was almost dictatorial, as though talking to very minor underlings on his staff. Lisa wasn't sure she liked it; he may have been the most gorgeous man she had ever seen, but he needed to learn some simple manners.

The door to the Embassy was huge; heavy, dark oak, carved with various medieval designs that suited the overall gothic appearance of the building. It reminded Lisa of a scene from an old Hollywood horror movie; she half expected it to be opened by a twisted dwarf named Igor.

Instead, the door swung slowly open to reveal the delightful form of a young black girl of about sixteen or seventeen, dressed in a tiny maid's outfit which revealed more than it hid. The beauty of the girl almost took Lisa's breath away. She looked like a tiny version of her friend and lover Sonia, her dark eyes large and hypnotic, the whites shining in stark contrast to her flawless, ebony skin. Her nose was tiny, her mouth large, with thick, pouting lips which jutted forward markedly, as though purposely made for nothing more than sucking cock.

She wore a white, frilly maid's hat and pinafore, the latter small and totally see-through, tied with a thin piece of material at her back. Her only other clothing was a pair of tiny, white panties, suspender belt and white, lacy stockings. Her breasts, small but firm, thrust arrogantly against the flimsy material, the long, almost jet-black nipples erect, seemingly begging for attention.

The maid welcomed the three guests and turned to lead them through the great hall. As Lisa watched the girl's near-naked, thrusting buttocks as she walked ahead of them, she couldn't help but wonder why the Ambassador needed the services of her and Janet, with such delicate loveliness at his command.

They were led through another pair of heavy, oak doors into a large, brightly lit room. In front of them stood a giant of a man, also black, naked but for a red, leather posing pouch which strained to contain obviously huge genitals. He stood, unsmiling, holding out a muscular arm. 'May I take your coats, ladies?' he said, in a clear, booming voice that seemed to echo around the building.

Lisa was suddenly reminded of the way that she was dressed. She waited with nervous excitement as Janet removed her heavy fur, draping it over the servant's muscular forearm.

She saw what her friend had meant as she looked at her gown; her back was completely exposed from her head to her feet, the material held together with thin strips of black lace, the gap in the dress being about four inches. Needless to say, Janet hadn't worn underwear, the resulting view being both beautiful and erotic in its tantalising subtlety.

Lisa began to wonder if she'd perhaps gone too far this time. Subtlety wasn't the word that would be used in her case, she knew. The massive African stood waiting patiently for her coat, which she unbuttoned slowly, gradually revealing her outfit. Finally, she removed the coat and draped it with Janet's, and stood back nervously as she waited for some sort of reaction.

Apart from her black stockings and suspenders she wore a pair of tight, black shorts in shiny PVC, split wide at the crotch, the puffy lips of her sex fully exposed. The shorts were held up by braces of lightweight chain, the silvery links straining on either side of her mountainous breasts, which jutted naked and unfettered before her. The outfit was completed by another, much thicker chain drawn tightly around her waist, the surplus links of this savage belt hanging loosely by her side, almost to her knee.

Frank whistled appreciatively and Lisa breathed a sigh of relief. She looked at the giant servant's face, but he remained impassive, probably used to such sights.

Janet breathed in her ear, lustily. 'No wonder you couldn't open your coat in the hotel!'

'You look pretty sexy yourself!'

'You both look wonderful,' said Frank, speaking with some gentleness for a change. 'I'm sure the Ambassador will approve.'

'The Ambassador *does* approve!'

The voice came from behind them, the girls swinging round to meet their host. He was a small man, quite chubby with dark hair and complexion, a thick, bushy moustache over his broadly grinning mouth. Lisa reckoned that he was about forty years old, but couldn't be too sure, his Latin looks maintaining an attractive youthful appearance.

'Welcome to my home, young ladies,' he said, holding his hand out in greeting. Lisa clutched his sweaty palm first and he gripped her small hand tightly with both of his, kissing her on the cheek. He greeted Janet in the same way, then warmly shook Frank by the hand, betraying affection for an old friend.

'You will have drinks, yes?' he said, motioning to the young maid, 'and then we will have some fun. Now, let me see you more closely.'

He caught Janet by the arms and turned her around, his eyes glinting as he examined her naked rear. 'Such a perfect arse,' he said, as though inspecting a fine piece of livestock, 'I will have much pleasure with that.' He ran his podgy hand over Janet's smooth buttocks, allowing his middle finger to probe gently between them. 'Yes, much pleasure.'

He turned to Lisa. 'And you now, my dear,' he said, 'such a sexy outfit. I can see where you want me to touch you.' His hand went straight for her sex, which was still wet and puffy from her experience with Janet in the car.

170

'Ah, she is wet for me already!' he boasted. 'You have done well, Frank.'

Frank just smiled. The little maid brought a tray of drinks and stepped back next to the other servant, his bulk dwarfing her, making her look extremely vulnerable. 'Now,' said the Ambassador, eagerly, 'before we start I will give you a little show, to get you in the mood, although I don't think the lovely blonde needs any help.' He leered at Lisa. 'Come, everybody sit.'

The four of them sat together on a large settee, Lisa and Janet on either side of the Ambassador. Once settled, he clapped his hands and the two servants walked in front of them, their faces showing no emotion whatsoever. The Ambassador leant over to Lisa and spoke into her ear, 'You watch these two; I could watch them for hours!'

The little maid stripped off her skimpy uniform and panties and stood before her audience, her fingers rubbing quickly at her hairy pussy, her eyes staring into Lisa's. She then turned to face the other servant. So small was she, and so large her partner her face came level with his lower chest, which she kissed gently, before running her tongue sensuously down over his powerful abdomen to the leather pouch which covered his obviously rising manhood. Although fully bent over she kept her legs straight, her perfect bottom thrusting provocatively in the air.

'Don't you just want to have that pretty, black ass?' said their host to Frank, who grinned in agreement. 'You will, my friend, before the night is over, but first, see what he does.'

The maid ran her tongue wetly over the straining pouch, chewing hungrily at the bulge, her hands groping the stiff sinews of the man's buttocks. Slowly, she drew the tiny garment down, pressing her mouth to the exposed flesh, concealing his secrets from the curiosity of the seated guests. She nuzzled at his sex, still hiding it from them, teasing them until suddenly she threw her head back, allowing his penis to thrust into view.

The size of his sex matched his enormous bulk and for

a moment Lisa feared for the young maid, knowing that she was probably about to take it inside her, but then surmised that such an event was probably a regular occurrence. For herself, she yearned to feel the big, black phallus forcing its way within her, filling and stretching her to the limit. She also remembered that they were there to please the Ambassador and not themselves, although she secretly hoped that a session with this huge man was part of the night's agenda.

The maid had clamped her thick lips over the end of the exposed cock now, unable to take more than a couple of inches inside her little mouth. She pumped at his steel-hard length with both of her hands as though trying to milk it, and occasionally paused to grip his heavy balls or stroke his firm bottom. The Ambassador, meanwhile, had started to probe at Lisa's pussy with one hand, whilst fondling Janet's bare backside with the other, an inane grin of self-satisfaction on his face.

After a couple of minutes the maid stood and walked over to the far side of the room, leaving her partner standing alone, his tool jutting ridiculously in front of him. Lisa wanted to rush over and clamp her mouth over it; to suck on him and taste his flesh. She was sure that Janet must be feeling the same way, but they had to stay where they were, as playthings for their host.

The tiny servant returned, carrying something by her side. Lisa's eyes shone with mounting lust as she realised that it was a long, vicious looking whip with three or four strands of harsh leather. The maid drew back the weapon and cracked it hard against the thigh of her lover, causing him to cry out in pain. She repeated the action over and over again, whipping his back, legs and buttocks with a wild ferocity, until he fell to his knees, whimpering. Lisa noted with incredulity that, throughout this vicious treatment he remained fully hard; clearly he was enjoying every stinging blow.

He fell on his back now, his manhood lying erect on his stomach, the thick, bulbous end resting against his navel.

172

His young tormentor whipped him across the chest, then the stomach; dangerously close to the stiff erection. She then played the strands around his cock, teasing him with them as he quivered in anticipation.

Suddenly she threw the whip to one side and leapt astride the prostrate figure, grabbing at his stiff tool desperately. Finding it, she guided the head to her tiny sex and sat down hard on the mammoth length, its hugeness slipping with impossible ease into her receptive sheath.

'Where the hell does she put it all?' mused Lisa, watching in astonishment as the big, black stalk disappeared into the young girl's wildly-stretched sex-lips as she forced herself to take every thick inch.

With cries of lust and pain, she rode her lover in the same savage way that she had beaten him: hard and without mercy until, with a bellow worthy of a rampaging bull, he threw his hips up to meet her downward pumping thrusts, coming inside her frail body with all the power he held.

As soon as he had subsided, the maid pulled herself from him, allowing his shrinking shaft to flop noisily onto his belly. She squatted over his face, forcing him to lick at her inflamed clitoris until, with a loud groan she orgasmed, grinding her sex into his mouth as his tongue flicked at her erect bud. Finally she collapsed at his side, sated and exhausted.

The Ambassador stood up and applauded. 'Did I not say that they are wonderful?' he said, proudly. He turned to look at his guests, as the two servants slipped quietly from the room. 'And now, for our pleasure, I will take you to my special room.'

'I will stay here,' said Frank, 'perhaps, when your maid has recovered . . .?'

'I'll send her to you. You will find she knows many tricks.'

'I'm sure she does,' said Frank, casually squeezing the prominent bulge in his trousers. 'Now, you girls, remember, do whatever His Excellency wishes.'

The girls smiled to indicate their acquiescence, and followed the Ambassador from the room.

He led them back through the great hall and to a small door at the far end. Opening it, Lisa saw that it led to some sort of cellar, the steep steps disappearing into the darkness. Their host turned on a light and bade them follow him as he proceeded down the staircase.

At the bottom of the stairs was another, smaller hall, the stone walls lined with many heavy, barred doors, reminding Lisa of a prison. She wondered what secrets lay beyond these portals, what terrible events took place within the cell-like rooms. She felt the excitement mounting inside her, sexual desire mixed with uncertainty and fear, a powerful combination.

Their host took a large bunch of keys from a hook on the wall, unlocked one of the doors and pushed it open, indicating to the girls that they should enter. Janet walked in first, Lisa following, her eyes peering into the darkness. The Ambassador joined them, closing the door with a thud before switching on a light.

Lisa gasped at the sight that met her eyes. The room resembled a medieval torture chamber, filled with all manner of wooden benches, shackles and strange instruments. Heavy chains were hanging from the walls, their purpose unclear. She looked anxiously at Janet, but her friend seemed untroubled by the scene, an expression of sheer lust and excitement playing across her face.

The Ambassador walked to the centre of the room, holding out his arms with pride. 'Welcome to my special playroom, ladies,' he said, smiling broadly. 'We will have much pleasure, I think.'

Janet stood by a large, rack-like bench, her fingers stroking one of four manacles attached to the sides by thick chains. Lisa trembled, remembering the force with which the young maid had laid into her lover, wondering if she was to undergo similar experiences. At the same time though, she felt the arousal increasing in her sex, her lust for the unknown coming to the fore.

The door opened, the sudden noise making her jump with shock. The massive form of the male servant entered, his head stooped slightly against the low ceiling. He was still fully naked, the thick phallus she had seen plunge into the maid just a few moments previously now hanging limp, but nevertheless still fearsomely large between his heavily-muscled thighs. He stood by the door with his arms folded, as though awaiting instructions.

The Ambassador threw off his robe, revealing his extremely hairy, rotund nakedness, his small cock firmly erect against his fat belly. 'Come, ladies, be naked with me,' he cried, licking his lips in anticipation of joys to come.

Janet removed her dress quickly and stood naked but for her high-heeled shoes, her hands on her hips, her legs slightly apart. Lisa followed suit, leaving on her stockings, suspender belt and the thick, silver chain around her waist; the latter touch seeming to her to match the circumstances and environment.

The Ambassador walked over to them and firstly caressed Janet's breasts. His jutting penis pointed directly at her hairy sex, while his thumbs teased her nipples to erection. She breathed heavily, shivering with excitement as one of his hands moved onto her back, down to her pert bottom, then round to the front, pressing his palm over her pussy.

'So wet, so ready,' he said, through clenched teeth, his eyes blazing with lust. 'Go, amuse yourself with my man-servant, I will take your friend first.'

Lisa watched with not a little envy as Janet smiled and went to join the huge, black stud, seeing her clutch his rising stalk with both hands, kissing and licking his massive, sweating chest. The Ambassador came over to her and took hold of the chain that hung by her side, pulling her to him. She trembled as the fingertips of his other hand fluttered over her breasts, then gasped as both hands cupped them, lifting them high.

'Lick your nipples,' he commanded, 'lick them hard.'

Lisa pushed her head slightly forward and stuck out her tongue, the tip easily touching her nipple, which became immediately erect in response. She repeated the exercise with her other breast, until both nipples jutted upwards, each over an inch long and very hard. The Ambassador let her huge breasts fall gently back and clutched her waist, staring appreciatively at her heaving bosom.

'You have the biggest tits I have ever seen on such a slim girl,' he said without taking his eyes from her thrusting mounds. 'They are superb!'

Using the chain around her waist again, he turned her round so that her back was to him. 'And such a perfect arse!' he said, his hands now rubbing her soft buttocks. 'Truly, an arse like this was made to be fucked!'

He knelt behind her and pressed his face against her bottom, his tongue lapping greedily between the cheeks. She opened her legs and bent forward a little, enjoying the sensation, allowing him to taste the saltiness of her anus, feeling the tip of his tongue prodding at her tight hole.

Suddenly he stood up, wiping the saliva from his chin. 'Enough!' he cried, 'I must have this girl!' He took hold of the chain and dragged her over to a large 'X' frame, fastening first her wrists and then her ankles to the heavy, metal manacles, so that her back was to him. He stood back for a moment, admiring his captive, then she felt him run his hands delicately over her shoulders, down her back and again onto her bottom, the fingers kneading her soft flesh.

She pushed her buttocks out as far as her restraints would allow, desperate to take him inside her. She felt him probe with his podgy fingers into the wetness of her pussy, drawing her juices onto her anus, lubricating the tiny sphincter; preparing her.

She felt one of his fingers snake inside her bottom, the feeling almost making her come with its suddenness. Then it was withdrawn, to be replaced with the thicker intrusion of his cock which, although small, still filled her tight hole adequately.

She sighed with pleasure as he began to pump in and out of her, the constraints of the shackles increasing her enjoyment, the knowledge that he could do to her whatever he pleased driving her mad with lust. She'd become used to taking the dominant role; this feeling of total vulnerability and submission was wonderfully erotic.

She heard Janet cry out and turned her head, just in time to see her friend accommodate the man-servant's huge, black stalk inside her pussy as she squatted over his reclining body. The sight must have attracted the Ambassador also, for he pulled himself away from Lisa's body and almost leapt towards the rutting couple, and quickly rammed his hard little prick straight into Janet's backside, making her squeal with shock and pleasure.

Lisa watched as her friend was double-fucked, frustrated at her inability to move, to join in. The Ambassador's fat thighs humped furiously against Janet's bum, eventually knocking her from the huge stalk that was impaling her pussy. The servant pulled himself from under her body, leaving his master to hammer away to his heart's content and walked towards Lisa, his manhood jutting proudly in front of him, causing her to gulp with terrified anticipation.

She prayed that he would not take her in the way preferred by his master. She knew there was no way she could painlessly accommodate such a monster anally. It was to her relief, therefore, that she felt him fingering her sex, opening the wet lips for his invasion. She braced herself as she felt the thick end of his knob touch her tender lips and his steel-hard shaft begin to slide inside her.

She was amazed at the ease with which he entered her, his hairy crotch touching against her bottom almost immediately. He pumped into her with long, slow strokes – the urgency taken from him by the session with Janet – filling her, stretching her in every way. She felt every nerve-ending; every sensation in her body was centred on his perfect tool, his steady shafting exciting her with its insistent demands.

He seemed to sense her need, the pace of his thrusting

increasing, his hard thighs bashing against her lovely bottom as he plunged into her greedy honeypot. Lisa felt the sensations tearing at her sex, and the waves of pleasure shooting down her legs to the tips of her toes as she struggled against the tightness of the manacles; so eager was she to wrap her arms and legs around her lover, to take him inside her body as deeply as possible.

The final surge nearly caused her to shout out involuntarily, as the orgasm ripped through her with a ferocity even these days she rarely experienced. The servant pumped heavily into her, the speed incredible, thrusting his gigantic stalk in and out like the piston of a well-lubricated engine. With a roar he pulled out of her, and she felt the spray of his come soaking her back and bottom. She began to cry with the sheer exhilaration of the moment, her ravaged pussy aching but sated.

After a few minutes, Lisa was released from her shackles, and fell to the stone floor, still weak from the screwing she'd just undergone. The Ambassador was lying on the bench; Janet was busily fastening his wrists to the iron restraints, his small tool glistening and erect. The man-servant joined her, fastening his master's ankles, then stood over him, seemingly glaring at the reclining figure, holding his still large, black penis in his hand.

Suddenly, he began to pee, the urine spraying all over the Ambassador's face and body. The flow seemed to go on for ages, the girls watching in astonishment as the chained man's cock grew even harder, his pleasure apparent.

Janet took the hint and climbed onto the bench, squatting over his face. With some effort the pee began to trickle from her, then gushed in a torrent, the effusion soaking her victim.

The man-servant finished, and motioned to Lisa to take his place. Following Janet's example she squatted over him, this time aiming to soak his genitals. She strained hard, and with some difficulty began to piss on him, just as Janet finished drenching his face. She felt a sort of perverse pleasure, an unusual sensation of power as she peed, happy that she had discovered another sexual practice to add to her repertoire.

Suddenly, with a mighty cry the Ambassador came, straining and struggling against his shackles, his seed pumping high into the air, soaking her. She had never seen or imagined such a copious amount of sperm from one ejaculation, his orgasm continuing for easily a full minute. Lisa watched as he pulled harder at the chains, his teeth gritted as he enjoyed his strange release; the sight of this powerful man in complete subjugation was oddly arousing.

Eventually, the Ambassador was finished. He lay exhausted as the girls unfastened the manacles, then meekly rose and followed them as they walked out of the room to return upstairs. The servant remained, already starting to clean up the remnants of their mutual pleasure.

Back in the large drawing-room they found Frank curled up on the floor with the little maid, obviously recovering from a long bout of sex. He looked meaningfully at the girls, saying nothing. They knew what they had to do.

Gently, they sat the exhausted Ambassador down on the settee, and sat themselves either side of him, stroking his head and kissing his fat face gently. Lisa could feel the powers building up within her, knowing she was transferring a hypnotic command of capitulation to the unsuspecting man. His eyes became heavy and he drifted off into a deep sleep.

Frank got up from the floor and motioned for the girls to leave. The maid lay asleep, unlikely to wake before the morning, so he could question the Ambassador as much as he wished.

Lisa and Janet left the room, to be met by the manservant in the hall, who was clearly aware of what was going on. He handed them their clothes and coats and led them to a sumptuous bathroom, where they showered and dressed in silence.

The girls took their coats and left the Embassy, happy

with the memory of some good sex, but both feeling a little uneasy. The limousine waited, ready to take them home.

Chapter Eight

The sleek limousine drew steadily into the London traffic, which was still surprisingly heavy despite the late hour. Janet sat back in the plush seat, enjoying the coolness of the leather against her virtually naked back, her coat draped over her lap. She gazed absently out of the window, musing about the events of the evening and her earlier conversation with Lisa.

Her friend was right, of course. What they and the rest of the Lust Angels were doing was wrong. They were being used by Frank, and through him the old man; used for purposes she knew to be illegal, and possibly dangerous. There was certainly more to it than she had supposed in the past; she had a sense of foreboding, a premonition of evil to come that she couldn't put out of her mind.

She looked across at Lisa, who was staring glumly at the floor of the car, obviously thinking similar thoughts. She'd kept her coat on, concealing the gorgeous body that Janet had grown to love.

'Did you enjoy yourself tonight?' she said, trying to sound cheerful.

'It was different,' said Lisa, moodily. 'That Ambassador is a dirty sod, isn't he?'

'You can say that again; I've a feeling that we only scratched the surface with him.'

Lisa smiled, looking back at the floor. Janet moved over to her, putting her arm around her shoulders, kissing her lovingly on the cheek.

181

'It'll be all right, Lisa,' she said, sympathetically, 'I'm sure we're not doing any harm.'

'Are you?' Lisa's question was delivered with obvious doubt.

Janet shrugged. 'No, not really, but what can we do? I like looking like this, and I know you do.'

'What scares me is that I could return to how I used to look, but still have the same sex-drive, condemned to satisfying myself with cucumbers and candles for the rest of my life.'

Janet kissed her on the cheek again. 'No matter what happens,' she said, gently, 'I'll still screw with you.' Even as she made this promise, she wondered if she meant it. Was she in love with Lisa, or just her perfect body and gorgeous face? In truth she had to admit to herself that it was the latter, but decided wisely to keep her thoughts to herself.

The two girls kissed passionately on the lips, Janet's hand snaking inside Lisa's coat, finding the warmth of her huge, bare breasts. 'You haven't half got a lovely pair of tits, Lisa,' she said.

'I know, and I want to keep them.'

They laughed and cuddled some more, enjoying the warmth of friendship. Janet unbuttoned Lisa's coat and began to suckle on one of her long nipples, her hand trailing smoothly between the beautiful blonde's legs, up over her stocking-tops to the familiar wetness of her hairless sex. Lisa responded by opening her legs wide, pushing her hips forward to admit Janet's probing fingers to her sex.

'God, doesn't it ever stop?' sighed Lisa. Janet sat up and looked happily at her friend, loving the way her eyes sparkled with lust as her thumb excited her clitoris.

'Do you want it to?'

'No, never! I want to fuck and be fucked every day for the rest of my life!'

Janet smiled in mock resignation. 'Well,' she said, 'it looks like that's the curse we've brought down upon ourselves, so we might as well lie back and enjoy it!'

Lisa said nothing, lying back on the soft, leather seat,

resting one leg on the rear window-ledge, the other against the back of the driver's seat. Janet realised her need and dived her face down to nuzzle at her wet pussy, her tongue fluttering over the puffy sex-lips, drinking the delicately perfumed juices and savouring the sweet taste of lust. She wanted Lisa to take her in the same way, but knew from her own experience that her young lover was still going through the particularly highly-sexed stage of metamorphosis and that her need was greater.

She concentrated her licking to the large, hard bud of her clitoris that poked angrily through the wet folds of her outer lips, as long and thick as the tip of her little finger.

Lisa started to buck her hips up and down, mewing like a contented cat. Suddenly she gave a shout, and grabbed tightly at her friend's head, ramming it hard against her pussy as she orgasmed. Janet continued to suckle and lick at her inflamed bud until the excruciating tenderness forced Lisa to push her head away.

They lay still for a moment, Janet licking lovingly at the smooth thighs wrapped weakly now around her neck. She was desperate for sex herself now, but Lisa would probably want to rest, to recover. Perhaps when they got to her flat, she would invite her friend in and they would spend the rest of the night in bed, making love.

She sat up slowly, wiping the wetness from her chin and mouth, and peered through the car window into the darkness. They were still in the city, but not on a road she knew. It was when the vehicle stopped at a traffic-light and she noticed a road-sign that she realised they were headed in totally the wrong direction.

'Driver,' she called out in alarm, 'you're going the wrong way. This isn't the road to Brighton!' She beat her fist against the glass partition that separated them from the front of the car, but the chauffeur ignored her. 'Driver,' she said with more anger than panic, 'can't you hear me?'

Lisa sat up. 'What's the matter?' she said.

'It's this stupid bastard. I can't make him hear. He must be deaf! We're heading in the wrong direction.' She hit the panel again and this time the driver turned his head slightly, revealing a sinister grin.

'He's not the driver who brought us here!' said Lisa, in alarm. 'What's happening?'

Janet tried the door, not surprised when she found it locked, with no way of unlocking it from inside. The car was moving swiftly now, through unlit streets where the houses, once grand and imposing, now showed the signs of years of neglect; many of them boarded up for demolition. Occasionally there was a break in the gloomy terraces where buildings had been reduced to rubble, and small fires illuminated sad, huddled figures of tramps and other flotsam and jetsam of society grouping together for comfort.

Despite the girls' oaths and threats the driver ignored them, heading for a mystery destination, just once glancing back at them and grinning with ugly malevolence.

Lisa sat back on the seat, wrapping her coat protectively around her body. 'Are we being kidnapped?' she said, her eyes showing her terror.

'Looks that way,' said Janet, trying to remain calm. She couldn't imagine why anyone should want to kidnap them; what would be gained? Was it something to do with the Ambassador, perhaps? Maybe Frank had been caught trying to interrogate him and he had implicated them as accessories to his crime. Thoughts raced through her head, alibis and excuses, as the car sped on its journey.

It was a good half hour before the car finally slowed down to drive through an even shabbier industrial area; the darkened, decaying buildings a testament to the latest economic recession; the once thriving factories now shelter to rats and vagrants. Janet and Lisa had resigned themselves to their fate and were sitting quietly, huddled on the back seat, staring anxiously into the gloom outside.

The vehicle inched through the narrow gateway to one of the factories, stopping in a small, scruffy yard. The driver switched off the purring engine and got out, walking behind them to close and bar the gates. Janet tried the door again; it was still locked.

The driver returned, still grinning evilly and opened the door from outside. At first the girls sat still, then reluctantly climbed out of the relative safety of the car, the coolness of the night making them shiver. The driver led the way to a small, steel door, opened it and gestured brusquely for them to enter.

Inside, the building was just as gloomy as its exterior. The smell of damp decay seemed to envelop them along with the darkness. They stood still, trembling.

The driver pushed them both forward, and Janet stumbled over some rubbish on the floor, heading deeper into the gloom. They rounded a corner and saw an almost welcoming shaft of light shining from beneath another door, to which they were roughly propelled. The man knocked heavily on the wood and waited.

After a moment, the sound of a metal bolt being withdrawn from its clasp was heard and the door swung open. The light streamed from within, so bright that Janet had to shield her eyes for a second, until she was able to focus on the room ahead of them.

In stark contrast to the rest of the building, the room was well furnished and carpeted, like a typical suburban lounge. The occupants of the room were anything but suburban, however. Including the driver, there were six men standing before them: large and nasty-looking characters, with a surfeit of muscle-power but probably little in the way of brains shared between them. They stood in a line, their arms folded, their expressions uniformly menacing.

'Who are you? Why have you brought us here?' Janet was amazed at her courage in speaking. Lisa said nothing.

'We have brought you to meet someone,' said one of the group, a huge man with a grotesquely massive head.

'Who?' demanded Janet, angrily. She'd decided that whatever was going to happen to them was unavoidable and she wasn't simply going to give in meekly.

185

'Mistress Druscilla wishes to see you. You have made her very angry.'

'I don't know what you mean! I've never even heard of her!'

'You have now!' The voice was strong and sharply female. The girls swung round, to see the owner of the voice standing at the back of the room, her massive frame silhouetted against the even brighter light emanating from the doorway through which she had entered.

'Are you Druscilla?' said Lisa, her voice trembling.

'*Mistress* Druscilla!' said the woman, walking towards them. Janet gulped as she came fully into view. She was well over six foot tall, very broad shouldered, and big in every way. She had dark, almost Latin looks; her cold eyes contrasting in steel blue, piercing with a glaring stare. Her black hair was cropped short and her face bore not a trace of make-up but, despite her fierce expression, she appeared strangely beautiful, in a powerful way. Janet remembered her occasional sessions in bed with Sonia; how the big African had dominated her when she'd fucked her with her huge dildo and how she'd enjoyed the feeling of total submission. She wondered if this was the fate that awaited them here.

The big woman walked over to Lisa and unbuttoned her coat, pushing it from her small shoulders, allowing it to fall to the floor in a crumpled heap. There were sounds and comments of appreciation from the men, but Mistress Druscilla just stared at the luscious young body revealed to her, naked but for the tiny, split-crotch PVC shorts and black stockings. Janet couldn't help but notice the contrast between the two women; Lisa, softly feminine and vulnerable, oozing sexuality with a kind of enigmatic innocence and their captor, butch and fearsome, dressed in a heavy, pin-striped suit that hid any curves and any other allusions to her femininity.

Mistress Druscilla ran the tip of her forefinger down between Lisa's breasts, over her stomach and lower abdomen, stopping to probe firmly in her tight sex, stirring and prodding at the dampening hole.

186

'You and your friends are costing me a lot of money,' she said, through gritted teeth, 'and you're going to have to be punished.'

'What have we done?' said Janet. Their captor walked over and stood in front of her, the look of evil lust obvious on her face. She reached out and, with one harsh movement ripped Janet's dress from her body, her eyes leering wildly as they feasted on the sight of her flawless, naked body.

'What have you done? What have you done?' Mistress Druscilla's voice was raised to fever pitch. 'I have over fifty girls working the hotels and streets of London and you are taking my best clients away.'

'But I don't understand; we're not whores,' Janet protested, wincing as the big woman gripped her sex hard, the fingernails digging into her tender flesh.

'No, indeed you're not . . . that's the problem! You and the rest of the so-called "Lust Angels" give the clients what they want, and much more, yet you do it for free. No wonder I'm losing custom. Now you must stop!'

'But you don't understand,' sobbed Lisa, 'we can't stop.'.

'Oh, but you will,' sneered Mistress Druscilla, grasping Lisa between the legs in the same way that she still held Janet, 'because, by the time we've finished with you, you'll never want to see a cock again, let alone do any fucking.'

She pushed the two girls back, the force causing them to stumble to the floor. The big woman stood erect with her hands on her hips, her legs planted firmly apart, a look of sheer contempt on her face. 'Tie them to the chairs!' she barked, turning and marching out of the room.

Her henchmen crept forward like so many lizards, eager to get their hands on the two young lovelies that were completely at their mercy. Hurriedly, they bent Lisa and Janet over the backs of the heavy armchairs, their faces pressed against the seats, their bottoms thrusting in the air. Janet felt her ankles being roughly tied to the castors at the back of the chair, her legs splayed apart, whilst she watched Lisa being stripped and bound in the same way. More rope was used to secure her wrists to the front castors, making any movement impossible. The two chairs were then pushed together, so that their faces were inches apart.

Lisa's face was flushed, her eyes shining with terror and lust. Janet felt the same way; full of fear of the unknown but with an agonizing need for sex. She knew they were both quite ready to take anything that Mistress Druscilla chose to offer.

One of the men stood behind Lisa, fondling her backside. 'This one's got a gorgeous arse,' he said, cruelly, 'I can't wait to get stuck up it.'

'Leave her! You'll get your chance.' It was Mistress Druscilla, returned to take control once again. The girls looked up at her as she stood before them, and gasped. She was now clad fully in black leather; a heavily-studded basque supporting her mountainous breasts, an extra chain corset around her waist drawn in tightly, emphasising the size of her bust and her large, naked bottom and hips, her legs covered by high-heeled thigh-length boots. From her extremely hairy crotch jutted a long, thick and very realistic dildo in shiny black plastic, similar in size to the one favoured by Sonia; in her hand she held what looked like a table-tennis bat, its surface covered in chamois leather.

She grinned evilly at her two victims, rubbing the dildo suggestively with her free hand. 'What do you think of this, then?' she sneered.

The girls said nothing, pretending terror. Janet was very aware that, like her, Lisa would be relishing the idea of being impaled by such an impressive instrument. Nevertheless, she also realised that their captor would be furious if she discovered that rather than instilling fear she was causing them to feel nothing but lust.

'First I will thrash you both, to get your little bottoms hot and raw. The leather on this bat will ensure that your skin stings terribly, but your pretty arses won't be marked; isn't that considerate of me? Now, who's first?'

'Oh, please don't spank us or fuck us with that great big

thing,' said Lisa, desperately trying to conceal her delight, 'we'll do anything you say.'

Mistress Druscilla walked behind Lisa, grinning. 'So, the little blonde has volunteered!'

'No, no!' cried Lisa, in mock terror.

Thwack! The bat came down fiercely on her plump bottom, making her squeal. 'Jesus Christ, oh God!' she shouted, staring into Janet's eyes. From where she was standing, their tormentor couldn't see the look of abject pleasure on Lisa's face. Janet meanwhile maintained a look of anticipatory fear.

Thwack, thwack, thwack! With each stroke Lisa shuddered, crying out loudly. Janet felt the creaminess between her own legs as she waited impatiently for her turn, a trickle of sex-juice running down the inside of her thigh.

'This one's so scared she's pissed herself!' shouted one of the men, gleefully, noticing Janet's emission. His Mistress ignored him, continuing to use all her strength to slap away with the leather-covered bat at the young blonde's beautiful and now bright red bottom.

Lisa stared directly into Janet's eyes, looking for all the world like she was high on drugs. 'I'm going to come!' she hissed, so that only her friend could hear. One more whack and she went over, crying out with her orgasm, making her screams sound as though from pain rather than erotic pleasure.

'That one really got to you, didn't it?' said Mistress Druscilla, whacking her twice more before walking away to stand behind Janet.

'Yes, Mistress,' said Lisa, trying to get her breath, 'it hurt tremendously.'

'Good! And now for your young friend!'

Janet braced herself to receive the first stroke, smiling at her friend who was sobbing in post-orgasmic ecstasy. After what seemed like an agonisingly long time it came, thwack! on her small, pert bottom, sending stinging shards of pleasurable pain throughout her lower body. 'Ow! Oh, God, that hurts!' she cried, knowing her protestation would cause Mistress Druscilla to hit her even harder. Sure enough, the blows rained down furiously, tears filling her eyes as she cried from the sheer bliss of the assault.

Just as she felt her orgasm was about to explode the spanking stopped. 'No, please, no more!' she shouted, knowing their cruel tormentor would ignore her pleas, desperate to come whilst being thrashed.

'No more, eh?' said the Mistress, raising the paddle once again. 'Well, perhaps just another six.' The bat came down again on Janet's sore bottom, the sound like the crack of a whip as it sent tremors of lust through her tortured flesh, her inner thighs wet from her lust. Three more strokes and she came, screaming with the sheer frenzy of the orgasm tearing through her, her backside humping uncontrollably as she rubbed her pussy against the hard back of the chair.

'I don't believe it!' said Mistress Druscilla, angrily. 'The bitch has actually come! Right you cow, let's see you deal with this!' The bat was thrown to one side and Janet felt the pressure of the big dildo being pushed against her well lubricated sex. Even if she wanted to, she wouldn't have been able to stop its intrusion into her body, her need for a good, hard fucking now paramount.

There was no gentleness, no care as Mistress Druscilla rammed into her; the full length of the plastic monster sliding fully inside Janet's aching sheath. The thrusting forced the chairs together, the girls' arms trapped between them, their faces touching. Lisa kissed her friend on the mouth.

'What's it like?' she breathed.

'Fucking wonderful!' whispered Janet, trying not to respond too pleasurably to the incessant thrusting. Mistress Druscilla seemed to sense that she was giving pleasure rather than pain, however and pulled angrily from Janet's greedy little pussy, walking quickly round the chairs to stand behind Lisa.

'It's going up me, it's going up me!' breathed Lisa, quietly to her friend, 'Christ, it's fucking lovely! I don't half need this!' Then, louder she shouted out for the benefit of the Mistress. 'Oh, please, Mistress Druscilla, it is too big, too thick. It hurts so! Please do not fuck my little cunt so hard!'

Needless to say, her protests caused much delight to the big woman, who hammered the huge dildo harder and harder into the gorgeous blonde's defenceless body. 'Is that gentle enough for you, bitch?' shouted the evil lesbian, pumping the full length in and out of her supposed victim, slapping her sore buttocks hard at the same time with her large hands.

'No, Mistress, please. It is so huge! You are splitting me in two!' She smiled blissfully at Janet, her expression giving a lie to her words. The apparent rape went on for ages, Lisa coming three times, each orgasm causing her to cry out as though in pain, begging her tormentor to stop, knowing that wouldn't happen as long as she continued to plead for mercy.

The fourth orgasm was too much, though. She squealed with the pleasure and exhilaration of it, crying out with unsubmissive joy, 'Oh, yes, fuck me, fuck me, more!'

Mistress Druscilla stopped dead, and pulled the soaked dildo from its ravaged sheath. 'I don't believe these two!' She unfastened the dildo from her crotch and threw it angrily to the floor. 'They're all yours, boys,' she shouted, as she stormed from the room, 'do what you like!'

As soon as she'd gone, the girls were pulled roughly apart, still tied to the chairs. One of the men had his erection out and rammed inside Lisa in a matter of seconds, his hips pumping ferociously, whilst Janet felt the warm wetness of a tongue lapping around her aching pussy. Another of the body-guards presented a thick, quickly hardening prick to her face, which she happily took into her greedy mouth, enjoying the stale, manly taste, whilst whoever was behind her started to push a not inconsiderable length inside her willing body.

Her expert use of her lips and tongue brought the man in front of her off very quickly, his sperm gushing to the back of her throat as she swallowed, her nose pressed against the sharpness of his zip-fly. When he pulled away, she saw that Lisa had now had her hands freed, and was sucking one man whilst rubbing the stiff erections of two more, her gaping pussy waiting for attention.

The sight proved too much for the guy who was humping Janet, who withdrew nonchalantly from the warmth of her vulnerable body and walked over to her friend, ramming his stalk hard into her, causing her to cry out and almost lose the cock from her mouth.

The other two men now pleasured themselves at each end of Janet's lovely body, the one whose come she had swallowed now happily erect again, pumping into her from behind.

After a while, the girls were released from their bonds and the six men stripped naked, and the orgy began in earnest. The girls used every trick they had learned in their short, but busy sexual lives to give pleasure to the men and, in consequence, joy to themselves. Lisa quickly adopted her now favourite position, with two men pumping into her pussy at the same time; one in her mouth and one more in each of her hands. Janet meanwhile sat happily on the remaining man's lap, his cock firmly up her bum.

Later, Janet decided to go one better than Lisa. She straddled the reclining form of one of the men, allowing his stalk to slide into her wet sex-lips, another man taking his place deep inside her bottom. The two men with the longest tools knelt in front of her, the tips of their erections touching. She opened her mouth wide and took both thick knobs inside her lips, whilst reaching out and grasping the two remaining shafts with her hands.

Lisa sat watching as the six men received the attention of her lovely friend. Clearly, it was Mistress Druscilla's intention that the session with these six bruisers, so closely following her own attack on the girls with her monstrous dildo, would finish them for good, putting them off sex for life. However, she had reckoned without the power of the old man's magic and the girls' remarkable staying-power.

Only when all the men were exhausted did the screwing stop. Mistress Druscilla returned some time later to find the girls happily lying amidst all this naked male flesh and was furious.

'Take them into the storeroom and chain them up,' she barked, 'I'll think of what to do with them later.'

The girls were hustled out of the room and down a long corridor to the rear of the building. A heavy door was unlocked and they were pushed into a remarkably warm room where the door was clanged shut behind them.

Janet found a light-switch and flicked it on. The heat was being generated by an old furnace at the far end of the room, a welcome warmth in view of their nudity. Lisa was made to kneel on the stone floor and started to sob.

Janet lifted her friend's tearful face and kissed her. 'Don't worry, we've had a nice time so far. All we've got to do is work out how to get out of here.' She began to collect her thoughts. The door was metal, far too heavy to break down and there were no windows. The situation looked hopeless.

The door burst open. Three strangers, clad in scruffy jeans and T-shirts walked in, carrying heavy, unlabelled boxes. They ignored the two beautiful, naked nymphets, and carried on with their labours as though alone, stacking the cases on top of each other in a corner of the room. This done, two of the men left, whilst the third approached the shivering girls. He was a large, menacing-looking character with thick stubble and a leering, almost insane grin on his face.

'Well, look at this,' he said, raising Lisa's tearful face with his stubby fingers, 'a couple of horny little tarts, if ever I saw any.'

'Leave her alone, you bastard!' Janet marvelled at her bravado, but she couldn't bear to see her friend upset in this way. The man moved away from Lisa and stood in front of her, his face inches away from hers. His grinning expression reminded her of one of the baddies in a cheap, Italian Western, and his breath was foul.

'And what will you do if I don't?' he said, nastily, running his filthy hand over her firm breasts, causing her to shudder with distaste. He misinterpreted her shiver as one of lust. 'Like that, do you?' His podgy hand trailed down between her legs, finding her still wet from the earlier session with the six body-guards. 'God, you're soaked! You're really ready for it, aren't you?'

With all the contempt she held within her trembling body, Janet summoned up the courage and spat in his face, her phlegm hitting his eye and running down one cheek. He reached back his hand ready to hit her.

'Leave those women alone!' It was Mistress Druscilla barking out the order, walking into the room with another of her henchmen. She threw some lengths of rope over to the grinning ape and instructed him to bind the girls' wrists together. That done, they were secured to some metal shelving, their arms high above their heads, their feet just touching the ground.

By the time both girls were tied to the shelving, Janet's terror had turned to hatred, determined to get her own back on these evil men. She watched as they secured Lisa's ankles to the shelves and tried to kick out as they did the same to her, causing the two men to hold her roughly until the bonds were tied.

Mistress Druscilla handed the key to the storeroom to the man she had entered with. 'Guard them until I return in the morning. I'll decide what to do then.' She and the laughing boy then left, the door slamming coldly behind them.

Janet watched as their jailer locked the door. Ordinarily, and under very different circumstances, she could have gone for him in a big way. He was tall, with dark, almost black hair like her own, a heavily tanned complexion with traces of stubble on his firm jaw-line. His shoulders were broad, his hips narrow, his superb body emphasised by the tight jeans and small singlet he wore.

He walked over to the two girls, looking appreciatively at the naked, female bodies standing side by side before him. Their arms were tied above them, their legs secured slightly apart, and the flesh of their pussies was clearly

194

visible to his eager gaze. He licked his lips and put his hand out to touch Lisa's cheek, then ran it slowly down onto her breast, working a finger round and round the nipple, watching it grow in response. Janet almost felt jealous, envious that he had touched her friend first, rather than caressing her own, lovely body; she felt unable to suppress the feelings of lust that were building up inside her.

This strange combination of emotions; hate, terror and lust was tearing at Janet, confusing her. She looked at Lisa's face; it remained impassive. The man was fondling both breasts now, tweaking the long, hard nipples between his fingers and thumbs, his face displaying a lust equal to her own.

He moved over to Janet and stroked her firm, apple-sized tits, her nipples already fully erect, then ran his hand slowly down over her flat stomach to her hairy pussy, his middle finger worming its way between the wet lips of her slit. She gasped more from sexual excitement than fear, although the trembling of her body could be interpreted either way.

'Jesus, you're dying for it!' he said. Janet said nothing, staring nervously into his eyes. 'I think I'm gonna fuck you, little girl!'

'No!' said Lisa. 'Leave her alone!'

'It's all right, Lisa, it's all right!' Janet looked at her friend, praying that her eyes gave away her meaning.

'Yes, Lisa,' said the man, 'it's all right, she wants fucking, and she's gonna get it, just like you will in a minute!'

Janet hated this man for the way he was acting, but she couldn't help feeling that he was putting it on, that it was all macho bravado. Nobody this gorgeous could be all bad, she mused. His fingers were still caressing her between her legs, not roughly but tenderly, like a new lover. She pushed her hips forward on his hand, taking all his fingers inside her, the wetness of her sheath enveloping them. She started to moan as his hand slid in and out of her, the thumb expertly flicking against her hardening clit. She licked her lips and rolled her head from side to side, arching her back

195

to try and make him push more and more between the puffy, very aroused labia, every conscious thought now between her legs. She pulled on the ropes that tightly bound her limbs to the shelving, the constriction heightening her feelings of vulnerability, and making her feel incredibly randy.

'D'you know,' he said, excitedly, 'I can do *anything* I want to you both!'

'Of course you can, darling,' said Janet, 'and we can't resist.'

She noticed Lisa watching her face and smiled to reassure her. Her friend smiled back, licking her lips. It was clear that she too was turned on by the situation. There was to be no rape here; although naked, bound and secured, *they* were dictating the rules; if anybody was going to be taken advantage of it was this poor sap pawing away at Janet's sex. They would fuck him senseless.

'What's your name?' asked Janet, as the man kissed and licked at her breasts, his fingers still caressing the puffy lips of her sex.

'Con,' he said, then suddenly looking concerned, 'I don't suppose I should have told you that!'

'Never mind, Con. Why don't you fuck me, like you promised?'

'No,' he said. 'Not yet. I can do what I want, when I want. And what I want to do is lick you both.'

'Yes, Con,' said Janet, 'whatever you say.' She was enjoying playing this game and she certainly fancied a good tonguing. Con knelt in front of her, parting her soaked sex-lips with his thumbs and pressing his mouth against them, gave a gentle, loving kiss. His tongue darted forward, plunging inside her, then withdrew sensuously to lick around the entrance to her vagina, drawing her labia between his suckling lips. Janet shook as he expertly drew her sex in and out of his mouth, his tongue constantly busy. She looked across again at Lisa, mouthing the word, 'Wow!'

He moved his attention to Lisa, licking greedily at her

shaven quim, the tip of his tongue flicking like a butterfly's wings covering her clearly visible clitoris. Janet watched with lust and envy as his head moved up and down, his rough tongue rasping against Lisa's sex, her friend mewing like a kitten from the pleasure she was receiving.

Con stood and walked back to Janet. '*Now* I'll fuck you.'

'Save plenty for me,' said Lisa, before turning to Janet and quietly whispering, 'remember Simon?'

Janet nodded. Lisa had obviously realised what was in her mind. Apart from fulfilling her immediate sexual needs, Con was going to be the way out of this mess. All they had to do was get the key . . .

Con unzipped his tight jeans and pulled out his already stiff erection. He bent his knees and aimed his thick shaft at Janet's waiting pussy, holding onto the shelving with his free hand. She felt the thickness of his bulbous end part her wet labia-lips, and groaned as he slid his length into her. He held still for a moment, their pubic hair meshed together, his hardness already throbbing deep within her loins. Then he began to pump slowly in and out, the roughness of his denim jeans rubbing against her tender flesh with each forward thrust.

Still holding the shelves with one hand, he gripped her pert, firm buttocks with the other, levering himself in and out of her, screwing her steadily. She pulled on the ropes that held her ankles. She wanted to wrap her legs around his heaving body, to dig her heels into his back, to let him know he was hitting the spot. Her orgasm was coming quickly, too quickly. She thrust her hips out to meet his movements, their pubic bones crashing together rhythmically, his shaft delving deep into the innermost recesses of her young body. Because her limbs were tied so tightly, the only part of her body that could respond to his steady lovemaking was her pussy; its wetness and warmth were clear indications of her pleasure.

He slowed his movements to a stop, then eased his hardness from her and walked over to Lisa, who smiled and closed her eyes, ready and willing to be taken. Janet watched as the young man's length disappeared into the folds of her friend's sex-lips and thrilled at the erotic sight of the two groins thrusting against each other.

The humping was much wilder this time; he had no patience or style and was soon ready to loose his seed. The muscles of his backside were stiffening; Janet wanted to reach out and stroke them, lick them; but all she could do was watch. The shelving shook as Lisa and Con hammered against each other, sighing, moaning, groaning as they both approached their orgasms.

A small jar fell from above their heads and crashed on the stone floor, spilling its white, powdery contents. It could have been talc, it could have been heroin – it didn't matter. Con grabbed hold of one of Lisa's heaving breasts with one hand, the other slipping between Janet's legs, cupping the wetness of her sex. He cried out as he came, thrusting heavily into his lover's body, making her squeal as she joined him in the heavenly oblivion of sexual release. He squeezed Janet's pussy, two fingers snaking into the open lips, his eyes closed from the ecstasy of the moment.

Gradually, he released his hold on her and pulled away from Lisa. His manhood hanging limply, he sat back on a small chair and stared, with not a little pride, at his beautiful conquests.

Nothing was said for some time as he recovered from the bout. Janet glanced at her friend. There was a small trail of sperm oozing from her reddened slit, slithering down her inner thigh. Janet wanted to lick it from her lovely leg, to kiss her friend's recently ravaged sex and to have the same done to her. The cream moved onwards, the trail of glistening juice reaching Lisa's knee. She could see what Janet was watching and the two girls started giggling uncontrollably. Con stood up, apparently thinking they were laughing at him.

'What's going on?' he said, angrily.

'Oh, nothing,' said Lisa, 'look, we really enjoyed that,

but we could have so much more fun if we weren't tied up and it's such a long time until morning.'

'I don't know, I . . .'

'Oh, come on,' said Janet, 'you're a brilliant fuck. Anyway, where could we go, dressed like this?'

Con may have had a gorgeous body, but he certainly wasn't very bright; then again, maybe it was the fact that his brains were once again descending metaphorically to his balls that caused him to release the girls from their bonds. They rubbed the soreness of their wrists and ankles, the recent session having caused them to tug hard at the ropes, and found a couple of large, cardboard boxes to sit on.

Janet knew that they wouldn't be able to overpower Con. Although there were two of them, he was clearly strong and could easily hurt them. They were going to have to exhaust him.

She turned to Lisa and whispered, 'Operation Simon, then.' The two, naked beauties stood up and walked over to the seated figure and pulled him to his feet. Deftly, they removed his T-shirt and revealed his powerful, muscular chest. Lisa knelt on the cold floor and pulled off his scruffy shoes, taking the socks with them, as Lisa unfastened and removed his tight jeans.

His tool was once again standing erect and ready, his scrotum pulled tight under the thick stem. Lisa planted her mouth firmly over the end, working her magic on him, rubbing both her hands around his shaft. She bobbed her head backwards and forwards as she gobbled him, making his thighs thrust involuntarily towards her beautiful face.

Janet went behind him and licked between his slim buttocks, running her tongue steadily up and down the crack, pausing as the tip touched his raspberry-like sphinter, forcing it forward into the tight hole, taking her customary pleasure from the anal contact. She stroked his firm thighs, waist and back, tasting his fresh scent of sweat. The muscles of his bottom clenched in response to the mind-blowing sucking Lisa was administering.

Janet slid her tongue round his thighs to the front, sliding the tip over his thick, hard stem. Lisa meanwhile slid a hand under his heavy balls, allowing a finger to tickle his anus, wet from Janet's licking. Both girls gobbled and suckled at his erection, alternately sucking the end or nibbling at the shaft, hearing him groan with pleasure. Lisa used her pouted lips and fluttering tongue to their utmost, although both girls were experts with their mouths and they knew exactly how to give the utmost in oral pleasure.

He groaned again, his hips beginning to buck. Janet grabbed hold of his stem and rubbed him furiously, watching with pleasure as a stream of sperm shot across Lisa's face. The remaining spurts she took in her own mouth, swallowing the fluid quickly as it gushed to the back of her throat.

They let him recover for a moment, leaving him to sit on the relative warmth of some cardboard that had been strewn over the floor as a makeshift carpet. To Janet's delight she saw that, although he wasn't fully erect he hadn't lost all of his hardness; she knew they'd get it up again. After all, that was the plan.

After a few minutes, Janet lay on her back, holding her legs open in the air, clutching her feet with her hands. 'Come on, Con,' she said, 'you've got two randy girls to satisfy!'

Con sighed and crawled between her legs. He wasn't up to intercourse yet, so he lowered his face between her lovely legs and started to lick at the folds of flesh, nibbling sensuously at the hairy outer lips, then running his tongue lightly over her hot little bud, making her raise her little bum from the floor to meet his oral caresses.

Lisa saw her chance and moved behind him, pressing her mouth against his upturned bottom, her tongue licking and prodding at his tight hole. She reached around his thighs and caught hold of his shaft, feeling it hardening within her grasp. Con's tongue worked wonderfully against Janet's eager sex, causing her to wriggle her hips suggestively, her hands clutching his hair, pulling his face closer to her accommodating warmth.

He pulled his head away from Janet's almost vice-like grip and grabbed Lisa, pushing her onto her back and lying across her body. He buried his face in the sensuousness of her hairless crotch; his erection once again the target of the lovely blonde's expert mouth.

Janet heard the sounds which told her that her friend was, once again, experiencing the same wonderful licking that she'd just had. Con's thighs started to make pumping motions, his hardness thrusting in and out of Lisa's willing mouth. Janet went behind him, kissed Lisa lightly on the forehead, then ran her tongue over his balls, drawing them in and out of her wet mouth, her nose pressed firmly between his thrusting buttocks.

Lisa seemed to be coming again and again, her gasps of pleasure stifled by the thick erection in her mouth. Janet was desperate for sex now, frigging herself wildly as she suckled Con's testicles. With great effort, she and Lisa pushed him over onto his back so that her friend was now lying on top, grinding her hips against his face.

Lisa sat upright and Janet squatted over Con's firm erection, taking the full length at one go into her aching pussy. She immediately started to hump up and down, feeling the hardness thumping into her, easing the lust and frustration that had been building up inside her. She took hold of Lisa in her arms and they kissed lovingly, both girls satisfying their lust on this man who, as far as they were concerned, could have been anyone.

Con was totally gone, his body completely controlled by the demands of these insatiable teenagers. He couldn't come again, but nor could he lose his raging hard-on. The girls fucked and fucked him, orgasming almost in turn, kissing and caressing each other constantly.

They changed places, Lisa taking his proud length again inside her sweet honeypot. Janet squatting with her delicious bum covering his face. She held herself down on him, feeling his tongue snaking at her anus, almost forgetting their plan. Then she remembered and nodded to Lisa. The other girl leant back, without for an instant changing her rhthym, and retrieved the door-key from the pocket in their captor's cast-off jeans, handing it surreptitiously to Janet.

Janet stood up and Lisa immediately fell forward to kiss Con on the mouth, her hips bucking against his like a steam engine. So occupied, he didn't see Janet walk quietly over to the door, unlock it and silently pull it open.

She slipped out of the room, waiting with heart thumping for Lisa to follow. She heard her friend's voice telling Con to close his eyes and wait, as she had a lovely surprise for him. Suddenly they were both outside the door, slamming it shut and turning the key.

'I don't think it's just prostitution that Mistress Druscilla's into,' said Lisa, as they crept quickly along the dark corridor. 'Did you see all that stuff in there? Looked like drugs to me.'

'Me too. Come on, we've got to get away. These people may like fucking, but they won't mess about when they find we're gone.'

The girls managed to find their way back to the yard, finding to their relief that the gate had been left unlocked when Mistress Druscilla and her cronies had gone off on their nefarious business. Despite their nakedness, they scurried out into the dark street and straight into the headlights of a parked police-car.

The two officers got out of their vehicle and walked casually towards the naked beauties. 'Well, well,' said one, in his best police-college voice, 'what have we here?'

The girls jabbered excitedly, telling the policemen of their kidnap and their suspicions about drugs. They sat, gratefully in the back of the car, whilst one of the officers radioed in for support.

'Seems that there's a big fight outside a nightclub down the High Street,' said one of the policemen, getting out of the car and joining the girls on the back seat, slipping his arm around Lisa's naked shoulders, 'they won't be here for over an hour.' He cupped her breast with his large hand. 'Still, no hurry, eh?'

Janet grinned and clambered over the back of the front passenger seat to join his colleague. Lisa sighed and unzipped the policeman's trousers, reaching in and taking out his already stiff erection.

'Oh, well,' she said, 'here we go again.'

Chapter Nine

The message had been short and to the point, the instructions clear. It had been waiting for Lisa when she arrived home from London; a type-written note in a simple, brown envelope accompanied by a rail-ticket and some cash. The signature was Frank's, but the style of the letter was very curt, even for him.

She was to join the other Lust Angels on the overnight train to Inverness, to attend a special meeting with others like themselves, an event which was to be addressed by the old man himself. What it was to be about remained a mystery, the only clear fact being that it was vital that all should attend.

So it was that Lisa packed her case for the trip; a formal trouser-suit for the meeting and a rather erotic black-chiffon dress for the evening. She decided to travel in a pair of tight but comfortable jeans and a simple check shirt completed by white socks and trainers and, of course, no underwear.

Brighton station was packed with commuters when she got there and it took her some time to find the correct compartment. When she did she found all five of her colleagues waiting for her, all dressed in a similar, casual way, either in jeans or track-suits, talking excitedly and perhaps a little apprehensively of the prospect of meeting the evil old man again.

She listened with some concern to their chatter; the power and control he held over them seemed total, unassailable. Why then did she feel so nervous? Janet had shown that she was not happy with the things that they were sometimes asked to join in with, particularly after the recent session with the Ambassador, but even she seemed as excited as a schoolgirl today.

Lisa decided not to pursue the matter for the moment, but to wait until after the meeting with the old man before deciding what to do next. Frank had apparently gone on ahead, so the girls were left to fend for themselves on the journey. This presumably explained why they had each been given money. He certainly looked after his Angels, caring for them like a mother hen.

Although the train was busy, the first-class compartment they occupied had only enough seats for the six girls. They were therefore left in peace for the trip to London where they would change onto the Scotland sleeper.

They passed the time by exchanging stories of their recent sexual exploits, and Lisa found herself becoming more and more turned on as the miles sped by. Sonia told of how she had entered (and won) a 'Miss Wet T-Shirt' contest at a local club and how she had been so turned on that she had ripped off the soaking shirt and her even wetter knickers and fucked the compère there and then, on the stage in front of over a thousand people, to much applause.

This story prompted Rani, the demure, innocent-looking little Asian girl to tell of how she had been dragged, not unwillingly by the five members of a pop group into their dressing room after a concert, where she persuaded them to tie her to a bench. She was not only screwed by them all, but had satisfied the needs of two roadies and their manager as well, all in the space of about an hour.

Kate, the bubbly little blonde and Jan, the devastatingly gorgeous Chinese girl had, like Janet and Lisa, been doing most of their screwing as a team and had seemingly had more lovers than the rest of the group put together; their penchant for a multiplicity of sexual partners being much in demand. They also admitted to falling in love with each other, describing their sex together in the most lurid detail.

It soon became too much for Lisa, who felt she would explode if she didn't get some sort of sexual relief quickly. She excused herself and went out into the corridor, the cooler air helping to soothe her almost uncontrollable lust.

There were three other people in the corridor, all of them men. She looked at each of them in turn, weighing up her chances of getting them into the toilet with her, so she could bonk her way to London.

One man, a little over-weight and middle-aged, seemed to catch her glance. He folded up his newspaper and walked towards her, steadying himself against the swaying of the train with a handrail. Lisa stood with her back to the window, so that he had to squeeze against her mountainous breasts as he pushed past, her eyes staring straight into his, willing him to grab her between the legs.

Although it was clear from his flustered expression that he would dearly like to have done just that, he carried on down the corridor, heading for the toilet. He looked back at her and smiled, indicating to her albeit hopelessly that he would dearly love her to follow and disappeared behind the small, wooden door, the sign on the lock remaining set at 'Vacant'. She glanced at the other two men, but they seemed preoccupied with their newspapers, so she walked slowly towards the toilet, acting as nonchalantly as she could.

As she walked past the second of the two men, a tall, distinguished-looking black man in the smart suit of a senior city-gent, he looked up from his paper and smiled at her. She returned his smile and felt his hand stroke her bottom gently.

'Me next?' he whispered. Lisa said nothing, but grinned and opened the toilet door slowly, slipping into the confined space and locking it behind her.

The businessman was sitting astride the toilet, his trousers unzipped, a short, stubby but fully erect cock in his hand. His face was sweating profusely. Lisa found him almost repulsive, but was so desperate for sex that she decided to sate her lust on this rather pathetic specimen. She knelt down as far as the cramped space would allow and took the man's tool in her hand, rubbing it gently. He began to shake, his breathing erratic. She looked up into his eyes and smiled seductively then opened her pouting mouth, licking the lips suggestively.

She slipped her wet lips over his hard little erection, her tongue slithering round and round the stem. He gave a short, breathless cry and she tasted the familiar flavour of sperm as he collapsed across her, his head hitting the wall noisily. She swallowed his copious offerings with both greed and disappointment, her fingers clawing between her legs, trying in vain to force her orgasm whilst she still had him there.

He recovered quickly however and pulled his tiny, wilted member from her mouth, stuffing it back into his trousers. Lisa stood up, wiping her mouth as he opened the door and left, without a word.

She watched him go, in furious disbelief. Her need for a come was now even more urgent and, without a partner she couldn't do anything about it.

She decided to take a pee, to calm herself down a little. She pulled her tight jeans down to her ankles and squatted over the recently vacated seat, feeling the soothing warmth of her urine as it trickled from her body.

Suddenly the door was pushed open; she had forgotten that it had remained unlocked when the businessman had left, and now she sat before the handsome, black gentleman, her legs wide open, unable to stop the flow that was now gushing from her.

He obviously realised her embarrassment. 'That's all right, my dear,' he said, locking the door, 'you carry on. I'll watch.'

Lisa knew there was no way she could stop whatever he said, but at least now she was beginning to enjoy the situation. She relaxed and looked straight into the big man's face, the gush increasing even more as she emptied her bladder. She was surprised that she'd wanted to go so badly, but had noticed in the past that when she was turned on her feelings of lust often took over from the more basic bodily needs.

As the flow turned to a trickle he unzipped himself and took out his length, the ebony head shiny with his juices. Lisa took it carefully into her mouth as she kicked off her jeans, licking it, enjoying the salty taste. Knowing the effect her mouth could have on a man, she took care not to use all her oral skills this time; she was anxious for full sex and soon stood up, turning her back to him.

'Fuck me, please,' she said – the very first words she'd spoken to this stranger – and raised one leg so that her foot rested on the toilet seat. At first she felt his big fingers probing at her sex, then at last his thick shaft slid effortlessly into her burning sheath and she pushed her bottom back so that she could accept every inch. He began to pump steadily into her and she felt the first twinges of her orgasm almost immediately. She moaned with the pleasure, his rate of humping increasing in response.

'Yes, oh yes. Fuck me, fuck me!' she cried, not caring if she could be heard all over the train. 'Oh, you've no idea how much I need it!'

The man just grunted, his stalk thundering in and out of her with a fearsome force, each thrust lifting her from the floor.

'That's it! Give it to me, harder, harder! Fill me with everything you've got!' Lisa's orgasm tore through her young body with intense ferociousness, causing her to scream deafeningly. Her lover simultaneously emptied his cream into her, the throbbing of his thick stalk against the tender flesh of her sheath sending wave after wave of climactic after-effects through her body.

As the throbbing slowed and he began to wilt inside her she felt the intense relief overcome her and sobbed quietly. She felt him slip from her, heard the sound of his zip as he made himself decent, then heard the door open and close as he left her, his last gesture a grateful, if patronising, pat on her bare bottom.

She stayed in the same position for a few minutes, recovering from her mind-blowing orgasm and at the same time wondering if the third traveller would come in to have her; she knew she would be quite happy if he did. After a while, however, she realised he was not going to join her and reluctantly locked the door again with a sigh.

She squatted over the toilet again and held her pussy lips open with her fingers, watching the erotic image reflected in the small, cracked mirror on the opposite wall. Despite her shattering orgasm, she was again feeling very randy, and wondered how long it would be before her insatiable needs for sex would start to diminish a little, as promised by Janet, so that she could begin to live a near-normal life again.

Cleaning herself up, she pulled on her jeans and, checking in the mirror that she looked presentable, unlocked the door and returned to the corridor. Her two lovers had disappeared, the third man, much younger and remarkably handsome, stood looking out of the window. He glanced at Lisa and smiled weakly. She wondered why he hadn't come into the toilet to take her after the African had left; he would certainly have heard her screams of pleasure and known exactly what she was up to. Perhaps he was the faithful, married type, or maybe he didn't go for girls.

It crossed her mind to use her powers. She looked hard at him, holding his gaze, willing him to lust after her. A quick glance at the front of his trousers revealed the telltale bulge already beginning to show; she knew she had him.

Suddenly, however, the train lurched sideways as it hit some points, and Lisa momentarily lost her balance and concentration. When she looked back, the stranger had turned his face away.

She shrugged. She could have resumed her hypnotic seduction of course, but somehow in this instance it didn't seem right. She wanted him to want her for herself, not because of some mysterious magical power. She returned to her compartment.

'Where have you been, then?' asked Janet as Lisa resumed her seat.

'Oh, I just needed some air.'

'We heard,' giggled Rani, 'we thought you were being murdered!'

'Oh, well,' said Lisa, smiling, 'you know how it is.'

'Yes, we know exactly how it is,' said Kate, who was sitting with Jan's hand firmly wedged between her legs, 'the first six weeks or so are hell, but it gets a little easier after that.'

'Six weeks!' Lisa was horrified. 'You told me it would only be a week or so! I don't think I'm going to be able to stand it. You wouldn't believe some of the things I've done and still I want more!'

'Oh, we would believe it,' said Jan, softly, her fingers playing gently against Kate's denim-covered sex, 'we've all been there. It does get better, I promise, although you'll still need it every day.'

Lisa sighed and sat back in her seat, taking hold of Janet's hand and placing it nonchalantly between her own legs, her friend responding immediately with a gentle caress. She closed her eyes and began to doze, the exertions of the previous minutes and Janet's expert fondling easing her into a peaceful sleep.

The girls arrived at the sleeper-train with little time to spare, the taxi-trip across London being delayed by horrendous traffic. Each of them had a small but comfortable compartment to themselves, and they were soon settled for the long journey ahead.

Lisa lay staring at the carriage roof unable to sleep, the short nap earlier having taken any feelings of tiredness from her. Her head was filled with strange thoughts, worries about the situation that she and her friends were in, and she wondered just how far she was prepared to go to keep her good looks.

She remembered the podgy little virgin she had been just a short time ago; the way boys had ignored her; how desperate she had become and how wonderful the sex had been since her transformation. She loved the way that men looked at her nakedness in total admiration; enjoyed the way they lusted after her, eager to sink their hard erections into her lithe, young body. She knew she couldn't do without that adoration, nor the sexual fulfilment.

She also knew that what they were doing was wrong. She worried about just how far it would go; to what lengths they would be asked to use their powers to control rich and powerful men. Then she remembered the orgy with the American businessmen and the session with the Ambassador. She knew she needed it; there was no going back now.

After more fruitless attempts to sleep, Lisa decided to get up and walk through the train. She was naked, so pulled on a long T-shirt to cover her modesty, checking her reflection in the mirror and seeing that it only just hid her pussy and that the outline of her massive breasts and erect nipples was clearly defined through the thin, white cotton. She shrugged. Everyone would be asleep and, even if she met someone in the corridor, she couldn't have cared less; she'd certainly got nothing to be ashamed of.

She stepped out into the coolness of the corridor, the sudden change of temperature causing her nipples to grow even longer. She walked a little way down the narrow passageway then stopped, peering pointlessly out of the window into the darkness. She felt much calmer now, more at ease with herself. Perhaps things weren't so bad as she'd imagined; why shouldn't she be beautiful and have fun? What's so wrong about that?

A door to one of the sleeping compartments nearby suddenly slid noisily open, making her jump. A man walked out, the same man who had avoided her attempts at seduction on the Brighton train. Despite it being in the early hours of the morning he was fully dressed. Lisa smiled in recognition, oblivious to the fact that she was nearly naked.

The man smiled nervously back. He seemed even more

211

gorgeous than she had remembered: tall, dark with a heavily tanned complexion and deep brown eyes. He looked to be about thirty years of age.

'Hi,' she said, 'can't sleep?'

'No, I always have trouble on these long journeys. In fact I don't even bother going to bed.'

'I saw you on the other train,' said Lisa, resting back against the window, feeling the cold glass pressing against her bottom, 'do you remember me?'

He grinned, his face reddening slightly. 'Oh yes, I remember you. You seemed to be having a good time.'

Lisa laughed, deciding to act the tart. 'Yes, I was. I always wanted to do it on a train. My name's Lisa, by the way.'

'I'm Phil,' he said, leaning against the opposite wall, the front of his trousers bulging noticeably.

'Are you married, Phil?'

'I was,' he said, the nervousness returning to his voice, 'but that finished over three years ago. There's been nobody special since.'

Lisa pouted seductively, running a hand over his strong chest. 'How sad,' she said, huskily, 'you must be terribly frustrated. Are you frustrated?' She caught hold of his hands and lifted them to her breasts, smoothing his palms over her massive mounds, knowing he would be able to feel her bullet-hard nipples pressing into his flesh. He nodded in answer to her question, his breathing shallow and difficult.

'Come with me,' she said, softly, taking one of his hands and pulling him towards her compartment, 'come on, I'll help you to ease your frustration.'

Phil pulled back from her weakly, shaking visibly. 'I–I'm sorry, I can't. You wouldn't enjoy it, I know.'

Lisa decided once again not to use her persuasive powers, preferring to rely on her physical attributes to bed this hunky man. With one quick movement, she caught the hem of her T-shirt and wrenched the garment over her head, throwing it to the floor to stand naked before him.

Phil gasped at the sight of her devastatingly beautiful body, his eyes darting backwards and forwards between her big breasts and her hairless pussy, the lips of which were wet and engorged with lust.

'Oh, my God, you're sensational!' he breathed, licking his lips quickly. She grabbed him again and pulled him into her compartment, slamming the door behind them.

She rested her hand on his chest, stroking lightly with her fingers, looking him straight in the eye. 'You're going to fuck me, Phil,' she said, 'and you're going to fuck me now!' She pushed her hand up into the shoulder of his jacket, intending to help him to remove it, but he pulled away. 'What's the matter?' she said, with genuine hurt and disappointment.

'Oh, Lisa, I *do* want you, I want to make love to you, but . . .'

'But what?' She sounded angry, because she was.

'It's just that, my wife and I had such a lousy sex-life . . . we were incompatible, she said. She never stopped moaning about it, and it ended up with me not being able to perform.'

Lisa smiled and pulled him back to her by the lapels of his jacket. She kissed his mouth gently, running her tongue over his full lips. '*I'll* get you to perform, don't worry.'

He seemed to relax, sitting down on the bed, and she managed to push his jacket off. She'd never wanted a man as much as she wanted Phil; she was going to take him and teach him, make him the best lover she'd ever had.

She deftly released the knot of his tie, pulling the thin strip of material sensuously from his collar, all the time kissing and licking his face, sniffing and tasting his subtle cologne. She knelt across his legs, seeing with pleasure the way he stared at her massive breasts, the nipples still hard and erect, awaiting stimulation. She unfastened the cuffs of his shirt, then one by one the front buttons, revealing a completely hairless and lightly muscled torso. He helped her to remove the shirt, then lay back, his head on a pillow, whilst she removed his shoes and socks.

213

She ran her hands up and down the full length of his legs, watching, fascinated as the bulge in his trousers grew dramatically. She would have no problem in getting him to perform, that was clear. She couldn't understand why he thought he had a problem.

She carefully unzipped his fly, then undid the top clasp, taking hold of the waistband and slowly, meaningfully, pulling his slacks from him.

He now wore nothing but a pair of red briefs, bulging at the front quite remarkably. She kissed his sex gently through the material, taking in the erotic, manly scent, then licked his genitals wetly over his pants, her tongue tracing the shape of his hardening penis. A patch of dampness appeared in the red material where the end of his steadily stiffening tool lay. Lisa reached into the waistband and gradually eased his briefs down, slowly revealing his half-hard cock and heavy balls.

Taking his pants from his ankles, she raised one of his legs into the air and kissed his heel. Then she ran her tongue slowly and deliberately up his calf, over his knee, then up his inner thigh until she was a fraction of an inch from his sex. She ran her hands smoothly over his stomach, chest and thighs, teasing him; not touching him where she knew he wanted to be touched. His hips started to buck slightly; he wanted to be stroked and fondled, he needed it as badly as she did. She sat back onto his leg, allowing him to feel the wetness of her naked, shaven pussy, and rubbed herself against his shin so that her juices smeared over his hard flesh, exciting her clitoris on the bone.

She kissed him lightly on his balls, taking his sex in her hand. He was still quite soft, but nevertheless very large, the shaft thickening steadily in her grasp. She sat up and started to rub him gently, watching in awe as his shaft began to take on monstrous proportions. The thick stem hardened like steel, the heavy, circumcised head almost the size of a fresh peach. Its girth was now too much for her to clasp her fingers completely around, and the sight of the gnarled hardness filled her mind with never before imagined feelings of lust. She'd often wondered if she'd ever find a man bigger where it mattered than the old man, and now she had, and wow! He was two, perhaps even three inches longer and much thicker; so large as to be almost comical. His balls, though of normal size, were dwarfed by the immensity of the monster phallus, which she now held firmly in both hands.

'Oh, my God,' she sighed, 'now that is what I call a *cock*!'

'Are you sure it's all right?' he said, sounding genuinely concerned. 'I'm sorry it's so big.' Sorry? What was he talking about?

'It's beautiful,' she said, with total sincerity, 'it's the biggest I've ever seen!'

'That was the problem with my marriage; my wife hated it. She said I hurt her.'

'Silly bitch!' Lisa dived down and kissed the large, bulbous knob-end, running her tongue wetly over it. At the same time she rubbed the stem roughly with her hands, marvelling at her good fortune. She was about to have sex with an overwhelmingly gorgeous man, a guy with a perfect body and a cock like a dream.

She opened her mouth wide and took the end inside, closing her full lips under the rim, lapping around it with her tongue as much as his size would allow. She couldn't get any of his shaft into her mouth, he was just too big. Instead, she had to content herself with gobbling and suckling greedily on the huge end, tasting his pre-come as it occasionally throbbed from the large slit.

She sat back, still astride his lower legs, allowing him to gaze in wonder at her nakedness for a moment, his eyes now concentrating on her shaven sex, the lips soaked with her juices. 'You are beautiful,' he sighed, 'absolutely beautiful.'

She smiled warmly and fell across his body, pushing him back onto the bed, kissing him heavily on the mouth, their tongues wetly worming themselves around each other as they rubbed their naked bodies together. She felt the hugeness of his erection as it pressed against her stomach, then moved her body downwards until the thick stem rested between her breasts.

She stiffened the muscles of her upper arms so that her breasts gripped him and rubbed him as her hands had done previously. She moved herself down further so that she could lap at the end of his penis with her tongue whilst it was held in its heavenly grip. She felt him prodding at her sex with one of his feet, slipping a couple of his toes into the warmth. He'd pressed the final button. She clamped her mouth over the end of him, making her soft but firm mounds grip him even tighter as she came; her muffled cries belying the intensity of her orgasm, her wetness soaking his foot.

After a moment she sat up and gazed lovingly at his splendour. The long, fat erection rested on his stomach, the tip just short of his ribs. She knew she wanted that monster inside her now; the waiting and the foreplay were over.

She lifted herself onto her heels, squatting over his crotch. Although she wanted him badly, she knew that she would have to be careful, to ease him gently into her until her body had got used to the monstrous intrusion.

She took hold of his beautiful phallus and pulled it upwards towards her, opening her already engorged pussy-lips with her other hand. His thick tip touched her wetness and she sank down slightly, taking the knob-end inside her body. For a moment she felt that he *was* too big, that she wouldn't be able to take it after all and that she would disappoint him. Then she remembered how she had taken the giant dildo Mistress Druscilla had impaled her with; that was about the same size as Phil's delightful offering and she'd loved that. There would be no problem.

She started to move gingerly up and down, taking two inches inside her, then letting an inch out, two inches in, one inch out; gradually accepting his full length into her stretched pussy. The end of his tool pressed against the entrance to her womb and there was still a couple of inches to go, but she persevered, wriggling her lower body to absorb the intruder, finally sitting triumphantly against his thighs, her sex pressing purposefully hard on his pubic bone.

She sat still for a minute, getting used to and savouring his size, resting her hands on his shoulders and breathing heavily. 'Are you OK?' he said, with real anxiety. She nodded, and started slowly to move her body up and down on his stiffness, shuddering each time it touched the roof of her vagina, stretching her in every way. She could feel every inch, every part of its gnarled shape rubbing, oh so gently inside her. He filled her completely, even more so than two cocks had done during past escapades.

As she pulled up, her puffy sex-lips clung tightly to the thick stem; its size drawing them out like a wet, pouting mouth. Gradually she increased her pace, having him in earnest, her clitoris rubbing constantly against his length, dragging her again towards the ecstatic oblivion of orgasm.

As she felt herself coming, she thrust her body heavily onto his, sighing and moaning as she shafted herself on him. She let her legs splay outwards, stiffening them at the knees. She balanced her body on her toes and hands, and as her bottom bounced up and down the huge tool slithered in and out with ease. Phil lay completely still, no doubt knowing that she had to be in control, that one wrong move from him could hurt her and ruin this most excellent sex. Lisa held her body well above his, so that only six or seven inches slid in and out of her accommodating pussy. Her thighs pumped madly as her orgasm tore at her loins, the shivers of lustful pleasure running down her stiffened legs to her feet.

She collapsed onto him, taking his full length inside her and lay still, sobbing with pleasure. Phil stroked her back and bottom tenderly as she recovered, kissing her lovingly on the face and neck. She felt warm, soft and vulnerable in his arms; she wanted this moment to last forever.

After a few minutes rest she sat up, still impaled on his hard shaft, and started to move up and down again. She let him watch as he slid in and out of her tight sheath. He fitted her easily now, like a hand in a glove and he was able to start moving his hips in response to her thrusts, stiffening his buttocks as he pushed his monster tool deep into her. She moved quickly, her breasts bouncing heavily, her hands behind her head.

There was no need for either of them to touch her little bud, the thickness of the intruder ensured that it was constantly in contact with his flesh, its tenderness replaced by lust as she humped herself towards another come. She squealed as she let go a gentler, easier orgasm, then pulled herself from his steel-hard erection.

She held it with one hand, rubbing it delicately, looking at it with the wonder of a child at Christmas. A thought suddenly occurred to her. 'There's a friend of mine who'd love to see this; she loves big cocks.'

'It's a pity she's not here.'

'She's on the train. I'll go and get her, if you like.'

From the look on his face, Phil liked. Lisa jumped off the bed, and opened the door.

'Are you going out like that?' he said, with a grin.

Lisa shrugged. 'She's only a few doors down the corridor,' she said and left, closing the door gently behind her.

As it happened, Janet's compartment was at the far end of the carriage and Lisa felt a little vulnerable as she stood, stark naked in this public place. She knocked lightly on Janet's door, then again, louder.

'Wha-what is it?' Her friend's sleepy voice came from behind the door. 'Who is it?' she said. 'What do you want?'

'Janet, it's me, Lisa. You must come up to my room. I've got something to show you!'

'Don't piss about, Lisa,' Janet sounded annoyed, 'I'm half asleep. What have you got?'

'How does about fourteen inches of hard, thick cock sound?'

'You're kidding!' Janet had suddenly woken fully.

'No, I'm not, I've just been sitting on it. It's far too much for one little girl to cope with!'

'I'm on my way.'

218

Lisa returned to her compartment quickly, leaping back into bed with her latest lover. 'You're really quite something,' he said, 'not many girls would do that.'

'A bloke with a cock like yours deserves two girls. You'll like Janet, she's nearly as randy as me!'

There was a light knock at the door. 'God, that didn't take her long!' Lisa hopped out of bed again and opened it. From where Phil lay on the bed he wouldn't have been able to see that she stood, naked and noticeably sexually aroused in front of one of the carriage porters, a tall, black youth of striking good looks, his large eyes gleaming with pleasure at the vision before him.

His gaze moved slowly over her body, feasting on the sight of her large breasts, slim waist and shaven pussy, its lips red and prominent from the recent sex she'd had.

'Sorry, miss, I think I got the wrong room.' He just stared between her legs now, his eyes bulging like a caricature of Uncle Remus.

'That's all right,' she said, for some reason stroking the side of his head with the back of her hand. He didn't need further invitation. He pushed his large hand quickly against her crotch, feeling her wet invitation. Lisa just stood there, her back against the corridor wall as this total stranger pawed at her, the fingers groping inside the loose lips, pressing against her with the palm of his hand.

She unzipped his trousers and reached into his pants, pulling out his hard erection, which was probably less than half the size of the one she'd just been enjoying. Without a word she pulled it towards her pussy, the hard end replacing his fingers, sliding fully into her. She could hardly feel a thing as he humped her, Phil had stretched her so much, but she still enjoyed what was happening, feeling so brazen, so debauched.

The railway-porter's hips pumped swiftly until, with a groan it was over for him. Lisa stood impassively, as though she was being raped, although in reality it could be said it was she that was doing the raping. She had no idea why she'd let this stranger screw her; it was as though her cunt had a mind of its own.

He pulled from her, put himself in order and stood, looking rather stupid. 'What are you waiting for, a tip?' said Lisa, anxious that he should go, to end the embarrassment that was creeping upon her. He wandered away with a bewildered look on his face, passing Janet as she came out of her compartment. Noticing her friend's nakedness, Janet looked back quizzically at the youth, but said nothing.

Lisa took Janet into her room and proudly indicated Phil, lying like some prize specimen at an exhibition, his monster phallus still firmly erect against his smooth body. He'd probably had it in mind to ask Lisa why she had been so long at the door, but the sight of Janet removing her woollen dressing gown and revealing her pert nakedness seemed to put any such thoughts out of his mind.

The bed was just big enough for the two girls to sit either side of their conquest, each holding his wonderful erection in one hand. Little was said, the electric atmosphere enough to inspire the moment. Phil lay back and watched, happy to let them do as they wished.

Janet leant forward and ran her tongue over his big knob, tasting the scent of her friend, her free hand pulling at her own pussy-lips, readying her for the onslaught ahead. Lisa licked him also, both girls running their tongues up and down the long length of his shaft, from balls to tip, the edges of their tongues sometimes touching, the sensation sending thrills through Lisa's body. She wanted to enjoy both of these highly sexed bodies: the firmness of Phil with his monstrous stalk, and the soft, fleshiness of Janet with her warm, wet and ever inviting pussy.

Janet wet her finger with saliva and pushed it gently into Phil's anus, causing him to raise his buttocks slightly. Lisa gobbled hungrily on the end of his sex, wondering if he was ever going to come. Janet's finger slid incessantly in and out of its tight sheath as she kissed and licked at his chest, chewing lightly on the nipples, then running her tongue back down to his erection. She slid her tongue wetly up the long stem until her mouth met Lisa's, still firmly clamped over the thick knob.

They pulled their mouths from the phallus, still gripping it tightly with one hand each and kissed each other passionately. Lisa felt her friend's tongue slithering over and over her own, her desires now giving themselves to Janet's beauty.

Without letting their mouths part for an instant, the girls manoeuvred their bodies so that Janet was astride Phil, his tool pointing menacingly at her fully aroused sex. She lowered herself onto him, taking almost two-thirds of it before having to stop, still smooching heavily with Lisa.

They pulled themselves apart, Janet now ready to concentrate on having Phil. 'He is a big fucker, isn't he?' she said, beginning to ride him, taking as much of his tool as her small body could accommodate.

She settled into a steady pumping motion and Lisa went behind her and knelt between their legs to watch as her friend's gorgeous bum moved up and down, relishing the sight of the enormous cock disappearing into Janet's tight sheath. She lay her head between the two lovers' thighs and gently licked at Phil's balls, running her tongue over the plum shapes and between, before playfully fluttering the tip over his sweating anus.

Lisa's ever-searching tongue slid back up, over the tight sack of his scrotum, up the long stem then onto the thrusting buttocks of Janet, licking around her sweet, hairless arsehole, dipping the thin tip of her tongue into the tight sphincter.

In response to her friend's delicate oral contact Janet slowed down her movements for a while, then her pumping became more urgent, and Lisa sat back as her friend hammered her hips down onto the mighty cock, taking almost the full length into her tiny body. Suddenly, Janet arched her back and held still, only the fat, bulbous end inside her, and panted heavily as she came. Lisa planted her mouth firmly against the other girl's bum, licking furiously at the hole, her arms wrapped round her hips.

Phil shouted out, 'Oh, yes, I'm coming!' and Janet leapt off him and grasped his thick erection, pumping it for all she was worth. Lisa joined her, four hands now wanking him into oblivion. He raised his bottom from the bed and his cock throbbed within their grasp, his first load of sperm shooting into the air before splashing down over his chest and stomach. Lisa and Janet pushed their mouths immediately to the spurting slit at the end, licking and swallowing as more and more cream shot their way, faces wet with his juices and their own sweat.

As his great rod subsided they licked the residue from him, occasionally kissing each other lovingly, before collapsing back on the bed, exhausted.

The three lovers lay staring at the ceiling. Lisa was considering that she had found perfection; sex with a well-endowed man and a beautiful girl. She knew that she would always want it this way, that she would never be satisfied with anything less.

Chapter Ten

The venue of the old man's meeting was a rambling but palatial Georgian house set in a vast estate in the Highlands of Scotland, close to Inverness. As the taxi-cab sped through the breath-taking scenery towards the huge building, Janet reflected that the old man may be many things, but hard up for cash was not one of them.

She was feeling very tired. The purpose of using the overnight train had obviously been so that they would all be rested for the morning meeting, but she and Lisa had spent the whole night enjoying themselves with Phil and were both now quite exhausted.

They'd said their goodbyes at Inverness station, and as Phil went off to his business in the town, he promised to keep in touch. She wasn't sure how Lisa felt, but she knew that she would contact him again when they returned; there was no way she was going to let a man with that much cock slip away.

The car finally drew up outside the large entrance to the mansion, a uniformed lackey opening the door to let the girls step out into the crisp air. He bowed in welcome, then signalled to three other male servants to collect their baggage.

The girls were ushered inside the great hall, chattering excitedly like a touring group of schoolgirls. The furniture, paintings and tapestries continued the image of opulence; the house reeked of wealth.

There seemed to be people everywhere. Men and women scurried about the place, some in uniform, others not, all with various and apparently important purposes. Janet looked around her in wonder, but nevertheless with a feeling of unease. Her conversations with Lisa had put doubts in her mind; just what were the old man's intentions? Perhaps today they would find out.

They were led upstairs to the bedrooms, two girls sharing each one. Initially, Janet was to have shared with Jan, but after a little persuasion from her and Kate a swap was made, so that the two lovers could be together. It also meant that she would be with Lisa and she certainly fancied another taste of her dear friend's pussy, if given the chance.

Like the rest of the house, their room was large and expensively furnished. There was one, massive four-poster bed which suited her plans perfectly, and she knew Lisa wouldn't object.

They showered quickly and dressed in their formal wear as had been suggested. Lisa wore a smart two-piece trouser-suit and crisp, white blouse, her amazing figure all but concealed in the loose folds of the garments. Janet had chosen to dress in a long skirt and blouse, even going to the trouble of wearing panties and a bra, something she hadn't done for years, unless dressing up for sex. Once ready, they headed back down to the hall, and met up again with their colleagues.

So far, there had been no sign of Frank. There were so many people here though, and the house was so vast, he could have been anywhere. Janet was surprised that he hadn't been there to meet them, however.

As they waited, she looked around at the other occupants of the large hall. Apart from the many staff members, there were a number of groups of young people, huddled together somewhat nervously, like themselves. Most of them were girls, but there were a few men. What all of them had in common was their devastating good looks.

'Have you noticed how gorgeous everybody is?' said Lisa, catching her thoughts.

'They must be Lust Angels, like us,' whispered Janet. 'There are loads of them.'

'God, I wish I knew what it was all about,' said Lisa, anxiously.

Suddenly, the conversation was interrupted by the crash of a large gong at the far end of the room. Everybody turned in the direction of the sound to see Frank standing there, holding his hands up for silence.

'Ladies and gentlemen, we are ready. Please follow.'

He led the way through two huge, open doors into another hall, even larger and grander than the first. At the far end was a stage, unoccupied for the moment, while the rest of the room was filled with chairs facing front. The guests filed between the rows of seats, sitting down where indicated by the many servants, who controlled the sudden influx with the precision of a military operation.

Janet and her group found themselves seated close to the stage and watched as Frank and three other smartly dressed men sat on the platform facing them, two on either side of a large, empty chair.

The hubbub of conversation carried on for a short while until the lights were suddenly dimmed, revealing for the first time the room's total lack of windows. A number of servants walked forward, solemnly carrying large candlesticks which were placed around the stage, the flickering flames casting eerie shadows against the walls and curtains.

Once again people began to talk, until Frank stood up and clapped his hands loudly. 'Welcome,' he said, his voice strong and confident, 'welcome to you all. This will be the first time that you will have met other groups such as yourselves and, no doubt, you are surprised at just how many of you there are.'

There were murmurs of agreement from the crowd. Frank held his hands up again. 'Truly, our leader is great and powerful, to have created so many specimens of perfect sexuality. Now you are to learn his wondrous purpose!'

Janet looked anxiously at Lisa and at the other girls in

their group. Frank was sounding more and more like a mad evangelist. Just what was going on?

'Let us welcome him,' Frank babbled on, 'come, stand and raise your hands in praise!'

The assembled throng did as instructed, more out of curiosity than deference. Suddenly there was a crash, like that of thunder and the room was filled with a blinding light. Janet clamped her eyes shut against the intensity of the brightness, feeling very afraid. She felt Lisa grip her hand tightly and returned the grip, taking some comfort from their shared terror.

The light dimmed and Janet opened her eyes slowly. The only illumination came from two large, black candles set on either side of the central chair, which was now occupied. As her eyes became accustomed to the dark she made out the occupant's features; the evil, gnarled expression of the old man, his eyes blazing with fearsome malevolence.

'Oh, sweet Jesus,' said Lisa, 'I've just figured it all out. You know who he really is, don't you?'

'Please, God, no,' said Janet, her voice trembling, 'not that.'

The old man suddenly stood up. A girl shrieked in fear, causing him to grin. He seemed much taller than Lisa had remembered him, his body unbent, robust and seemingly immensely powerful.

'Welcome, my Angels,' he said in a cracked, sinister voice, leering round at them, apparently able to see them all despite the darkness of the room. 'Some of the more intelligent amongst you will have at last realised my identity, but for the more stupid, let me introduce myself.

'Some know me as Nick, some the Devil, the Anti-Christ. You will, nevertheless know me as your benefactor, to whom I gave the gift of beauty, in exchange for simple compliance. The time has now come for you to show me your gratitude!'

A number of the girls began to sob; Sonia suddenly shouted out 'Never!' The old man rounded on her, glaring at her with his foul eyes.

'Oh, but you will, my pretty,' he said, 'because if you don't you will revert to your original, ugly state, but with the sexual appetite of a nymphomaniac. You are all completely in my power; you must know that those who have intercourse with the Devil become his Angels, and so it is with you all, male and female.

'Each one of you has tasted my shaft within your bodies and accepted my fluids. I am within you always . . . and control you.'

Sonia sat back in her chair, shaking visibly. The old man faced front again. 'Now for your instructions. Each one of you has been allocated a different politician, world leader or other influential person to deal with. You will be taken from here tonight and flown to various locations around the globe, where arrangements have already been made by my able assistants for you to meet your prey.

'At exactly the same time, every one of you will have sex with his or her chosen victim, using your full powers to dominate them completely. Once they are fully in your control, I will take over, entering their minds through your delicious bodies, subjugating them to my will.

'In short, at last and thanks to you all, I will rule mankind for ever, in full command of the world's affairs through the puppets you will help me to control. Now, go my Angels and do not fail me!'

There was a second, blinding flash of light and he was gone. The room was silent for some time, the servants busily removing the candles, the normal lighting having been switched back on. Gradually, people began to speak, the noise of conversation building up louder and louder, until Frank again called for silence.

'Angels, you have been told the truth and you have your instructions. The task before you is vital and I know you will not fail. You may have your doubts at the moment, but I ask you to put them aside. Ahead of you lies a future of wealth and satisfied lust; take it with both hands, I implore you!

'Tonight you will all be sent on your missions; as for today, I know the yearnings will be building up inside your insatiable bodies. The servants are here to pleasure you in any way you desire; use them, abuse them as you will. The day is yours!'

There was a short, silent pause, broken by a sudden cry of elation; then another, and more. Janet looked around her in horror. Everybody seemed more interested in getting out of their clothing than the terrifying prospect that had been presented to them by the old man. She looked at Lisa, noticing that she was slowly unbuttoning her jacket.

'What are you doing?' shouted Janet, grabbing her.

'I can't help myself,' said Lisa, pulling away, 'I've got to have it! I've never wanted sex so badly as I do now!'

'But it's the old man – he's making you do it!'

'I don't care! I need a fuck!' Lisa ripped off the jacket and trousers of her suit, standing now in just a pair of black stockings and a suspender belt. She looked around her with mad eyes, hungrily searching until she saw one of the many servants standing by the stage. She rushed over and grabbed him, clawing at the front of his trousers, ripping them open to get at his sex.

Janet watched in terror as the servant stood impassively whilst Lisa sucked his erection. All around her others sucked and humped at the stone-faced members of staff, like an attack of wild dogs on a herd of wildebeast. Some of the male Angels were gay and they were happily satisfying each other, whilst those who were heterosexual ran from girl to girl, ramming their uniformly huge shafts deep into pussy after pussy.

Lisa had pushed her conquest back onto a chair now and was bouncing up and down like a thing possessed on his knee, his stiffness ramming in and out of her gaping vagina. She screamed almost with each thrust, as though she were having constant orgasms. Around her all the other girls were acting in a similar way.

Janet couldn't understand why she remained unaffected. Perhaps it was because she'd been beautiful before and that

228

the limited change she'd undergone was reflected by the lack of the old man's power over her. The sight of all these rutting people was turning her on incredibly, but she knew that she wasn't possessed with the same frenzy that held the others.

She looked around for her other friends. Sonia and Rani were squabbling over who could sit on the stiff length of one of the male Angels, whilst Kate and Jan were happily lying on the floor together, lapping content-edly between each other's legs. The room was filled with the scents of arousal, the cries of orgasm and release deafening.

Janet began to shake with lust; not induced by the old man's spell, but the genuine need for good sex that she experienced every day. Being the only one in the room who was dressed, she quickly stripped off her clothing and underwear and went in search of a willing victim, soon finding a handsome male Angel who was about to impale the bottom of a beautiful Swedish-looking girl. She grab-bed hold of his erection and pulled him to her, much to the annoyance of the other girl who uttered an oath in some unintelligible language before storming off to find a re-placement.

Janet turned her back to him and bent over, keeping her legs straight and apart, and guided his thick knob to her waiting pussy. He entered her and slid easily to the hilt, gripping her waist as he began to pump in and out of her body. She rested her hands on the fronts of her thighs and pushed her backside out to meet his thrust, gritting her teeth as the steady rhythm brought her quickly to the point of orgasm. She felt him slide a finger into her anus and that was enough to bring her over, the shock waves of her come causing her legs to buckle as the stranger hammered into her from behind.

She gradually slid down to kneel on her hands and knees on the floor, her lover still firmly embedded inside her tight sheath, his finger pumping in and out of her other love-hole. She looked around her, at the throng of beautiful, naked people sucking, fucking and buggering each other and, for a moment, she felt as though she were in heaven.

She saw Lisa nearby, busily being serviced both orally and anally by two servants, her virtually constant orgasmic squeals muffled by the fat penis in her mouth. The sight of her friend in such an erotic pose started Janet's build-up to orgasm again and she knew that the old man's spell was beginning to work on her. She also knew also that she had to break away, to fight against these feelings of perfect ecstasy. She closed her eyes, the pleasure intense. 'Just one more come,' she thought, 'just one more.'

She turned her head and looked back at her lover, seeing his face for the first time. He really was absolutely gorgeous; clearly the old man's magic worked as well on men as it did on girls. She had to get him to make her come quickly, before the power took over her mind completely, and there was one way she knew that would do the trick.

'Fuck me up the bottom!' she cried. 'Fuck me up the bottom, and frig my clit!'

The young man didn't need telling twice. He pulled his long stalk from her wet sheath and withdrew his finger from her anus, replacing it immediately with his thick, bulbous cock-end. He was big, but she'd had a lot of experience at this type of sex and he slid into her tight hole easily. He resumed his steady movements, his hand trailing under her body to paw at her sopping pussy, the fingers expertly fondling her engorged clitoris.

'Yes! Give it to me hard!' she shouted and he responded to her cries by hammering his full length quickly in and out of her backside, his fingers frigging her at an alarming rate. She came with a mind-tearing explosion, her fingers digging into the palms of her hands, almost drawing blood.

Immediately it was over, she pulled herself from him, leaving him sitting back on the floor looking astonished, his big dick waving about ludicrously in the air. She rushed over to Lisa, pulling her away from the attentions of the two servants roughly.

'What are you doing?' Lisa asked, angrily.

'I've got to get you out of this room,' said Janet, fighting to hold on to her friend's struggling body, 'come on!'

'No, no! I need sex! Please leave me! I've got to have sex!'

'I'll give you sex,' said Janet, dragging Lisa out through the sea of humping bodies, 'I'll give you the best tonguing you have ever had – come on!'

Lisa followed obediently. 'Do you promise?' she said, coyly.

Janet smiled at her friend. 'I promise,' she said, meaning it.

The two girls ran up the stairs, Janet in fear, Lisa filled with lust. They ran into their bedroom, Lisa flinging herself onto the big bed, her legs wide open, her fingers pulling at the lips of her wet and ravaged pussy.

'Come on, Janet,' she pleaded, 'lick it, lick it!'

'In a minute,' said Janet, peering through the half-open door to see if they had been followed. She breathed deeply, her heart beating quickly, praying that they hadn't been spotted as they left the scene of the orgy. To her relief, nobody came up the stairs, the only sounds being the distant squeals of orgasm from the main hall.

She turned and looked at Lisa, who was lying quietly now, looking a little confused. She sat next to her on the bed, and stroked her thigh gently. 'Are you OK?' she said, tenderly.

Lisa put her hand to her forehead, sitting up slightly. 'What happened to me? I don't understand.'

'It's all right. The old man's power doesn't seem to stretch beyond the hall. Just relax.'

'I knew there was something wrong in all this,' said Lisa, a tear beginning to trickle from her eye, 'what are we going to do?'

'I don't know, but whatever happens, we mustn't go through with his plans.'

'But we'll lose our looks.'

Janet smiled, benignly. 'Then so be it,' she said, lying next to Lisa, cuddling her softly. There was no lust, just

231

genuine love and friendship between the two girls as they lay with their limbs entwined, wondering if this was to be their last time together.

Frank stood looking at the two naked girls on the bed, his face betraying a concerned curiosity. 'What happened to you two,' he asked, 'why did you leave the party?'

Lisa sat up, pretending exhaustion. 'We just fancied a good session together,' she said, 'so we thought we'd come up here. That was allowed, wasn't it?'

Frank grinned. 'Yes, I suppose so. Good session, was it?'

'Brilliant,' said Janet, joining in the deception, 'the best yet.'

'And there'll be plenty more like that,' said Frank, sitting on the end of the bed, 'I promise. Now, I've come to tell you about your assignment.'

The girls sat up, their smiles suggesting enthusiasm. 'Are we going to be together?' asked Lisa, desperately hoping they were.

'Yes. Your target is a very important one, the President of Europe, no less.'

Lisa's eyes widened with genuine awe. 'The President!' she said. 'But how . . .?'

'It's all arranged,' said Frank, confidently, 'he's expecting two hookers to visit him tonight. You will be flown to Brussels, taken to his apartment and left to serve him. But remember, he *must* be inside one of you at exactly six o'clock, to coincide with all the other couplings that will be occurring world-wide.'

'Six o'clock,' repeated Lisa, as though making special note of the important time.

'Correct,' said Frank, rising to leave the room, 'many of the others have already left. A helicopter will arrive to take you in about an hour. Please be ready.' He walked out of the room, closing the door. They heard the sound of the key turning in the lock.

Lisa looked at her friend, and smiled weakly. She knew that Janet had saved her from completely losing her mind

232

earlier that day, and she also knew that she had fallen in love with this beautiful girl. She reached over and took her head in her hands, and kissed her mouth wetly, running her tongue sensuously over her friend's lips. 'Don't worry,' she said, not convinced, 'we'll think of something. Come on. Let's get ready.'

They got up off the bed and walked into the plush bathroom, Janet turning on the shower, and stepping under the soothing warm flow of the water. Lisa joined her, soaping her friend's body liberally with both hands, the two girls kissing and cuddling like the lovers they had become.

Lisa rubbed the bar of soap between Janet's legs, and her friend returned the compliment to her. Their mouths joined in a passionate kiss; their tongues played around each other deliciously. The foam bubbled around their aroused pussies as they rubbed furiously at each other, their bodies pressed tightly together.

'I'm coming, my darling,' said Lisa, softly, 'I'm coming; please come with me.'

'I am,' said Janet, kissing Lisa lightly on the tip of her nose, 'I'm coming as well. I love you, Lisa.'

'I love you too.'

Lisa sat nervously looking out of the window as the helicopter sped over the English Channel towards their destination. Janet sat on the other side of the cabin, also gazing out into the clouds. The girls had chosen similar evening-wear for the occasion: long, figure-hugging dresses that moulded themselves around the perfect shapes of the lovely girls; Janet's in black, Lisa's in red. Both dresses were slit up to the waist on one side, revealing their lack of panties and the black hold-up stocking they both wore. They looked like the part they were to play; high-class prostitutes, en-route to service an important client.

Lisa was already feeling the now very familiar twitching between her legs; the need for sexual fulfilment. The old man's power was strong, that was certain, but she knew she had to fight it, if they were going to find a way out of this mess.

Brussels was wet and dismal, the President's apartments suitably grand. The journey from the airport had been in a limousine with smoked-glass windows, and the chauffeur was silent, obviously used to making such deliveries to his employer. Although afraid, Lisa couldn't suppress the feeling of excitement at playing the part of a whore, knowing her body was to be used at the whim of a great man. She crossed her legs in anticipation, feeling the wetness of her sex against her thighs.

They were led hurriedly into the building, up a long staircase to a large bedroom at the back. They were left alone, the doors closed.

'Oh, well,' said Lisa, nervously, 'this is it. What time is it?'

Janet looked at her watch. 'Five-thirty,' she said.

'Perhaps he'll not get here in time,' said Lisa, hoping.

Suddenly the doors opened and a man entered, dressed in a long, flowing robe. Lisa recognised the handsome, distinguished features as those of the President himself.

'Welcome, ladies,' he said, his voice betraying a slight, mid-European accent. 'I trust your journey wasn't too arduous?'

'No, sir,' smiled Lisa. He looked even more wonderful in real life than on the newsreels; middle-aged but very attractive, oozing sexuality. She wondered why he had the need of hookers, being so good-looking, but then surmised that this way there would be no come-backs, no complications, or at least so he thought.

'I must say my contacts have done me proud this time,' he said, standing in front of them, his hands stroking their faces gently. 'You really are the most beautiful girls I have ever seen.'

His hands strayed to the clasps on their shoulders, unfastening them simultaneously. The dresses fell to the floor, the girls now wearing nothing but high-heel shoes and stockings. 'Beautiful,' he repeated, breathing softly.

234

He began to run his hands over Janet's body. 'What we have here is perfection,' said the President, as though making a speech to some invisible audience, 'small, apple-firm breasts, soft belly, gently-curved bottom and,' both his hands slipped between her legs, 'a soft, wet and hairy cunt, begging for a fucking . . . isn't it?'

'Yes, sir.'

Lisa could see that her friend was trembling; was it lust, or fear of what was to happen at six o'clock?

'And here,' the President now moved in front of Lisa, his hands cupping her huge breasts, 'here we have possibly the largest pair of tits in the world, at least on such a small, young girl.' He tweaked her nipples between his thumbs and forefingers, then bent his head and sucked each one in turn, making them stand out like organ-stops. His hands trailed down, over her waist and round her back, sliding down to grip her bottom.

'Oh, and such a perfect arse! An arse like this was made to be fucked, was it not?'

'Yes, sir,' said Lisa, shivering.

The President ran one of his hands round to the front of her body, his palm covering her sex. 'And here, the object of all men's desire . . . the most perfect, hairless cunt. Lie on the floor! I must lick you!'

Lisa did as commanded, lying on the soft-carpeted floor, her legs open. The President knelt between them, bringing his face in line with her wet pussy, gazing lovingly at its beauty. He slowly ran his fingertip between the outer-lips, parting them gently, before pushing in to the knuckle. He stirred her wet honeypot sensuously, causing her to raise her hips from the floor, then he removed his finger and pressed his face against her soaked mound, his tongue flicking and darting around the puffy lips.

He took hold of her heels in each hand and raised her legs so that her knees pressed against her head as his tongue delved deeper into her pussy, suckling greedily. His technique was expert and well practised and she found herself relaxing under his gentle but insistent oral caress.

Lisa groaned in ecstasy as his licking moved down to her anus, prodding at her tight sphincter with the tip of his tongue, the extra sensation sending her into heaven.

The President sat back and removed his robe, revealing his naked body to the girls. His erection stood up, long and proud. Janet knelt and took the thick end into her mouth, rubbing the stem quickly, her free hand groping at his bottom.

She raised her head and kissed the swollen tip lightly. 'Come on, Lisa, help me,' she said, almost pleadingly.

Lisa suddenly realised her plan. She was trying to make him come before six o'clock, so that he wouldn't be inside either of them at the fateful hour. She dived over and joined her friend in licking the large phallus, her tongue tracing his length then running, greedily over his tight scrotum, suckling at his balls and lapping wetly at his anus, using all her oral expertise.

Despite Janet's frantic rubbing, the President held back, his self-control astounding. Both girls now held his stalk, masturbating him steadily, their tongues playing around the thick, circumcised end. 'Such a big one, Mr President,' said Lisa, seductively, 'such a monster that needs two girls to rub it.'

The President grinned, enjoying the praise, his erection stiffening. 'What a whopper!' said Janet, joining in the game. 'Quite the biggest I've ever seen! I can't wait to have it pushed inside me, especially up my bum.'

His shaft throbbed, but still he managed to hold back. The girls started to pump him heavily with their hands, feeling that his time was near, but he drew them away.

'Hold on, ladies,' he said, laughing, 'you'll have me shooting on the floor! This monster's going up you right now!'

Lisa glanced at the clock, the time nearly six. She looked at Janet in panic, her friend's expression one of terror. The President pushed Lisa onto her back, preparing to impale her, pointing his hardness at her wide-open sex-lips. Suddenly, she knew what she had to do.

236

With a quick movement she wriggled from under his body, and stood by the door, her fingers rubbing madly at her pussy. 'You can't have us! We're not going to let you fuck us!'

Janet shouted over to her. 'What are you doing, Lisa? You mustn't bring yourself off!' Her face showed that, as she uttered the words she realised exactly what Lisa was trying to do. Her fingers immediately went between her own legs, rubbing frantically at her already engorged clitoris, steadying herself by holding the back of a chair.

The clock began to strike. The President stood up, his erection jutting forward, his face a picture of confusion. 'What the fuck d'you think you're doing?' he roared. 'Get those pussies over here now!'

'No!' cried Lisa, desperately clawing at the folds of her sex. 'We are making ourselves come. We don't need you!'

'The hell you are!' He made a grab for her, but she scurried over to the other side of the room, standing next to Janet. The clock began to strike the hour. Janet's eyes suddenly took on a startled expression.

'Jesus, I'm coming!' she shouted. Lisa rubbed harder at her own sex, feeling the beginnings of orgasm building inside her aching loins.

'Me too!' she yelled. 'Me too!' The girls purposely stood apart, knowing that they mustn't touch as they both went into convulsive, shattering orgasms, brought on entirely by their own hands.

There was a blinding flash of light; furniture was thrown about the room, as though by unseen hands, pictures were ripped from the walls.

'You stupid bitches! You've ruined everything!'

It was the disembodied voice of the old man. 'You could have had eternal life, eternal sex! You've ruined my plans, you fucking fools!' There was another, even brighter flash of light, the old man's voice screaming in anger and pain as his powers seemed to be sucked from him. Lisa clamped her eyes shut against the light's intensity and to hold back the tears.

237

After a moment, all was quiet, the terror was gone. Lisa opened her eyes and looked at Janet, blinking. She didn't seem to have changed, but then she'd always been beautiful, just vain.

'Janet,' she said, trembling, 'it's over. We've won.'

Janet opened her eyes and looked at her friend. Lisa bit her lip, building up the courage to ask her the question. 'How do I look?' she said, fearing the answer.

Her friend looked at her for what seemed like an age. 'Beautiful, Lisa, just beautiful!'

Lisa ran to a mirror over the dressing table. Her face, although tear-stained and flushed was as lovely as before, her figure still perfect. She turned to her friend, grinning. 'Then he was lying, he was lying!' Janet nodded, smiling broadly, and they rushed into each other's arms, hugging tightly.

'I don't know what the fuck was happening just then, but I don't half need a screw!' The President was sitting on the floor, looking a little shaken, but with his sex still firmly erect. Janet and Lisa looked at each other and grinned, then dived onto his reclining body, determined to give him the best seeing-to he'd ever had.

Lisa lay dreamily on her bed, watching the prismatic patterns reflected from the mirror on her dressing table playing across the stippled, white ceiling. It felt good to be back home, in the security of her own little flat, after their incredible adventure.

She felt the reassuring warmth of Phil's naked body next to hers and glanced at his sleeping face, glad that she'd kept his phone number after their session on the train. He looked so beautiful, his eyes tightly shut, his breathing heavy, exhausted from the previous night's indulgences. His wonderful length lay impassively across his stomach, so harmless now, its languid state belying its size and power when aroused.

Lisa touched herself between the legs, remembering the perfect pleasure this wonderful phallus had given her, the

238

way it filled her completely, totally sating her lust. No man could satisfy her like Phil; big, and he knew how to use it, what more could a randy young girl want?

She raised herself up on her arm and looked over Phil to the other side of the bed. Janet lay half awake, staring at nothing. She smiled when she saw Lisa, who motioned for her to keep quiet as their lover hadn't yet woken. Their relationship was ideal, she thought. Three young people, fully compatible sexually, free of inhibitions and old-fashioned prejudices, perfect lovers in every way.

Lisa took hold of Phil's long shaft and squeezed it gently, as Janet lazily ran her hand over his thigh. He stirred, but remained asleep, his erection nevertheless rising slightly in response to her touch. She let it fall heavily back onto his stomach and climbed off the bed, heading for the bathroom.

As she washed and dried her body she thought again of her two lovers in the other room: Phil's strong, firm body, the wonderful way he made love; Janet's softness, the taste of her wet pussy, the feel of her tongue against her own sex; the massive hardness of Phil's steel-like erection as it penetrated her; the soothing warmth of Janet's mouth on her ravaged cunt. Their sex sessions were wild but loving, completely free of barriers . . . perfect.

She returned to the bedroom, her eyes meeting the delightful view of Janet's bottom pumping up and down on the now hard and very awake man beneath her. Lisa sat on a chair at the foot of the bed and watched, content to savour the sight of her two lovers as they pleased each other, seemingly oblivious to her presence. Janet humped herself on the magnificent tool steadily, still unable to take the full length inside her, the thick, heavily veined shaft glistening as it penetrated her.

Lisa gently traced the line of her own, wet lips as she watched her friend's small, hairy hole being stretched monstrously, even the tight sphincter of her anus opening slightly with the force of the downward thrusts. Eventually, the vision was soon too much for her to resist. She left the chair and knelt on the bottom of the bed, between the rutting couple's legs and ran her hands over Janet's pumping buttocks, feeling their soft firmness. She leant forward and kissed lightly between them. her friend slowing her movements to take advantage of the new feeling, sliding herself gently up and down on the top half of Phil's immense length.

Lisa ran her tongue down the crack of Janet's bum, over her anus, onto the fleshy lips of the base of her pussy, forced out by the thickness of the stiff intruder, then onto the erection itself; the tip of her tongue tracing the six or seven inches down to his balls. She licked greedily at the plum-like shapes, between them and under, drawing them individually between the pouting lips of her wet mouth.

She pulled her mouth away and Janet's movements started again earnestly, humping hard on the phallus they both loved so much. Lisa pressed her wet crotch against her friend's bottom and rode with her, wishing she had a penis with which she could impale the gorgeous bum under her, knowing her friend would love the sensation. Phil didn't need to move, he just lay there as Janet hammered her small, little body onto his, using him for her own pleasure.

She came with a shout, her fingernails clawing at the pillows, sandwiched between her two lovers, sobbing quietly with pleasure.

Lisa sat back, allowing Janet to climb off Phil, his sex smacking firmly against his stomach as it fell from the grasp of her pussy. She lay to the side and Lisa immediately dived down onto him, licking the full length of his rod, tasting Janet as she sucked his massive hardness. She ran her tongue up one side, from his balls to the top, over the thick, peach-shaped end and down the other side, nibbling gently with her teeth at the wonderfully gnarled fucking machine.

She knelt on the bed beside him, resting her elbows on a pillow and pushing her bottom out. She knew it might hurt this way, but it was what she wanted. 'Fuck me, do it from behind,' she ordered. 'Fuck me, *now!*'

Phil got up immediately and positioned himself to face Lisa's beautiful buttocks, staring lustfully at her open, hairless pussy. From this position she could see their full reflection in the dressing-table mirror, as well as a view of Janet, lying at their side, watching.

She was turned on by her vulnerability, presenting herself as she was to this man, his length waving menacingly in front of his slim thighs, looking as though it would split her in two. She felt him open her sex-lips with his thumbs and watched as he pushed his erection towards her, unrelenting, unforgiving. She sensed the now familiar immenseness of him as he entered her, the massive, bulbous end widening her to the limit, until her labia lips closed over the ridge, trapping him within her honeypot.

Then came the wonderful feeling of stretching, his shaft filling every part of her, her abundant juices being forced out by the sheer size of the monster. Gradually, more and more went in, until she felt his pubic hair touching her buttocks.

He moved just slightly for a while, until she again became used to him, then began to fuck her steadily. He pulled almost completely out each time, letting her savour the full length with every thrust. She watched the image in the mirror, transfixed.

Janet had moved round behind Phil and was licking his bottom, her hands caressing his firm thighs. Her face was forced away as the pace became more urgent, and Lisa was pushed heavily by the incessant pumping of her lover, her breasts bouncing back and forth, the nipples rubbing against the sheet on the bed, causing them to harden even more.

Janet moved round and crouched in front of Lisa, allowing her to bury her head in the warm wetness of her crotch, running her hands lovingly over her friend's sweating body. Lisa licked hungrily at the hairy pussy-lips, chewing on them, running her tongue between them, drinking from the sweet chalice before her. Phil was shagging her mercilessly now, there was a little pain but it was nothing compared to the immense pleasure she felt from the rubbing of his thick flesh against her clitoris. She was coming . . . coming with the biggest dong in the world inside her and her tongue firmly inside her best friend's pussy; it was all too much.

She started a long, low moan and stiffened her buttocks, the action gripping Phil's rutting tool like a vice. She pulled her face away from the tender confines of Janet's sex and arched her back, stiffening her entire body this time, her moan becoming a loud sigh of pleasure. 'Fuck me hard, now!' she cried, 'Don't hold back! Give me all you've got!'

Phil started to buck like an animal, thumping heavily into the willing receptacle, his fingers gripping hard onto her bottom. His tool seemed to grow even thicker within her as she felt the firm, rhythmic throbbing as he shot his sperm deep into her womb. The feelings of her orgasm shot down her legs to her toes, causing her to raise her knees from the bed, allowing him to ram every single inch inside her, his balls grinding against her soaking wet lips. They humped wildly on the bed, draining every bit of pleasure they could from the moment, until they gradually began to ease off, their genitals becoming sensitive and tender.

Phil pulled his drooping manhood from within Lisa, who had by now pushed her face back between Janet's legs. She kissed and licked gently at her friend's sex, but hadn't the energy to do more.

The three lovers lay, kissing and caressing each other for ages, their unison complete. Lisa looked lovingly at Janet and smiled. She knew that she had found happiness. Two lovers, always ready to please her, but with the freedom to indulge her sexual needs in any way and with whomsoever she chose, without hang-ups or recriminations. Phil would satisfy her, his long, thick erection filling her when she needed it; Janet would please her, the taste of her sweet pussy and the feel of her lapping tongue a source of endless joy.

The three of them would find and share other lovers, have new and varied experiences, never inhibited, always ready.

One thing was certain, she thought. The fun was only just beginning.

NEW BOOKS

Coming up from Nexus and Black Lace

Fallen Angels by Kendal Grahame
July 1994   Price: £4.99   ISBN: 0 352 32934 3
A mysterious stranger sets two young ladies the ultimate lascivious challenge: to engage in as many sexual acts with as many people as possible. Rich rewards await them if they succeed – but the task proves to be its own reward!

The Teaching of Faith by Elizabeth Bruce
July 1994   Price: £4.99   ISBN: 0 352 32936 X
Until she met Alex, Faith had never experienced the full range of pleasures that sex can bring. But after her initiation into his exclusive set of libertines, a whole new realm of prurient possibilities is opened up for her.

The Training Grounds by Sarah Veitch
August 1994   Price: £4.99   ISBN: 0 352 32940 8
Charlotte was expecting to spend her time on the island relaxing and enjoying the sun. But now, having been handed over to the Master, she has discovered the island to be a vast correction centre. She'll soon have a healthy glow anyway . . .

Memoirs of a Cornish Governess by Yolanda Celbridge
August 1994   Price: £4.99   ISBN: 0 352 32941 6
As Governess to a Lord and Lady, Miss Constance's chief task is to educate their son Freddie. But word soon gets about of her unusual techniques, and before long, most of the village is popping in for some good old-fashioned correction.

BLACK lace

The Gift of Shame by Sarah Hope-Walker
July 1994   Price: £4.99   ISBN: 0 352 32935 1
Helen had always thought that her fantasies would remain just that – wild and deviant whimsies with no place in everyday life. But Jeffrey soon changes that, helping her overcome her reservations to enjoy their decadent games to the full.

Summer of Enlightenment by Cheryl Mildenhall
July 1994   Price: £4.99   ISBN: 0 352 32937 8
Karin's love life takes a turn for the better when she is introduced to the charming Nicolai. She is drawn to him in spite of his womanising – and the fact that he is married to her friend. As their flirting escalates, further temptations place themselves in her path.

Juliet Rising by Cleo Cordell
August 1994   Price: £4.99   ISBN: 0 352 32938 6
At Madame Nicol's strict academy for young ladies, 18th-century values are by turns enforced with severity and flagrantly scorned. Juliet joins in her lessons enthusiastically; but whether she has learnt them well enough to resist the charms of the devious Reynard is another question.

A Bouquet of Black Orchids by Roxanne Carr
August 1994   Price: £4.99   ISBN: 0 352 32939 4
The luxurious Black Orchid Club once more provides the setting for a modern tale of decadence. Maggie's lustful adventures at the exclusive health spa take an intriguing turn when a charismatic man makes her a tempting offer.

Nexus

NEXUS BACKLIST

Where a month is marked on the right, this book will not be
published until that month in 1994. All books are priced £4.99
unless another price is given.

CONTEMPORARY EROTICA

CONTOURS OF DARKNESS	Marco Vassi		
THE DEVIL'S ADVOCATE	Anonymous		
THE DOMINO TATTOO	Cyrian Amberlake	£4.50	
THE DOMINO ENIGMA	Cyrian Amberlake		
THE DOMINO QUEEN	Cyrian Amberlake		
ELAINE	Stephen Ferris		
EMMA'S SECRET WORLD	Hilary James		
EMMA ENSLAVED	Hilary James		
FALLEN ANGELS	Kendal Grahame		
THE FANTASIES OF JOSEPHINE SCOTT	Josephine Scott		
THE GENTLE DEGENERATES	Marco Vassi		
HEART OF DESIRE	Maria del Rey		
HELEN – A MODERN ODALISQUE	Larry Stern		
HIS MISTRESS'S VOICE	G. C. Scott		Nov
THE HOUSE OF MALDONA	Yolanda Celbridge		Dec
THE INSTITUTE	Maria del Rey		
SISTERHOOD OF THE INSTITUTE	Maria del Rey		Sep
JENNIFER'S INSTRUCTION	Cyrian Amberlake		
MELINDA AND THE MASTER	Susanna Hughes		
MELINDA AND ESMERALDA	Susanna Hughes		
MELINDA AND THE COUNTESS	Susanna Hughes		Dec
MIND BLOWER	Marco Vassi		

MS DEEDES AT HOME	Carole Andrews	£4.50	
MS DEEDES ON PARADISE ISLAND	Carole Andrews		
THE NEW STORY OF O	Anonymous		
OBSESSION	Maria del Rey		
ONE WEEK IN THE PRIVATE HOUSE	Esme Ombreux		
THE PALACE OF FANTASIES	Delver Maddingley		
THE PALACE OF HONEYMOONS	Delver Maddingley		
THE PALACE OF EROS	Delver Maddingley		
PARADISE BAY	Maria del Rey		
THE PASSIVE VOICE	G. C. Scott		
THE SALINE SOLUTION	Marco Vassi		
STEPHANIE	Susanna Hughes		
STEPHANIE'S CASTLE	Susanna Hughes		
STEPHANIE'S REVENGE	Susanna Hughes		
STEPHANIE'S DOMAIN	Susanna Hughes		
STEPHANIE'S TRIAL	Susanna Hughes		
STEPHANIE'S PLEASURE	Susanna Hughes		Sep
THE TEACHING OF FAITH	Elizabeth Bruce		
THE TRAINING GROUNDS	Sarah Veitch		

EROTIC SCIENCE FICTION

ADVENTURES IN THE PLEASUREZONE	Delaney Silver		
RETURN TO THE PLEASUREZONE	Delaney Silver		
FANTASYWORLD	Larry Stern		Oct
WANTON	Andrea Arven		

ANCIENT & FANTASY SETTINGS

CHAMPIONS OF LOVE	Anonymous		
CHAMPIONS OF PLEASURE	Anonymous		
CHAMPIONS OF DESIRE	Anonymous		
THE CLOAK OF APHRODITE	Kendal Grahame		Nov
SLAVE OF LIDIR	Aran Ashe	£4.50	
DUNGEONS OF LIDIR	Aran Ashe		
THE FOREST OF BONDAGE	Aran Ashe	£4.50	
PLEASURE ISLAND	Aran Ashe		
WITCH QUEEN OF VIXANIA	Morgana Baron		

EDWARDIAN, VICTORIAN & OLDER EROTICA

Title	Author		
ANNIE	Evelyn Culber		
ANNIE AND THE SOCIETY	Evelyn Culber	Oct	
BEATRICE	Anonymous		
CHOOSING LOVERS FOR JUSTINE	Aran Ashe		
GARDENS OF DESIRE	Roger Rougiere		
THE LASCIVIOUS MONK	Anonymous		
LURE OF THE MANOR	Barbra Baron		
MAN WITH A MAID 1	Anonymous		
MAN WITH A MAID 2	Anonymous		
MAN WITH A MAID 3	Anonymous		
MEMOIRS OF A CORNISH GOVERNESS	Yolanda Celbridge		
TIME OF HER LIFE	Josephine Scott		
VIOLETTE	Anonymous		

THE JAZZ AGE

Title	Author	
BLUE ANGEL DAYS	Margarete von Falkensee	
BLUE ANGEL NIGHTS	Margarete von Falkensee	
BLUE ANGEL SECRETS	Margarete von Falkensee	
CONFESSIONS OF AN ENGLISH MAID	Anonymous	
PLAISIR D'AMOUR	Anne-Marie Villefranche	
FOLIES D'AMOUR	Anne-Marie Villefranche	
JOIE D'AMOUR	Anne-Marie Villefranche	
MYSTERE D'AMOUR	Anne-Marie Villefranche	
SECRETS D'AMOUR	Anne-Marie Villefranche	
SOUVENIR D'AMOUR	Anne-Marie Villefranche	
WAR IN HIGH HEELS	Piers Falconer	

SAMPLERS & COLLECTIONS

Title	Editor	Price	
EROTICON 1	ed. J-P Spencer		
EROTICON 2	ed. J-P Spencer		
EROTICON 3	ed. J-P Spencer		
EROTICON 4	ed. J-P Spencer		
NEW EROTICA 1	ed. Esme Ombreux		
NEW EROTICA 2	ed. Esme Ombreux		
THE FIESTA LETTERS	ed. Chris Lloyd	£4.50	

NON-FICTION

FEMALE SEXUAL AWARENESS	B & E McCarthy	£5.99	
HOW TO DRIVE YOUR MAN WILD IN BED	Graham Masterton		
HOW TO DRIVE YOUR WOMAN WILD IN BED	Graham Masterton		
LETTERS TO LINZI	Linzi Drew		
LINZI DREW'S PLEASURE GUIDE	Linzi Drew		

Please send me the books I have ticked above.

Name   ....

Address   ....
          ....
          .... Post code   ....

Send to: **Cash Sales, Nexus Books, 332 Ladbroke Grove, London W10 5AH**

Please enclose a cheque or postal order, made payable to **Nexus Books**, to the value of the books you have ordered plus postage and packing costs as follows:

  UK and BFPO – £1.00 for the first book, 50p for the second book, and 30p for each subsequent book to a maximum of £3.00;

  Overseas (including Republic of Ireland) – £2.00 for the first book, £1.00 for the second book, and 50p for each subsequent book.

If you would prefer to pay by VISA or ACCESS/MASTERCARD, please write your card number here:

Please allow up to 28 days for delivery

— — — —   — — — —   — — — —   — — — —

Signature: _____